Bounty of Vengeance: Ty's Story

BOUNTY OF VENGEANCE: TY'S STORY

PAUL COLT

FIVE STAR
A part of Gale, Cengage Learning

Farmington Hills, Mich • San Francisco • New York • Waterville, Maine
Meriden, Conn • Mason, Ohio • Chicago

Five Star™ Publishing, a part of Cengage Learning, Inc.

LIBRARY OF CONGRESS CATALOGING-IN-PUBLICATION DATA

Names: Colt, Paul, author.
Title: Bounty of vengeance : Ty's story / Paul Colt.
Description: First edition. | Waterville, Maine : Five Star Publishing, [2016]
Identifiers: LCCN 2015037318 | ISBN 9781432831776 (hardback) | ISBN 1432831771 (hardcover) | ISBN 9781432831707 (ebook) |ISBN 1432831704 (ebook)
Subjects: | BISAC: FICTION / Historical. | FICTION / Westerns. | GSAFD: Western stories.
Classification: LCC PS3603.O4673 B68 2016 | DDC 813/.6—dc23
LC record available at http://lccn.loc.gov/2015037318

First Edition. First Printing: February 2016
Find us on Facebook– https://www.facebook.com/FiveStarCengage
Visit our website– http://www.gale.cengage.com/fivestar/
Contact Five Star™ Publishing at FiveStar@cengage.com

Printed in the United States of America
1 2 3 4 5 6 7 20 19 18 17 16

For Trish

This book is dedicated to my first reader, best friend, research partner and wife, Trish. She's put up with my dreaming and scheming since we weren't much more than kids. I owe her a great debt of gratitude for that kind of support. She raised two talented kids we are proud of. Melissa and Jamie have given us families and grandchildren that are a credit to both of them. It took a while, dear, but here you go. This one's for you.

LP

PROLOGUE

Las Vegas, New Mexico
November 14, 2010

Retired police detective Rick Ledger rocked back in his desk chair. Cold gray light filtered through the curtains to his home office from the small pool deck in the backyard. He gazed at the antique tintype in the filigree frame atop his desk. A tall rugged cowboy with a dark rough shave stared back at him. Great-great-grandpa Ty had a story all his own. He was a rancher and deputy US marshal in Lincoln County, New Mexico, in the 1880s. He investigated the death of Billy the Kid. Rick's Grandpa Brock told him the story as a boy. He'd been fascinated at the time and remained so ever since.

He'd taken up the cold case a few years ago. He followed the trail of his grandpa's boyhood tale to his own conclusion. He was surprised at the intense controversy stirred by events that happened a hundred and thirty years ago. He shook his head. History, he concluded, affords a cloudy portal through which we view the past. Legend is fashioned by people. History, it seems, is sometimes written by the devious or uninformed. Nonetheless, some of it becomes history. When it does, it is accorded the stature of fact, not to be questioned even in the face of uncertainty or contradictory evidence. Rick knew from his career as a police officer, sometimes the law got it wrong. Sometimes Lady Justice truly could be blind. He took the controversy in stride. He felt no need to defend his work. He did wonder what Great-great-grandpa Ty would have thought. He would have understood Rick's conclusions. He'd struggled with some of the same evidence himself and he hadn't even had the whole of it. Most likely, though, he'd have been surprised that anyone still cared after all these years.

The story Great-great-grandpa Ty told his grandson Brock captured Rick's imagination when he heard it those long years ago, working on Grandpa's ranch for the summer. His only connection to the story was the picture of the cowboy in a filigree frame on the side table in the parlor. No one seemed to care about it after Grandpa Brock passed away. His dad had gladly given it to him when he asked. As it turned out Great-great-grandpa Ty had his own story. He might never have pieced it together if it hadn't been for the journal. He found that in an old trunk in Grandpa's attic. It seemed like it belonged with the picture. Rick's dad agreed. The journal belonged to Ty's wife, Great-great-grandma Lucy. Actually as it turned out, she was his second wife . . .

Chapter One

Number 10 Saloon
Deadwood, Dakota Territory
March 1877

Patch sat alone at a dark corner table, fighting the effects of winter with a whiskey bottle. Squat and wiry he had a deceptively powerful build with sloping shoulders, long arms and gnarled hands. Straight black hair hung to his shoulders in greasy plaits, courtesy of his Comanche mother. The dim flicker of yellow light rendered his features a twisted mask. He covered the empty socket that had been his left eye with a black patch. It gave him the only name he claimed. His one dark eye glittered cold as it followed the powdered pink flesh in the scarlet dress across the room. Kerosene lamps hanging from the ceiling bathed her in islands of smoky light. She moved from gambler to miner, offering invitations, her eyes dulled by disinterest and the numbing effects of the brown liquid in a small flask she carried in her garter. She laughed here, let another paw her there with a pinch from a third last of all. A familiar demand stirred beneath the whiskey warming his belly. Pain cursed his medicine as a boy. The curse haunted him.

He owed his lighter shade of dark skin to a white father. Mostly it saved him from the half-breed stigma when he moved among the whites. It hadn't been so with his mother's people. He didn't remember much about the man that fathered him, only the whiskey bottles, the cursing and the sickening sound of the blows when the man beat his mother. He felt no sorrow the night she killed him. The man passed out after beating her near senseless. He remembered her face, a bloody smear as she sat by the dying fire. Motionless she gathered her anger against her pain. He watched her through a child's eyes.

She struggled to her feet and staggered across the cabin dirt floor to the door and the big knife, hanging in its sheath on a peg. The blade turned orange in the firelight as she crossed the room to the bed where the man lay. Patch knew what she was about to do. It held no terror for him, only a curious fascination. She stood over the man lost in shadow. His slack jaw revealed a maw gaping in rows of yellow teeth. Her chest rose and fell. She clenched the knife in her fist, summoning her hatred, summoning her thirst for vengeance. The blade flashed. His throat gashed, coursing bursts blackened in firelight. The murdered man's eyes shot round white with disbelief. He made a wet sucking sound, drowning in gouts of blood. She stepped back. He struggled to rise. His body shook. His eyes clenched. The body fell back, lank and still.

She finished her work, slicing his belt and stripping away his britches. She took his manhood for a medicine pouch she would wear tied to her belt. They left the ranch that night and went to live with her people.

Chero, the tribal chief, took her for a wife soon after they joined the band. He gave her the Comanche name Winter Moon. Her new husband treated her not much better than the last. He hated her half-breed son. Patch learned to stay away from this husband. He grew up an exile among his mother's people.

He lost his eye in a knife fight at sixteen. Chatto, Chero's son by another wife, took it. In a wounded black rage, Patch gutted the boy. They banished him for his crime. It suited their purpose. It mattered little. They'd driven his spirit away many moons before. He remembered his mother, watching as they drove him out of the village. She fingered the leathery bag that spawned him, watching while her people pelted her son with sticks and stones. This memory of his mother proved an endless fountain of hatred. It stirred his blood lust to vengeance.

Women like the one in the red dress found him repulsive. He could see it in their eyes. They drove him away with his mother's contempt. He hated them for it. He found relief in their terror. Their screams made his medicine strong. This night he would once more wash the stain of humiliation in blood. This night, he would hunt. He would spend his anger in her screams and ride south. Yes south, away from the cold. No more cold, he would find warmth in the south. He would search for the witch Winter Moon. He would find her there and banish the demons that haunted him in her blood. But first he would slake this thirst.

Fort Laramie
April 1877

REWARD

Clarence Sanders, President, First Laramie Bank, offers $1,000 reward dead or alive for the person or persons responsible for the murder of his wife Ophelia Sanders. Mrs. Sanders's body was discovered in the Sanders home . . .

Johnny Roth closed the newspaper. He squinted against the bright morning sun. The sign up the street read First Laramie Bank. Tall and muscled, Roth dressed his lean frame in black. His hatband sported twists of fine Mexican silver work. Flashy, but then Roth didn't much care if folks saw him coming. He wore a pair of black-leather-rigged, ivory-handled Colts slung low on his hips. A man didn't wear a rig like that unless he could use them. Roth made his living using them. In his late twenties, cool gray eyes told some of it. He had a small scar that split his lower lip. Ladies found him fetching, in a dangerous sort of way. The men he tracked found him competent. Those fool enough to try found him deadly.

He started up the boardwalk. His boot heels clipped the planks to the ring of his spurs. He crossed mud ruts on Grand still stiff with night chill. He clumped up the boardwalk to the bank. The window sign said open. He stepped inside. The expansive lobby echoed the way bank lobbies do. Sunlight spilled through the front windows to a gleaming floor and teller cages that smelled of wood polish and the thin scent of money. He spotted Sanders easily enough. The banker sat at a big desk at the back of the lobby beside the vault door. His bushy gray brows knit in suspicion. Heavily armed strangers provoked that reaction in bank lobbies. Roth favored him with a half smile as he crossed the lobby. He opened a gate in the low wood rail that separated the vault from the lobby. The banker eyed him with sober uncertainty. Roth removed his hat to set him at ease.

"Mr. Sanders?" The banker nodded and stood, extending his hand. He took it. "Johnny Roth. I'm here about the reward for your wife's murderer."

Clarence Sanders looked older than his years in his dark suit and tie. Maybe grief had something to do with it.

"Have a seat, Mr. Roth." He gestured to a pair of barrel-backed chairs drawn up in front of his desk. "Are you a law-man?"

"Bounty hunter."

"I see."

"What can you tell me about your wife's murder?"

Sanders blinked back a painful memory. His confident demeanor shrank. His voice strained. "I came home for supper. Ophelia was in the parlor. She'd been . . ." He dropped his chin to his chest, groping for words. "Cut something terrible, blood, her clothes." He looked up, his eyes moist. "She'd been . . . molested."

Not much got past Roth's shell. Sanders's story did. "I'm sorry, Mr. Sanders. I don't mean to make this difficult for you. I just need to ask a few questions."

He nodded. "I understand."

"Did anyone see anything that might be helpful?"

Sanders shook his head. "Not much to go on I'm afraid."

"It isn't. Anything else come to mind?"

"The sheriff got a report of a similar killing last month up in Deadwood."

"What made the sheriff think the murders were similar?"

He paused, collecting himself. "The cutting. The victim in that case was a prostitute. She was seen with a dark-skinned man who wore an eye patch. My Ophelia would never have had anything to do with such a person. She was a pillar of virtue. I don't see the connection."

"They're both women."

"My Ophelia and a prostitute? I don't see it. I can think of reasons why a man might kill a prostitute, but a total stranger in her own home?"

"It may not make sense to you. But if he killed like that twice, chances are he'll do it again. If it is the same man, we have a one-eyed, dark-skinned suspect who traveled south from Deadwood. Maybe next time we'll get something more."

"You think he might kill like that again?"

Roth met the banker's eyes. "I'd say it's a pretty good bet."

"I see. Are you going after him, Mr. Roth?"

"It's what I do, Mr. Sanders."

Chapter Two

Wyoming Territory
May 1877

Cheyenne Sheriff Ty Ledger led his steel dust out of the small stable behind a neat whitewashed clapboard house and led him around to the front porch. Tall and wiry with dark wavy hair and a rough shave, he had the look of needing a barber most of the time. He had an easy way about him that might cause a man to miss the steel blued in his eyes. Those eyes didn't miss much. He punched cattle up from Texas, caught gold fever in Abilene and moved on to the Colorado gold fields in '67. He arrived too late for the big claims and drifted on to Cheyenne. The city fathers handed him the sheriff's star six years ago after a renegade outlaw tomahawked his predecessor while breaking the notorious Clay Lassiter out of jail. He'd soon shown himself fast enough with a gun that he seldom had to use it. He'd been reelected twice. At twenty-eight, he'd grown confident in the job. He looped a rein over the worn hitch rail and clumped up the step to the front porch. He paused at the door. The first flares of sunlight fired the eastern horizon tinting the bright blue sky pink. It promised a fine spring day for a ride. He opened the door to the smoky warm smells of bacon, coffee and fresh biscuits.

Victoria stood at the potbelly stove frying eggs. Her rich auburn hair hung in curls, framing a delicate profile. The small swell growing in her belly didn't show much yet, beyond an inner joy that gave her a radiant glow. She glanced over her shoulder and smiled.

"Hi, handsome. You hungry?"

"Smells mighty good in here, I guess I better be."

"Pull up a chair. Biscuits and preserves are on the table. Coffee's hot in the pot. Fatback and eggs will be up in a minute."

"This kind of treatment's likely to spoil a man, Victoria." He poured two steaming cups of coffee and scraped a chair away from the table. He set the coffee at their places and settled down next to a basket of warm biscuits and a jar of raspberry jam.

"You started spoilin' the day I fell in love with you, Ty Ledger."

A smile creased the corners of his eyes around a mouthful of biscuit and jam. Victoria carried two steaming plates to the table. She placed one in front of Ty and took her place across the table.

"You headed out to Lucky and Dove's place?"

He nodded. "Got a telegram from Washington to deliver."

Victoria scraped her plate with a forkful of fatback. "I thought he resigned from the marshal's service."

"He tried. The chief marshal refused his resignation. He put him on administrative leave at half pay. Nice work if you can get it."

"I never heard of such a thing."

He washed down a forkful of fried egg with a swallow of coffee. "The chief marshal didn't want to lose him. Lucky solved some pretty tough cases for him. Besides Lucky bein' a friend of the president probably didn't hurt either."

"What's the telegram about?"

"No idea. I expect Lucky will tell me about it after he opens it. Well, darlin', I best get on my way if I expect to be back in time for supper." He wiped his mouth with a napkin and scraped his chair away from the table.

Victoria followed him to the door. She tipped up on her toes to give him a kiss. "You be careful and hurry back."

"You have a good day and take care of that little bundle you're workin' on."

The man came out of the house. He collected the dark horse at the hitch rail and stepped into the saddle. He tipped his hat to the shadowy figure of a woman on the front porch and wheeled away to the northwest at the easy lope of a long ride.

Sun lit fire in the white woman's hair as she hung clothes on a line behind the white house. He'd watched the man ride away early that morning. He'd seen no sign of any other men about. She was alone with the promise of all that white flesh. The prairie wind tossed her hair. It played with the folds of her blue dress, pressing it against the shape of her ankles and the swell of her breast. The urge to hunt rose in his blood with the sun at mid morning.

He drew his skinning knife. The long blade held a keen edge. He liked a fine edge for his work, but that would come later. He turned back to his prey. She bent to pick up the wash basket, taunting him with the spread of her hips. He savored the promise, knowing what he would do. Planning a hunt gave him a taste of the pleasure he would know in taking his prey.

She climbed the worn wooden step to the back door and disappeared in the shadows beyond. The step might make a sound. The door would creak. No matter. With no one to help, he would have her.

He sees dim light inside the house. It is neat and clean. It smells of white people. She starts at the sight of him and backs away, possibly toward a weapon. She asks what he wants. Women were foolish in this way. They ask what they already know. He approaches her as he might a skittish horse. She backs into another room, a parlor. She has no weapon. He stalks her. She smells sweet. He is close now. She pleads. She will give him whatever he wishes if only he will leave her and go. Such a foolish thing to ask when they know he will not. He reaches for her. No, she says no, please. He can taste the tang of terror. She stumbles and falls back. He is on her. She strikes wildly with a fist. She tries to twist away scratching at his good eye. He catches her by the wrist. He hears the smack. His blow snaps her head back. She screams, her features twisted in anguish that excites him.

She struggles. They always do. He feels her heat. The smell of fear is sour. It makes his medicine grow strong. It stirs his blood. It courses through his veins, rising hot with power. Dress fabric rips in his fist. Buttons scatter across the plank floor like the seeds of a broken rattle. Thin muslin rips like paper.

She cannot resist his power. He drags her to her feet and pushes her across the room. The next room is dim light, the bed a dark shape. She twists and screams. She tries to kick him. He slaps her hard. It feeds his rage. She screams until no more sound comes from her voice. No sound where his hands close on her soft slender throat. No sound to sing his pleasure. No sound when he draws his blade.

He grunted. Sunlight swam red before his good eye. Ragged breath, thick with anticipation, caught in his throat. He rose from his hiding place. His shadow loomed before him. He hunched his shoulders and stalked toward the back of the house.

Slanting rays of last light warmed Ty's back as the steel dust crested a low rise, nearing home. The ride out to Lucky's place on Willow Creek took most of the morning. It turned out the telegram he carried was from Chief Marshal Bryson. It offered Lucky appointment as US marshal for Wyoming Territory. It was a plumb job. You got paid to appoint deputies to do most of the field work. Lucky's Cheyenne wife, Mourning Dove, fed him a fine lunch. They had a nice visit before he started for home. Now he could see the house, white painted pink in the distance. He smiled to himself and squeezed up a lope. He had time enough to see to his horse and wash up for supper.

Long purple shadows crept across the yard as he rode in. The house stood strangely quiet in the falling dusk. No light in the windows. No smoke rose from the stovepipe. A sense that something was wrong invaded his gut. He tried to put it aside. Maybe Victoria lay down for a nap and slept longer than she planned. He wheeled the steel dust around the house to the corral and stepped down. He looped a rein over a fence rail and turned to the house. Wash still hung on the line. Something was definitely wrong. A surge of alarm seized his chest.

He hurried across the yard and bounded up the back step to the door. "Victoria?" No answer. He scratched a match and lit the table lamp. Light bloomed in the darkness, revealing a chair tipped over in the darkened parlor beyond. His heart jumped in his throat. "Victoria." He called again. Still no answer.

He crossed the parlor to the bedroom door. A sweet, sickly smell announced the worst before his lamp lit the dark form staining the rumpled sheets.

The scene in the small bedroom hit him with the force of a mule kick. Dark bloodstains and rumpled bedclothes masked the remains of his wife and unborn child. His head turned light. His knees went weak in a flood of denial and grief. He dropped to the floor and retched. The lamp slipped from his fingers. It did not break. It rolled on its side, spilling oil and flame across the bedroom floor. He froze in dazed disbelief as the pool of flame spread like a carpet. Fiery tongues licked the dresser and curtains.

Burning oil spread toward the bed. *Victoria!* He reacted

instinctively. He leaped to his feet. Flames spilled around his boots. Smoke burned his eyes. Intense heat enveloped him. He ripped the bedclothes free of the mattress and wrapped her in them. He gathered her in his arms and staggered from the bedroom. He choked as he felt his way across the parlor rapidly filling with smoke. He fumbled for the front door latch. It clicked. He flung the door open and lurched onto the porch. Clouds of black smoke engulfed him, released from the hell gate opened in the place he called home. He staggered across the porch, his knees barely able to support the burden he bore effortlessly in happier times. He carried her away from the house he'd built for her and the family they'd planned. Soot and tears stung his eyes. He carried them blindly to safety in the yard. He gulped fresh air through raw sobs. *Why? Who? But God why?* He dropped to the ground, cradling her body in his arms as he watched his life destroyed in flames.

Cheyenne

Fat raindrops splattered the dusty earth, falling slowly with the promise of more to come. Wind whipped the small gathering of somber-clad mourners clustered around two freshly dug graves. They stood silhouetted against a dark pall of gray cloud in the fenced cemetery behind the little white church on the hill south of town. Parson Williams stood beside the grave markers, one smaller than the other.

"The Lord is my shepherd. I shall not want. He maketh me to lie down in green pastures . . ." The familiar passage trailed away in the wind.

Ty heard little of it. Grief had turned to rage in the last days. The murderer would pay. He did not know how or when. He only knew the murderer would pay.

Jedediah Chance stood beside his friend as he had since the news of Victoria's death. His Cheyenne wife, Mourning Dove, did her best to comfort a disconsolate Jon Westfield. Victoria was his only daughter. They were joined at the graveside by Blanton Collier, Cheyenne mayor, and his wife, Abigail. No one noticed the tall dark stranger, standing beside his horse beyond the cemetery gate.

"Lord God, we commend these souls to your everlasting care." Parson Williams brought his memorial to an end as the rain gained strength. He handed Ty a shovel.

He took it, wiping a raindrop from his cheek on the back of his hand. He scooped up a shovel of dark soil and let it spill into her grave. Clods of wet dirt sounded hollow concussions on the raw wooden lid. He handed the shovel back to the parson and turned away.

He squared his shoulders. No time for more tears. If he had any left, he pushed them aside. Grief resolved to a determined set to his jaw. His eyes narrowed as he glanced at the sheriff's star on his chest. He removed the badge and handed it to Collier. "I'll be leaving, Mr. Collier. You're gonna need a new sheriff."

"Ty, why not take some time to think it over? After all, this is your home."

"Not anymore. My home is gone. My job is finding Victoria's killer." He turned on his heel, discussion at an end.

Collier closed his fist on the badge and shook his head. Chance hurried after his friend, leaving Mourning Dove at the grave with a sobbing Jon Westfield.

Ty paused at the cemetery gate, noticing the dark stranger for the first time.

The man held a sturdy black horse. "Ledger, Chance." He nodded to each. "Sorry about your wife, Ty."

Johnny Roth hadn't changed much as Ty remembered him. He'd deputized Roth a time or two in years past. Had him act as sheriff the time he and Chance led a posse after the Lassiter gang. Word was he'd gone into bounty hunting in recent years. They hadn't seen anything of him for quite a spell. Like all of them, Roth was a few years older. Ty remembered eyes the color of mountain ice. They'd gone some colder. Cool and measured, he had an edge to him.

"Roth, what are you doin' here?"

"Followin' the man I expect killed her."

"What makes you think you know who killed Victoria?"

"I heard what happened. It fits him. He killed a whore up in Deadwood and a banker's wife in Laramie. The banker put a thousand-dollar bounty on him. That got my attention. The man's been headed south for as long as I've been followin' him."

"That does fit." Ty nodded. "I found tracks. He hid a horse near the house and rode south, after . . ." His throat caught.

Roth recognized the killer's trail. He tried not to let business get personal, but he couldn't help feeling the need to kill this son of a bitch.

Chance filled the awkward pause. "What do you know about him, Johnny?"

"Not much. Someone saw a dark-skinned, one-eyed man with the whore. He might be Mexican, maybe a half-breed."

Ty recovered his composure. "It may not be much, but it's more'n I had a minute ago."

Roth eyed him beneath his hat brim. "You fixin' to go after him?"

"I am."

"What about the bounty?"

Ty clenched his jaw. "I don't give a shit about a bounty. I want the son of a bitch dead."

"We might make a good team, then, as long as we don't fight over the pleasure of putting a bullet in him."

Chance understood grief. Revenge sometimes got a man in

trouble. "How about dead or alive?"

"What about it?"

"Deputy US marshals bring outlaws to justice not revenge."

Ty lifted an eyebrow. "I don't understand."

"Let me deputize you. Then you'll have the force of law behind whatever happens."

"Thanks Lucky, but I got no interest in takin' alive the animal that done this."

"Not so fast." Roth turned to Ty. "There's another reason you might want to pack a shield. Sometimes local law will help a bounty hunter and sometimes they won't. If you was a duly sworn deputy, we could pretty much count on full cooperation."

Ty nodded. "Makes sense. Come on down to the office, Lucky. We can do our swearin' out of the rain."

The rain stopped by morning. Heavy gray clouds drifted out of the west, promising more rain. Ledger and Roth rode out to the rain-soaked ruins of Ty and Victoria's house. The smoky smell of charred wet wood hung heavy in the air. Ty turned his back on the painful memory. He led Roth to the spot where he'd seen sign of the assailant's horse. The men stepped down. They left their horses to crop and prowled the area searching for sign. Two days of rain left little to mark the spot.

Roth cut off the search with a shake of his head. He scratched his chin as he squinted at the southern horizon. "He's been driftin' south since Deadwood. Hasn't hit town for a spell," Roth mused.

"He's headed to Denver."

Ty had a hard determination about him since the funeral. Nothing seemed left of the laid-back Texan Roth remembered from years ago. "Could be, what makes you think so?"

"I just know." Ledger collected his steel dust.

Roth shrugged and followed. "Man with one eye gets noticed.

Ask enough questions, we'll pick up his trail."

They stepped into their saddles. Ty wheeled the steel dust and squeezed up a lope south.

Chapter Three

Rio Pecos Valley
New Mexico Territory

Thin clouds scudded east on a warm breeze. Filtered moonlight splashed ripples of light across a shadowy sea of cattle sprawled along the grassy river bottom. Deacon Swain's head bobbed. Dozing in the saddle made light work of night watch. If anything needed doing, Tawny, his sturdy chestnut cow horse would see it got done. With Tawny on watch, the herd's quiet night sounds soon enough sang a man to sleep. On nights like this the big man might even snore.

A former South Carolina slave, Swain ran away early in the war. He fought for the Union, serving with distinction in an all-black unit. He drifted west after the war, catching on with the cattle trade moving herds north from Texas to the railheads. The trail boss, Wade Caneris, befriended him. Caneris respected the quiet competence of the dark giant so much he took Deac with him when he set off for New Mexico. They drifted onto John Chisum's South Spring Ranch and caught on with the crew running his Long Rail brand. Opportunity and competence soon made Caneris Chisum's South Spring foreman.

North of Swain's position, Axel Dunbar kept watch at the riverbank. The cattle were quiet. Dunbar was not. It was quiet all right, too quiet. Rustlers had been a problem for months. Raid after raid hit the Long Rail herds. Chisum made no secret of the fact he thought the small ranchers were behind it. Likely they were. Small ranchers objected to the size of the Long Rail herds. They numbered near a hundred thousand head. Some of those small ranchers, known as the Seven Rivers boys, led by Jesse Evans, accused Chisum of crowding them out of available public grazing land. Dunbar suspected they did more than accuse the boss man. Rustlers used guns. That made him nervous.

Cattle lowing behind him sounded the first alarm. Dunbar twisted in the saddle, straining his eyes at the darkness in the hills north of the river. Something had the herd unsettled. *Coyote,* he thought hopefully as he drew his Winchester from the saddle boot. He wheeled his horse toward the disturbance. *Easy,* he reminded himself, resting the butt of the rifle on his hip. He let his horse pick its way along the stony bank toward the sound of moving cattle.

A star burst out of the darkness over the backs of the milling herd. Dunbar's left eye exploded, shattering the back of his skull in his hat. He never heard the rifle report. His horse shied. His body toppled into the stream on the rocky bank.

The gunshot snapped Swain awake. All hell broke loose around him. Rustlers rode in from the north, shooting in the air to spook the herd. Swain counted muzzle flashes. *Must be four or five of 'em.* The panicked herd bolted south ranging over the river valley. Their frightened bellows and pounding hooves made a ruckus like to wake the dead. He searched the dark for some sign of Dunbar. If he was out there, God alone knew where. Swain spurred Tawny into a lope, trailing along with the herd, lost in the dust cloud rising on left swing. There wasn't much he could do with a stampede other than ride along to see how this played out. If he could identify the rustlers, at least he'd have somethin' he could tell Mr. Chisum.

Slowly he let the herd pull away, disappearing in the dust cloud left for drag. He swung in behind the dark shadowy horsemen driving the cattle south. With no resistance offered they'd holstered their weapons to concentrate on the herd. Swain took little comfort, hanging back to avoid detection. A spooked herd made for easy following. With any luck he'd find out who was behind the raid.

South Spring Ranch
Rio Pecos Valley

Wade Caneris clumped out of the South Spring bunkhouse to the rough-cut plank porch. He hitched his bracers over a clean cotton shirt and stretched. A big rawboned Texan with an unruly shock of sandy hair, drooping mustache and alert blue eyes, he had the weather-lined features of a man who handled storms, stampedes, river crossings and anything else the trail threw at his herd. Cowboys followed his quiet lead, knowing he'd pull them through to payday.

He tapped a gray felt hat on his head and squinted at the sun rising over juniper studded hills, tinting the bright blue sky pink. He picked up movement off to the south. He watched the speck grow taking on recognizable shape. A riderless horse jogging for home was never a good sign. He stepped down from the porch and headed for the corral gate. The horse picked up a lope in anticipation of water and grain. He recognized the lathered piebald as it turned up the ranch road. The horse broke down to a trot and pulled himself up at the corral gate. He stomped a demand for food and water with a snort. One rein trailed in the dust, the other had broken off at the bit. A crusty brown bloodstain on the horse's rump confirmed trouble. Caneris opened the gate and let the horse trot to the trough. He closed the corral and set off for the ranch house at a jog. He took the front porch steps in one stride. His boots announced him without much need to knock. Still he pulled off his hat and rapped on the door.

The door swung open a moment later. Chisum's Navajo

housekeeper Dawn Sky greeted him with expectant question in her eyes. The young woman's deep copper beauty never failed to have its effect on Caneris. Her wide-set dark eyes might flash like summer lightning or turn soft and liquid like a river eddy as they were now. She had a short straight nose, high chiseled cheekbones and full lips drawn taught in a bow. She carried her lean frame with the proud bearing of her people. She wore a plain cotton blouse and brightly colored skirt like most peon women, though her simple dress gave full measure to the flower of her womanhood. Caneris shuffled his feet, recovering himself. "John in?"

Chisum appeared behind her in answer to his question. He arched a questioning brow over a steaming cup of coffee. Lean and angular Chisum possessed a rugged, no-nonsense demeanor. He had wavy brown hair gone gray at the temples, neatly trimmed around prominent ears. Lively brown eyes with bushy brows set in lean features. He wore a neatly waxed mustache with a patch of whiskers below his lower lip. He favored plain spun shirts with a black ribbon tie that gave him the look of authority he commanded. It took singular purpose to run three ranches with herds approaching a hundred thousand head. "What is it, Wade?"

"The piebald Axel Dunbar rode last night just come in by itself."

Chisum combed his cropped brown hair with his fingers. "Where was Axel workin' last night?"

"He and Deacon Swain had night watch on the river valley herd. No sign of Deac either. I'm worried."

Chisum set his jaw. His mustache turned down at the corners. He furrowed his brow and nodded in unspoken agreement. "Have a couple of the boys saddle some horses. We'll ride out there and have a look around."

★ ★ ★ ★ ★

Thirty minutes later Chisum and Caneris rode out accompanied by Bill McCloskey, Henry Brown and George Coe. Chisum set a brisk pace southeast toward the Pecos. The beauty of desert flowers and a warm spring morning were lost on grim-faced men, fretting over the fate of their friends. Two hours later they rode into the grassy river valley and turned south along the west bank. They saw plenty of cattle sign, but no cattle.

A mile down the valley Caneris spotted a dark shape on the riverbank partially submerged in the water. "There." He pointed, drawing attention to the spot. They angled southeast to the riverbank, drew rein and stepped down. Caneris and Chisum exchanged knowing glances. The foreman pulled Axel Dunbar's body from the river and knelt beside it. He shook his head. The shattered skull told the story. "At least he didn't suffer none." He rolled the body in a blanket.

Chisum studied the ground along the riverbank and squinted south and west into the hills. "Cattle run off to the south. Looks like rustler's work to me. No sign of Swain either, you don't suppose he sold us out?"

Caneris straightened up. "Not Deacon, John. I've ridden with him a long time. I trust him like a brother. If we don't find him dead or wounded, it's more likely he followed them."

"Well it ain't easy hidin' a thousand head of cattle. I reckon we can follow that trail too. George, give Henry a hand puttin' poor Axel there up on Henry's horse. Henry, take the body back to the ranch and see he gets a proper burryin.' The rest of you spread out and ride south. Let's make sure we aren't leavin' Swain down here somewhere. Now come on, boys, mount up."

A mile downriver, Chisum called the boys in. They'd found nothing of Swain amid all the cattle sign. Grim jawed he picked up the pace on the ride south. His anger smoldered with each passing mile. His gut told him this trail led to Seven Rivers and the thieving bunch of small-time ranchers who made their business living off stolen cattle. They had a ready market for stolen beef. Doctor up the brands and they could get a quick sale to Murphy & Dolan up in Lincoln. The House, as the partners were known, had contracts to supply beef to Fort Stanton and the Mescalero Reservation. As long as the price was right, Murphy and Dolan weren't particular about where the cattle came from. That was the big problem. He just couldn't prove it. The Seven Rivers crowd figured to turn a quick profit at his expense and reduce the Long Rail grazing pressure in the bargain. He couldn't prove that, either. This time might be different though. They'd run off a thousand head and murdered Axel. Hidin' a thousand head wouldn't be easy. Murder made for an offense even Murphy and Dolan's hack sheriff couldn't overlook. Maybe this time they'd get the thieving skunks.

The sharp reports of three distant gunshots snapped Chisum out of his thoughts. He threw up his hand and drew his horse to a halt. The big buckskin pranced in a circle. Two more shots rang out, closer this time.

"They're comin' from up there." Caneris pointed up the trail.

A rider broke into view in the distance, little more than a dark speck in a cloud of dust, galloping toward them. Moments later two riders resolved out of the dust, giving chase. Pistol shots charged again.

"Follow me!" Chisum wheeled his horse and galloped into a covering wash west of the trail. They didn't have long to wait for the chase to play out. The shooters pursued a big black man on a blown chestnut.

"It's Deac, John." Caneris pointed as Swain and his laboring horse galloped past.

"Likely them two chasin' him is part of the gang that rustled my herd." Chisum set his jaw and drew his Winchester. He jacked a round into the breech. "Come on, boys, let's give 'em hell."

Chisum spurred his horse up out of the wash followed by Caneris and his men. The shooters slid their horses to a halt at the sight of Chisum and his men. One of them leveled his gun to fire. Chisum and Caneris both fired. Red gouts blossomed in the shooter's chest. He pitched back off his horse, dead before he hit the ground. The other wheeled his horse and spurred away south at a gallop.

"I got him," Caneris shouted. He spun away after the man raking his horse with his spurs. The shooter's horse didn't have much left. Caneris ran him down quickly. He pulled his riata free of the cantle thongs and let out his loop. He gave it two turns for balance and let it snake through the air. He dallied the rope around the saddle horn as the loop settled over the startled rustler. He cued his horse to a sliding stop, jerking the shooter off the back of his horse. The renegade rancher hit the hardscrabble, knocking him senseless.

Caneris stepped down. His horse backed a step holding the rope taught on the motionless form. He had the rustler disarmed and hog-tied by the time Chisum rode up with Deacon and the boys. "Good work, Wade. We got one of 'em alive." He turned to Swain. "Why were these men chasin' you, Deac?"

"Rustlers run off the herd last night. I followed 'em down toward Seven Rivers. Once the herd stopped runnin', they cut out what they wanted and left the rest. I come across these two, clearin' off the back trail where they split up the herd. They saw me and started shootin'. I didn't stay 'round to ask questions. Sorry, Mr. Chisum."

"No apology necessary, Deac. You done the right thing. Now we got one of the scum who can name the rest of 'em." He turned back to Caneris and stepped down from his saddle. "Get him on his feet, Wade." He scowled at the surly prisoner, trying to clear his head. Caneris dragged him to his feet.

"What's your name?"

The man spit through a dark scruffy beard showing yellow teeth.

Chisum hit him hard with the back of a gloved fist. A trickle of blood showed at the corner of the man's mouth. "I asked your name, boy."

"Real tough when a man's tied, ain't cha."

"I'd rather turn you loose and beat the shit out of you. Now, what's your name?"

"Go to hell."

He hit the man with a crack that snapped his head. "Now talk, before we fit you for a hemp necktie."

"Frank Baker."

"That's better. Who rode with you when you stole my cattle, Frank Baker?"

No answer.

"All right boys we're wastin' time here. Hang the son of a bitch."

"A man's got a right to a fair trial, Chisum," Baker said.

"We got your fair trial. Deacon here caught you red-handed."

"Hold on, John." Caneris stepped between his boss and the rustler. "Hangin' him won't get your cattle back. It'll only bring the law down on us. I say we take him to Lincoln and hand him over to Sheriff Brady. Let him get the truth out of him and round up the rest that's responsible."

Chisum set his jaw. Reason did nothing for his anger, but the pause did. Still he had his doubts. "Brady ain't never done nothin' about any of our other complaints."

"We ain't ever had an eyewitness to a murder before."

Chisum smoothed his mustache in the web of his thumb and

forefinger. “All right Wade, we’ll try it your way. Get him and the body over there on horses. We’re goin’ to Lincoln.”

Chapter Four

Lincoln

"Well, what have we got here?" Lawrence Murphy stood at his office window, gazing through the dusty film. The feisty Irishman coughed into a stained handkerchief. His thin body racked with the rattle. The ravages of disease shocked his once-fiery hair gray and thin.

Jimmy Dolan set down the papers he was reading and sat back in the barrel-backed chair beside Murphy's desk. Dolan had a modest wiry frame. He possessed a dashing demeanor women found attractive. He could be volatile, even violent, a trait Murphy found useful when the situation called for it. He also admired Dolan's ruthless business sense. "What is it, Lawrence?"

"Chisum's ridin' into town." He coughed.

"So?"

The fit passed. "He's got Frank Baker trussed up like a Christmas goose and a body in tow."

Dolan joined his partner at the window. Chisum jogged his horse down the dusty, sun-soaked street toward the sheriff's office. His men surrounded Baker. The body tied to a horse trailed along behind. "We're due for a delivery from the Seven Rivers boys. You don't suppose it has anything to do with that, do you?"

"Likely." Murphy turned away from the window and returned to his desk. "It'd be some coincidence if it didn't."

"I'll go see Brady later. If there's a problem, I'll take care of it. Now let's talk about the terms of this agreement, Lawrence. It seems McSween has it pretty well drawn."

Chisum and his men stepped down at the rail in front of the small adobe that served as the sheriff's office and jail. A breeze swirled across the river from the north, cooling the promise of summer heat. Chisum looped a rein over the rail. He had a bad feeling about turning a murdering rustler over to what passed for the law in Lincoln. He'd listened to Caneris. He respected the man's common sense. That didn't change Sheriff Brady. If he was right about the Seven Rivers boys doing Dolan's business, Dolan wouldn't be happy about the charges against Baker. His gut told him Baker would never come to justice. Dolan would get him off. That's what his gut told him, but Caneris had a strong point. They had a murder charge to go along with rustling and a witness.

"Get him down and bring him along, Wade." He stomped up the step to the office.

Sheriff William Brady had a small outer office. A wooden door led to a three-cell jail. The sheriff sat at his desk. A man of average stature, he had salted gray hair that hung to his coarse spun shirt collar. Watery blue eyes set in wrinkled sun-hardened features. Bushy mustaches covered tobacco-stained teeth. A slight paunch, gathered in his middle years, protruded over his gun belt. The cross-draw-rigged Colt on his left hip fought with the arm of his chair as he rocked back. "Afternoon, Mr. Chisum, what brings you into town?"

"I got a prisoner for you, Sheriff. You'll find the body of an unidentified rustler outside." Chisum jerked his head toward the door as Baker came in followed by Caneris and Swain.

"Prisoner you say, why, this here's Frank Baker. What's he done?"

"He and some of his Seven Rivers pals run off a thousand head of my cattle night before last. Killed Axel Dunbar doin' it. I don't know how many they got away with. Couple hundred head I reckon."

"That's a serious charge, John. What makes you think Frank done it?"

"My man Deacon Swain here was ridin' night watch with Axel. Deac caught him red-handed."

Brady pursed his lips under his mustaches and furrowed his brow at Swain. "I see. And he'd be your witness to a complaint?"

"He would." Chisum leveled a hard steady gaze at Brady, confronting the unspoken disregard for Deacon's testimony. "Now you go on and draw up any papers you need for me to file a complaint. I want this man locked up. There's a thousand head of Long Rail cattle somewhere in Seven Rivers I expect you'll be goin' down there to find. If you need any of my boys to form a posse, we'll be happy to help."

"I'll take your complaint, John. I'll also need a statement concerning the circumstances of the deceased."

"I told you, Baker and them rustlers killed Axel."

"Not him, the one outside."

"He and Baker was shootin' at Deacon here when we caught up to them. He threw down on us. We shot him in self-defense."

"And I suppose these men are all witness to that."

"These men and some others. I want Baker here charged with murder and rustlin'."

"I didn't kill nobody. He ain't got no proof."

"Shut up, Frank. Make out your complaint, John. It'll be up to the circuit judge to charge him. I'll send a couple of deputies down to Seven Rivers to have a look around first chance I get."

"First chance you get?" Chisum's voice rose in frustration. "Murder and a thousand head of cattle is an urgent matter, Brady. This isn't the first time these people robbed me. You sit up here pickin' your ass for a couple of days and them brands'll be changed. Hell, they'll be on their way to somebody's dinner table by then."

Brady bristled at the outburst. "Simmer down, Chisum. This ain't South Spring. You're in my office. I give the orders here." He jerked a sticky desk drawer open and drew out paper, pen and ink. "Here, write your complaint on this." He slid the paper across the table. "I expect you'll have to do it for your witness. Be sure to have someone witness his mark."

Chisum took the pen and bent over the desk. He dipped the pen in the ink pot and scratched across the page.

Brady got to his feet and ambled to the jail door. He stuck his head inside. "George!" Bedsprings squeaked. A sleepy-eyed Deputy George Hindman appeared in the doorway.

"Sir?"

"Lock up Frank here. We got a rustling complaint on him."

"And murder."

Brady gave Chisum an annoyed scowl. "Your man see Frank shoot Dunbar?"

"One of 'em did it. That makes Baker an accessory, unless he cares to tell us who done the killin'."

Hindman nodded. "Come on, Frank. We got a vacancy just about your size." He led Baker into the cell block.

Chisum stood. "Sign here, Deacon." He handed the pen to Swain. The black man bent over the desk and made his mark. Chisum spun the paper around and pushed it across the desk with the pen. "I'm sure you'll be pleased to witness Deacon's mark, won't you, Sheriff?"

Irritation flared in Brady's eye. Chisum fixed his gaze in stony silence. Brady picked up the pen and signed.

Late afternoon sun slanted through the office window. "Afternoon, Bill."

Brady looked up and stood. "Mr. Dolan, come in, come in. What can I do for you?"

Dolan swept the office with his eyes, making sure they were alone. "I'm curious, Bill. Who did Chisum bring in this afternoon and why?"

"Frank Baker. Chisum claims he helped steal a thousand head of Long Rail cattle. Says he killed one of his night watch men too."

"That's quite a charge. He got any proof?"

"Black hand he's got workin' for him saw Frank cuttin' the herd."

"Black you say." Dolan paused in thought. "Mind if I talk to Frank?"

"Suit yourself, Mr. Dolan. He's back there, second cell."

The jail door opened with a creak. He found a foul-tempered Frank Baker sitting on the bed in his cell. "Afternoon, Frank. It looks like we have something of a problem here."

"No shit." He spat.

"Take it easy. We'll take care of things. Now here's what I want you to do. You give Sheriff Brady a statement. I want you to tell him you caught Chisum's man trying to steal your cattle. That way it'll be your word against his. I'll have my friends in Santa Fe put in a word for you with the district attorney. You bein' white and all, I'm guessin' he won't press charges. We'll have you out of here in no time."

Baker brightened. "Much obliged, Mr. Dolan. Much obliged."

"I'll send the sheriff in directly. You give him your statement."

Chapter Five

Denver

Lucy Sample stepped out of the sweat-soaked smell of tobacco smoke and beer. She filled her lungs with sweet fresh air. Starlight gave the dusty street a pale blue glow. The action in the Silver Dollar dropped off with the drunks in the small hours of the morning. A few hard-case gamblers continued their game, but they were no prospect for a working girl. Her feet hurt. It'd feel damn good to get her shoes off. Her footsteps tapped a hollow tattoo along the boardwalk. She rounded the corner to the alley and climbed the creaky stairs to her small room. Building shadows blotted the stars. She climbed slowly too tired to notice the glint of a dark eye lurking in the alley below.

She paused on the landing, fumbled for a match in her purse. The door creaked open to darkness beyond. The match flared, giving off acrid sulfur smoke. She lit the lamp beside the door, trimmed the wick and kicked the door closed. She leaned against it with a sigh. A wisp of a girl, she retained a petite childlike figure that owed its curves to a tiny waist. Lamplight and fatigue shadowed a once-innocent beauty hardened some by the sporting life. Tendrils of sable hair escaped the ribbons and curls piled high on her head. Highlights caught red in the flicker of lamplight. Soft, knowing brown eyes looked like they came with a story. They did.

A stair creaked beyond the door at her back. Warily she thought some sport must have followed her home. A boot scraped a stair, closer this time. She slipped the bolt across the door frame. Someone breathed heavily outside on the landing. "Who is it?"

No answer.

"Who is it?"

"Patch." The voice sounded thick and hoarse.

"I don't know anyone by that name. I'm done for the night. Go away." She backed away from the door. The knob turned. The latch released against the bolt. "I said go away!" She lifted the hem of her dress as she backed into the side of her bed. Something heavy pressed against the door. The bolt held. A cold realization caught at the back of her throat. *He's going to try to break it down.* Her hand closed around the pepperbox derringer tucked in her garter. "Go away!"

The bolt exploded into the room. The door crashed open. A brutish hulk lurched out of the darkness, a shadow framed in harsh lamp glow. Raw fear choked her breath. She made out very little of him in the shadows. Shoulder-length black hair hung in greasy plaits. He wore a long buffalo coat. Lamplight flashed on the blade of a knife. It reflected in one eye, the other lost in shadow. He took a menacing step toward her.

She cocked her pistol. "Stop right where you are."

He chuckled humorlessly at the sight of the little gun. He glanced menacingly at the knife held point upright ready to strike. He took another step.

She leveled the gun onto a firing line. "Get out or I'll shoot."

His eye fixed on the little gun. A guttural sound rose in his throat. He lunged.

The muzzle flash exploded across the small room. The confined concussion reverberated in waves, magnifying the power of the little weapon. The intruder shrieked like a wounded animal. He staggered back, grabbing the side of his neck. Blood coated his fingers slick and dark. His features twisted in an angry snarl. He shook off the pain, straightened himself and hefted the knife prepared to strike.

She cocked the little pistol and stepped toward her attacker. The move took him by surprise. Doubt flickered in his eye for an instant. He turned and bolted out the door. Lucy followed him out to the landing and fired at his back as he bounded down the stairs. The bullet bit a chunk out of the stair railing. Her attacker reached the bottom of the stairs and disappeared down the dark ally.

She heard boots pound the boardwalk. Someone was coming fast. Sheriff Ben Prentice skidded around the corner gun drawn. "Lucy, what the hell's goin' on?"

"Man tried to attack me with a knife, Sheriff. He run off down the alley."

Prentice ran after him. Minutes later he returned. He climbed the stairs to the landing. "He's gone, Lucy. What'd he look like?"

"Ugly son of a bitch, looked like he might be a half-breed. He's got one eye and a bullet wound in the neck."

Prentice tipped his hat back and smiled slow. "You do know how to use that little pop gun don't you."

"Girl's gotta look after herself."

Ty and Johnny rode into Denver two days later under a sunny, cornflower-blue sky. They short loped through the dusty swirls on Colorado Street among a seething flotsam of miners, freighters and drummers. Roth turned in his saddle. "Here's where your badge comes in handy. We'll stop by the sheriff's office. If our boy's in town, he might just know where to find him."

"Ben Prentice is an old friend. He'd help even if I wasn't packin' this shield." Ty drew rein in front of the sheriff's office down the block from the Palace Hotel. They hitched the horses at the rail and stepped up to the boardwalk.

Prentice stood at his desk when they came in. He extended a sober hand in greeting. "Ty, I heard about Victoria. I'm sorry."

He took the offered hand. "Thanks, Ben."

"What brings you to Denver?"

"We're lookin' for Victoria's killer. This here's my partner, Johnny Roth."

Roth and Prentice shook hands.

"What makes you think you'll find him in Denver."

"We don't know that he's here. He was headed this way."

"What can you tell me about him?"

"He's got one eye. Most likely a half-breed."

Prentice arched an eyebrow. "He's not here now, but he was. Feller fitting that description attacked one of the whores down at the Silver Dollar a couple of nights ago."

"That fits," Roth said. "He killed one up in Deadwood."

"Well he didn't kill this one. Plucky little thing, gave him a taste of a pepperbox. Hit him too. He was gone by the time I got there."

"I'd like to talk to her," Ty said.

"Name's Lucy Sample."

"*Lucy Sample.* I know that name from somewhere . . ."

"Most likely you'll find her up the street at the Silver Dollar. If not she's got a room upstairs in the back. I'll take you."

Ty followed Prentice out the door still trying to place the name. Roth trailed behind, boots clipping the plank walk. A block up the street they swung through the Silver Dollar bat wings. It took a minute for Ty's eyes to adjust to the dim late afternoon light. The place smelled like saloons everywhere. Exposed to daylight all the stains and scars lay bare. The place was pretty deserted. The evening crowd wouldn't start to build for a couple of hours. Three of the regular girls, lounging at a back table looked up as they came in. Ty picked out the little one right off. Lucy Sample, he did know her though he couldn't recollect why. She seemed to recognize him too and stood to meet him as he followed Sheriff Prentice to the back of the bar.

"Lucy, this here's Ty Ledger. He wants to talk to you about the man who attacked you the other night."

"I remember. Ty Ledger, it's been a while."

That's it. He remembered the voice and the eyes. "Dodge wasn't it?"

"It was."

She still had some of that childlike innocence that seemed so out of place in her line of work. He remembered the honeyed tone of her voice, a light scent of lavender and soft brown eyes a man might take a swim in. It all came back in an instant from one easy conversation more than three years ago.

"You was chasin' Clay Lassiter back then. Don't tell me you're after the son of a bitch tried to kill me the other night. That'd be too much like a bright shiny knight ridin' to the rescue of a damsel in distress." She flashed a smile full of even white teeth and dimples that came with a twinkle in her eye.

"I am. He killed my wife."

Lucy's playful smile disappeared. "Oh my, I'm . . . I'm sorry." She held him in her eyes.

She meant it. "I'd like to ask you a few questions if you don't mind."

"Sure, sure." She took his arm and led him off to a corner table, leaving Roth and Prentice to stare at one another. Roth shrugged. He tossed his head after Lucy and Ty. "It looks like them two might be a while. Buy you a beer?"

Prentice nodded.

Lucy waved at the bartender who followed them to the table with two glasses. The bartender poured drinks and left the bottle. "I am sorry, Ty. I know what that ugly bastard had on his mind. I imagine it's been hard for you."

Ty nodded. "At least he didn't have his way with you."

His choice of words said a lot. "What can I tell you that might help?"

"I don't rightly know. Start with what happened."

"I left here late that night after the action died down."

The memory sounded painful, thin and tight.

"I got a room up the alley stairs in back. He followed me. I heard him on the stairs and bolted the door. He busted in. He had a knife. I told him to leave. He come at me. I shot him with my pepperbox. My aim wasn't too good. I nicked him in the neck. He got mad. I ain't never seen a killin' face like that before. I knew he was gonna use that knife. I cocked my gun and made a move toward him. I don't think he was expectin' that, 'cause he stopped. Then he turned and run. I followed him onto the landing and took another shot at him. He run off down the alley. Sheriff Prentice showed up about then and chased him, but he got away." She paused. "Don't suppose that helps much does it?"

"Did he say anything?"

"No. No, wait, he did say one thing. When I heard him at the door, I asked who it was. He didn't answer right off. Then he said, 'Patch.' Right then I knew he was going to break in. Don't ask me why. It makes sense, though. Patch, I mean, him havin' one eye and all."

Ty held her eyes in his, his mind imagining a similar scene in his own house. That scene ended differently. His eyes burned. He could feel them turn watery. His fists clenched against the rough cut of the tabletop. Lucy wrapped them in hers.

"Sorry," she whispered. "I didn't mean for it to hurt."

He shook his head. "No, I know. I asked. You told me. You done the right thing." He closed his eyes tight. A moment passed.

"You're a brave girl, Lucy Sample. That's to be thankful for."

"A girl in my line of work had better take care of herself.

Your wife didn't need to. She had you." She squeezed his hands, comfortable with more silence. "I knew you were special that night we met in Dodge. She was a lucky woman. What was her name?"

He slid his hands out from under hers and took them in his. "Thank you for understanding. Her name was Victoria."

"Like I said, she was a lucky woman."

They sat there for a time without speaking. After a spell Lucy took charge. "We got some right fine whiskey here goin' to waste, Sheriff."

He came back to the moment and smiled. He lifted his glass. "Yes, I believe we do." He knocked his glass back.

Lucy did hers with that mischievous twinkle in her eye. "That's better. A girl like me might doubt her charms if we was to stay serious much longer." She refilled their glasses.

"Actually it's not sheriff anymore. I quit."

Lucy swirled the whiskey in her glass. "Quit to kill a killer."

"I reckon."

"You could throw away a lot of life over that, Ty Ledger."

"He killed my wife and our child." He took his drink in a gulp.

"This story don't improve none with the tellin'." She poured him another.

"No it don't. This time it could have been you."

"You say that like it might matter."

He thought a moment. "It does."

"Shit! You're a shiny knight after all."

"Not so shiny. I just mean to kill that son of a bitch."

They lapsed into their own thoughts again.

"You must have loved her very much."

"I did."

"I remember that night in Dodge. I was so young then. I still thought I might find a shiny knight. You walked into the Long

Branch like a thousand other cowboys; but right off I knew you were different. I thought you might have felt a little something too when we talked that night. She must have had your heart back then already."

"She did."

Lucy half lowered her lashes. "Well, for what it's worth, Ty Ledger, I still think you're something special."

He met her eyes. "I do remember that night. I did feel somethin.' I believe I do now."

"Maybe we can make something of that, someday."

"Maybe someday, when that bastard is dead."

She suppressed a smile at what might have been the hint of a blush. "I'd like that. Just don't throw too much future away over the past."

"I'll try; but first I've got some unfinished business."

"Was she able to help?" Prentice asked on the walk back to his office.

"Some," Ty said. "Our boy calls himself Patch."

"Did she have any idea where he might be headed?" Roth asked.

"It wasn't exactly a social call."

"No I suppose not. So where does that leave us?"

"South I reckon. We haven't gone wrong with that so far."

"That makes Santa Fe the likely next stop."

"We'll need supplies and a place to stay tonight."

"I got bunks in the jail. It ain't fancy, but the price is right."

"Thanks, Ben."

Roth suggested a drink after supper. Ty didn't object. The Silver Dollar just happened to be handy. Johnny got his drink. Ty ended up at a table with the Sample girl. Roth wasn't surprised.

"So where to from here, cowboy?"

How do you fit a velvet voice in such a petite little thing? He'd have time enough to think on that later. He shrugged. "He's been driftin' south since Deadwood. From here it looks like Santa Fe."

"Santa Fe." Her eyes remembered.

"You know it?"

She shook her head. "My family was headed there when we crossed the Arkansas."

He remembered. She'd told him the story in Dodge, the story that came with those big brown eyes. "We'll be heading out in the morning." Her eyes shaded something that looked disappointed.

"I hope you get what you're after, Ty. I hope you get it soon."

He nodded.

"I'm pleased you stopped by tonight. At least now I'll know where to think of you."

Lamplight splashed across the writing table, casting shadows about the small room. She couldn't sleep. Her mind churned, schoolgirl silly. She couldn't stop it. She fingered the leather bound journal. She thumbed pages written in an even hand to the entry and read it again.

> *It figured for just another night at the Long Branch until he came in. A handsome devil I took him for just another cowboy at first. I asked him to buy me a drink. Strictly business it was. He didn't look at me like it was business. Ty Ledger is his name. Turned out he's sheriff in Cheyenne, come to town looking for Lassiter. That gave us something to talk about. The more we talked, the less it felt like business. There is something special about him. I felt it. He looked at me like he felt something too. That's usually good for more than a drink. Not this time, maybe next time. Maybe he has a girl. One thing is sure. He's something special.*

He is special. He did have a girl. She turned out to be a wife and mother. Now she was dead. That had a feeling too, pain, his pain. She felt it, that and something more. He felt something too. It felt like unfinished business. *Maybe next time?* She turned to a blank page and dipped her pen in the ink pot.

It's been quite a spell since I had anything fit for these pages. I saw him again today. He came out of nowhere, just like the last time. You remember that night in Dodge. That time he was a sheriff looking for an outlaw. He didn't have a story. This time he came with a story. He's a man on the trail of a killer. That man tried to attack me a few days ago. I was able to fight him off. Ty Ledger's wife and unborn child were not. Now he's looking for the killer. I hope he gets him, for the sake of the killer's victims and for Ty's sake. I hope that brings peace to his heart.

The first time we met I said he was something special. He still is . . .

Chapter Six

Office of the Territorial Governor
Santa Fe, New Mexico Territory

A soft knock sounded at the office door. Axtell's appointments secretary stuck his head in. "Mr. Elkins to see you, Governor."

Territorial Governor Samuel Axtell looked up from the day's stack of correspondence. Morning sun splashed across the spacious tile floor. He grimaced at the interruption. *Fine way to ruin a man's schedule.* He kept the irritation to himself where Elkins was concerned. "Send him in, Bates."

Axtell rose to greet his guest. "Stephen, welcome, to what do I owe the unexpected pleasure?"

"Sam, thank you for seeing me unannounced like this."

"Don't give it another thought. You know I always have time when you need it. Is there something I can help you with?"

"A small matter for our friends in Lincoln."

"Sit down, sit down," Axtell waved to one of the wing chairs arranged in front of a large ornate desk. "Care for a cup of coffee?"

"That would be nice, Sam. Thank you."

"Bates, coffee please." The aide stepped out of the room and closed the door.

Patrician of bearing, Stephen Elkins filled a room with understated presence. He wielded great influence in the territorial capital, despite having given up his congressional seat at the end of his last term. Elkins held sway as kingmaker in the smoky back rooms of New Mexico Republican politics.

"How are you adjusting to private life, Stephen?" Axtell made small talk waiting for the coffee.

"I manage. But you know that don't you, Sam?"

Tall and handsome with soft waves of graying brown hair, Axtell made a thoughtful, capable impression. Behind closed doors, he could be volatile and arbitrary. Like most in the Santa Fe elite, he put his best face forward where Elkins was concerned, respectful of the former congressman's inexplicable power.

"Care for a cigar, Stephen?"

"Don't mind if I do." Elkins selected a cheroot from the silver box Axtell offered. He bit the tip and spat it on the carpet.

Axtell struck a match and lit Elkins's cigar before puffing his own to light in a cloud of blue smoke. Bates appeared with two cups of coffee, steaming on a tray. He set the cups on the desk and left the office. Axtell turned confidential as the door closed. "So Stephen, what have Murphy and Dolan got up to this time that requires our assistance?"

"It's not them, at least not directly."

"Who then, nobody else down there counts for much?"

"John Chisum." Elkins released a mask of cigar smoke and took a sip of coffee.

"That son of a bitch, what help would we possibly want to give him."

"Who said anything about help? Chisum accused a small ranch hand named Frank Baker of rustling and murder. He turned him over to Sheriff Brady."

"What's that to us?"

"Nothing really, other than Dolan doesn't want Baker charged. I suspect he may be one of Dolan's, shall we say, suppliers."

"So what do you want me to do, Stephen?"

"Dolan told Brady to refer the complaint to Judge Brystol," Elkins said, referring to Circuit Judge Warren Brystol. "That puts the case in Bill Rynerson's jurisdiction. Have a talk with Bill. See if you can figure out some way to make Mr. Baker's little problem go away."

Axtell took a swallow of his coffee. "If you say so, Stephen, I'm sure we can come up with something. Bates!"

"Sir?" Bates's mousy bald head and smudged spectacles appeared owl-like in the doorway.

"Send for Bill Rynerson. I'd like to see him, at his earliest convenience. Tell him to bring the Baker complaint with him."

Elkins took a satisfied draw on his cigar. "I knew I could count on you, Sam. I knew I could count on you."

A Week Later

"You wanted to see me, Governor?"

Axtell glanced up from the current draft of his Territorial Assembly Agenda. "Why yes, Bill, come in, come in." He motioned Lincoln County District Attorney William Rynerson to the wing chair Stephen Elkins had occupied in regard to the matter at hand.

Rynerson crossed the office in heavy strides. At seven feet tall the man carried the frame of a giant. His long horsy features knit in sober concentration. He folded his frame into the chair's Lilliputian confinement.

"What prompts your interest in the Baker case? It's only come in a couple of weeks ago."

"I've been asked to look into it. Let me see the complaint."

Rynerson slid the file across the desk. Axtell flipped it open.

"Not much to it really," Rynerson continued. "John Chisum brought the complaint. It claims his man identified Baker as part of a group that stole Long Rail cattle and killed one of the night watch riders. The complaint is signed by Chisum and the witness, one Deacon Swain. Brady witnessed his mark. Baker claims it was the other way around. He says he caught Swain stealing his cattle."

"Sounds like one man's word against another's. Who is Swain?"

"Freedman, works for Chisum."

"Freedman, you mean he's ex-slave?"

"That's right."

A slow smile tugged at the corners of Axtell's mouth. "Baker's white, Bill."

"Swain works for John Chisum, Governor."

"Who gives a shit? You can't possibly press charges on such a flimsy complaint."

"Isn't that for a jury to decide?"

"Only if it's a good use of the territory's judicial budget. This case looks like a waste of time and money." Axtell pressed his fingertips into a steeple at the point of his chin. "If I was you, I wouldn't bother pressing charges." He paused, locking Rynerson's eyes. "You get my meaning?"

"I hear you, Governor. What do you want me to tell Brady?"

"Tell him to let Baker go."

Chapter Seven

Colorado Territory

Patch let his paint pony pick its way down the mountain pass toward the well-trodden way they called the Santa Fe Trail. The wound in his neck burned. He'd cleaned it as best he could. The bleeding had stopped, though he could still feel the loss of blood. As wounds went, it wasn't near as bad as the one that cost him his eye. Still, it made a constant reminder of the insult done him by the little whore. She had grit. He hadn't expected the gun. He hadn't thought she would use it. He should have killed her, but he couldn't risk another shot at close range. She meant to kill him. She might have. If it hadn't been for the sheriff, he could have gone back and finished her. Part of him still wanted to. He could see her white skin, almost like a child. Bright sun turned the vision blood-red. His medicine ran hot with a powerful urge to hunt. He needed to spill blood and more. He needed prey. He must find prey.

The mountain path leveled out. His vision of the whore faded. He drew rein. Off to the east, the Santa Fe Trail wound its way southwest. Ahead, the trail climbed toward the toll road through Raton Pass. The toll road would be faster. His instinct scented prey on the wagon trail southwest. His thirst ran strong. He swung his pony south and squeezed up a lope.

Santa Fe Trail

The day grew warm with the promise of summer. The wagon

creaked, rocking along the north bank of the Cimarron east of Raton Pass on the trail to Taos. Henry Figg walked beside the oxen. He flicked at the team with a stiff buggy whip, urging them to keep up. Oxen were a good choice when it came to clearing land and settling down to farm. On the trail, they struggled to keep up with the wagons drawn by mules or horses that made up the rest of the train. Wagon masters recognized this and positioned ox-drawn wagons at the end of the train where they could fall behind without disrupting the rest of the train. They could always catch up at the end of the day. It made for long days, requiring an extra hour or more of travel for ox-drawn wagons to reach camp each evening.

Rebecca Figg, Henry's young wife, dozed in the wagon box as the dusty miles of yet another long day rocked by. She wore a bonnet over long blonde curls to shade her pale blue eyes from the sun. She had a pleasant face and noticeable curves even in the simple homespun dress she wore on the trail. She married Henry in Saint Joe, a safe match with a family friend. The couple left family and friends to move west in search of opportunity and a better life. An unremarkable man in many respects, she found him steady and caring if somewhat stern in his demeanor. A few years her senior, his bushy unkempt beard and perpetually dusty trail clothes accented the difference in their ages.

High overhead the sun had begun to sink toward the mountain-strewn horizon. Soon the wagons ahead would consider suitable places to camp for the night. In a few hours they would rejoin the others. Rebecca's thoughts turned to preparations for supper. Fare on the trail proved maddeningly dull. Fatback, beans, biscuits, canned tomatoes or peaches and coffee made do unless by some unexpected good fortune game provided fresh meat. Now even the fatback was running low with no chance to replenish supplies before Taos.

★ ★ ★ ★ ★

Patch crested a low rise in the trail. The plain below fell away in a shallow valley. Far up the valley a lone wagon plodded along, its canvas covering set in a vast expanse of sand, scrub and rock. It gave the appearance of a colorless beetle crawling across the floor. The scent of prey drifted to him on a breath of hot breeze. He twisted his cracked lips in a crooked smile and squeezed up a lope along the north wall of the valley, trailing the wagon below.

A short time later he drew even with his quarry. He searched the horizon south and west along the trail looking for sign of a larger party that might come to the aid of their companions. He saw none. A lone man drove a team of oxen. A woman sat in the wagon box. They could not run to escape him. He saw no weapons, though the man at least must be armed. Others could be hidden in the wagon. Best approach it from behind.

He nudged the paint down the ridge to the valley floor angling behind the wagon out of sight of the man and the woman unless they turned to look back. They did not. He reached the valley floor and fell in behind the wagon a quarter mile ahead. He checked the trail as far as the horizon, still no sign of a larger party. Time slowed. His senses sharpened. He tasted blood lust. He fingered the hilt of his knife in its sheath. It fed his urge. He nudged his pony forward at a slow lope, closing on his prey.

Rebecca heard hoofbeats. She turned to the trail beyond the canvas tunnel. A lone rider on a paint horse approached at a lope. She saw only one man, still she felt alone beyond the safety of the wagon train. "Henry, someone's coming."

The man turned to his wife. He saw the approaching rider. With no one to drive them forward the oxen plodded another few steps and stopped. The wagon box came to rest even with where the man stood. "Hand me the Winchester." His voice remained calm, his stomach tightened, instinctively wary.

Patch drew rein beside the wagon. The man held a rifle. He could see the face of the woman in the wagon box as she leaned around the canvas. She wore a bonnet to shield her eyes. He saw fearful whites in the shadows. She was pretty and blonde. She would do.

"What can I do for you, friend?"

The man's question brought Patch back to the moment and the problem of the rifle. His eye flicked over the water barrel lashed to the side of the wagon. "I thought you might spare me a drink of water."

The man hesitated. "Sure." He hefted the rifle. "The ladle is hangin' beside the barrel. Help yourself."

Patch slipped down from his pony and ducked under the horse's head toward the water barrel. With his back to the man and the pony between them, the man didn't see him go for the .44 at his hip. He spun, dropping to a knee in one fluid motion. The woman gasped too late. He fired. His pony shied from the muzzle blast.

The man never brought his rifle to a firing line. The bullet hit him in the chest. He staggered back. Patch rose from his crouch. The woman screamed. He fired again and again. He liked it when she screamed. The bearded man fell back against the meaty rump of an ox. Gouts of blood turned his plain spun shirt bright red. Blue smoke drifted off on the hot breeze. The man slumped to the ground.

The woman's screams sang in his ears. The death song reminded him of his unmet need. Grief and fear twisted her face. She shrank from the glint in his eye. Her features etched hard like those of his mother. His chest tightened. His breath came thick and heavy. He drew his knife and slowly dropped his pistol belt, never taking his eye from the prize. He started for the wagon box. She disappeared inside.

He climbed into the wagon. Canvas muted the light inside golden in shadow. She cowered behind a trunk beside the pallet that served as a bed. She raised her hands before her as if to ward him away. He climbed over the seat, dropped his suspenders and stepped out of his britches. She fell back against a crate in a swoon. He cursed. She must scream. She must struggle. She would. He lifted her limp body and laid her on the pallet. He stood over her knife in hand. Her eyes fluttered behind their lids. A vein beat in the soft flesh at her throat. The swell of her breast heaved with her breathing. He lifted the hem of her dress and cut a small slit and tore it. Her eyes shot wide flooded in fear. She screamed and fought as she should.

Chapter Eight

Denver

Late morning sun found its way between the buildings, spilling through yellowed lace curtains into her small room. Lucy lay awake facing the prospect of another day. Her day led to another night, in an endless succession of days and nights since she'd lost her family crossing the Arkansas. It seemed a lifetime ago. In some ways it was. Now it seemed that this succession of days and nights led only to more of those same days and nights.

She'd been all of seventeen when she found herself alone in the wide-open cow town called Dodge. She had the clothes on her back. She had no family, no friends, no money and no prospects. Nothing stood between her and starvation. She did the only thing she could. She went to work. Life's lessons came fast and hard. They took her from Dodge to Denver, Denver to Deadwood and back to Denver.

She'd done right by herself when she sold her interest in the Lace Garter to Belle Bailey. Her fling with Billy Cantrell bankrolled her buy into the house Belle ran in Deadwood. Belle needed the money to get started. By the time Lucy was ready to cash out of the partnership, Belle had the money to buy her out and wanted to run her own place again. Deadwood had worn out its welcome for Lucy. She'd been ready to move on. Moving on meant coming back to Denver without knowing what she planned to do. She went to work at the Silver Dollar out of boredom. That worked for a time, but now she found herself restless again.

Maybe it was the trouble with that one-eyed brute. She'd handled rough types before and she'd handled him too. That wasn't it. Deep down, she knew what she wanted. She didn't want to admit it. She felt foolish for it. She tried to dismiss it, but it refused to go away. She wanted more. She wanted the normal life she'd grown up to expect. The human wreckage that soiled doves became in the sportin' trade scared her. She wanted no part of it. She could still avoid becoming another broken-down, diseased whore taking her prospects from whiskey or laudanum. She still had the last of her youth if she got out now. She might yet attract a decent man and a real life.

It was a silly schoolgirl notion brought on by a dream she couldn't shake. He haunted her dreams, tall and dark and in need of a shave. She couldn't help thinking. He was special. He had a quiet strength about him. There was something good and right and honest in him. He knew how to love. She wondered about his wife. What she'd been like? They were having a baby. Family was no foolish notion to him. At least the man he'd been before his loss. He had a burning need to avenge that loss. She understood that. Some of it scared her. That kind of vengeance could change a man. She hoped it didn't. She hoped he'd get it out of his system before it did.

Hope, as long as you had it, you could keep going. Sometimes good things came from small beginnings. Funny how they both remembered that little spark of something unexpected in one chance meeting way back in Dodge. He admitted he felt it. She felt it again even now. Maybe in time Ty Ledger would feel it again.

Well, he's gone and that's the truth of it. She tried to rid herself of such silly romantic ideas. She had told him that he could waste the rest of his life over the past. True enough. She too could waste her future clinging to the past. She still had her stake from the Lace Garter along with some money she'd saved from her earnings at the Silver Dollar. She had more than enough to pay her way to Santa Fe. Her family had been headed there when she lost them. Maybe at least one Sample should make it that far. Far-fetched as it may seem, maybe she'd find the chance of a normal life there. It was a silly schoolgirl notion. Maybe, but a girl could always hope. Hope only went so far. Hope without action went nowhere.

She glanced at the journal resting on the bedside table. The entries in it were written in the past. New entries were yet to be written. She let her mind's eye drift to the future. The choice seemed clear. Stay in the endless succession of days and nights that led to a certain future; or take a chance. She was no stranger to chances. Life had been one big chance ever since she climbed out of the Arkansas River and realized she was alone. Take a chance. She smiled. Sometimes a girl had to do what a girl had to do. Silly as the notion sounded, something felt right about heading south.

Santa Fe Trail
Colorado Territory

The black picked his way down the steep, rock-strewn trail under a blazing sun. Hot breeze swirled unpredictably in the rugged mountain pass. Johnny let the horse have his head along the twisted turns. Ty followed along behind. His steel dust dislodged a stone, sending it rolling down the trail. It bounced over another rock at a point where the trail made a sharp switchback to the east. The stone tumbled out of sight into mossy gray-green shadows in the canyon beyond. He looked over the edge.

"They call this a road?"

"Not yet. We make that choice when we cross the Santa Fe Trail."

"What choice?"

"We can follow the old trail or we can take the Wootton Toll Road over Raton Pass."

"Toll road, you mean we got to pay to use it?"

"That's right."

"Who the hell's gonna do that?"

"We are. I figure our boy won't pay. The toll road's a lot shorter. I expect we'll make up some ground on him."

"If the bastard is still movin' south," Ty said. "The only thing we know for sure is that he passed through Denver."

"He's been headed south since I first picked up his trail. You got anything better to suggest?"

"If I did, you'd hear it."

The trail switched back to the south and leveled out. Roth squeezed up a lope. A mile further on the irregular ruts of the Santa Fe Trail meandered out of the northeast in the distance. He drew a halt.

"Beside bein' shorter and faster Wootton runs an inn and tavern at the end of his road."

"A drink, a good meal and a bed, I like the sound of that." Ty picked up the steel dust's lope south toward the looming heights of Raton Pass.

Lincoln
June 1877

Chisum and Caneris jogged the length of Lincoln stirrup to stirrup under a blazing midday sun. A stiff breeze chased puffs of dust down the street behind them. Chisum drew rein at Brady's office and stepped down. He looped a rein over the rail and led the way to the boardwalk step. Caneris hurried to keep pace with the boss man's purposeful stride. The office door swung open. Bright sunlight muted to a shadowy amber glow. Brady sat at his desk.

"Afternoon, John, what can I do for you?" Brady knew the question was pointless. He knew what Chisum had on his mind. The big rancher wasn't going to like what he was about to hear.

"Afternoon, Sheriff. One of my boys tells me you let Frank Baker go. Is that right?"

"It is."

Chisum bent over Brady's desk, inches from his nose. "You let a murderin' rustler go just like that. What the hell's goin' on?"

Brady rocked his chair back defensively. "District attorney dropped the charges for lack of evidence."

Chisum went scarlet. "Lack of evidence? Bullshit! We caught the son of a bitch red-handed. You got the sworn statement of my man on that."

"I also got a sworn statement from Frank says it was the other way around. He says he caught your man tryin' to run off some of his stock. That's why he was chasin' him when you caught up with them."

"Baker's lyin', Brady, and you know it. That Seven Rivers bunch makes a business out of stealin' my stock. We finally catch 'em at it and you're tellin' me the law's going to look the other way."

"It's one man's word against another's, Chisum. That's how the district attorney sees it."

"The word of a murderin' rustler you mean."

"The word of your freedman." Brady folded his arms across his chest bringing the matter to a close.

Chisum straightened, clenching his fists at his sides. A small vein throbbed at his temple. "The next time I catch some of those boys stealin' my cattle, we'll deal with 'em my way. Murphy and Dolan got a sweet deal sellin' my cattle to the army and the reservation. I can smell their stink all the way to Santa Fe. They own you, and their friends own Rynerson. You best watch your step, Brady. I've had about as much of you and your handlers as I'm gonna take."

"Don't threaten me, Chisum! You take the law into your own hands and you'll find out you ain't near so big as you think."

"Why you no-good two-bit tin star, I got a mind to beat the livin' hell out of you here and now."

He started around the desk. Caneris stepped in front of him. "Easy, boss. Not here. Not now. The House holds all the cards."

"I listened to you the last time, Wade. Look where it got us."

"I understand. I'm just tellin' you dustin' the floor with the likes of him ain't gonna improve matters."

Chisum glared at his ramrod. He eased back and cut his eyes to Brady cold as ice. "You get my message and you get it good, Brady. I've had all I'm gonna take from the lot of you. You tell Murphy and Dolan. They keep tradin' in stolen beef, they're gonna have a war on their hands."

Chapter Nine

Raton Pass

Wootton's twenty-seven-mile toll road wound its way over Raton Pass. Ledger set a good pace for the promise of a drink, a good meal and a bed. The road made the passage possible by wagon and an easy ride on horseback. Still the mountain remained a demanding climb, the fatiguing effects of the heights noticeable to man and beast alike. They stopped to rest the horses more often than usual. Setting sun lit the western peaks crimson and purple as they drew rein at the tollgate that marked the end of Wootton's road. Beyond the gate a two-story adobe inn and tavern stood to the side of the road. Further down the slope in the shallow valley where Wootton's turnpike rejoined the overland trail, a small wagon train bedded down for the night shrouded in blue shadow.

A boy of about twelve ran across the yard to greet them. "That'll be twenty-five cents each," he said as he worked the gate latch to let them through.

Ledger fished the coins out of his pocket and tossed them to the boy. "You can buy us a drink, Johnny."

Roth nodded at the suggested bargain.

"Stable's back of the inn." The boy pointed to a rough-cut log outbuilding and corral. "I'll put your horses up if you like. Fifty cents each for the night."

Roth smiled picking up on the pattern. "You're a right enterprising young lad, aren't you, boy." He squeezed up a trot through the gate.

They crossed the yard and stepped down at the corral as the boy ran up to take their reins. Ledger produced a dollar and handed the steel dust's rein to the boy. He untied his saddlebags and slung them over his shoulder. "Drink's gettin' more expensive by the minute."

Roth laughed. "Let's get to it."

They clumped up the steps in the gathering gloom to a broad covered veranda that stretched the length of the inn. Inside oil lamps gave the tavern and registration desk a warm glow. A stout man of stern countenance stood behind the desk. Long graying hair bobbed above the shoulder receded from a broad forehead and prominent nose. Penetrating dark eyes sized up the arrivals. His wide mouth turned down at the corners, forming the suggestion of a dour disposition. "Wootton's the name, Richens Lacy Wootton. My friends call me Uncle Dick." Nothing about Wootton's appearance suggested the comfortable familiarity of an uncle. "What can I do for you?"

Ty extended his hand. "Ty Ledger, this here's Johnny Roth. We could use a drink, a room and a hot meal."

"We got all that." Wootton spun the guest register around for them to sign. "The room's a dollar each. Drinks and food are served in there." He jerked his head toward the tavern room on the right. A small group of travelers sat at a cluster of tables eating their evening meal. "You're in room two, top of the stairs on the left. Stow your gear and I'll see you in the tavern."

Minutes later Ty and Johnny ambled into the tavern room. The adobe walls gave off a warm glow of candlelight and evenly spaced wall lamps. Uncle Dick stood behind the bar polishing a glass he held up to the light. A clean white apron circled his girth softening a stern demeanor that could have stood for a brimstone preacher. "What'll it be boys? Folks around here favor Taos lightning." He managed a smile.

"Whiskey." Ledger glanced at Roth.

He shrugged. "Make it two."

Uncle Dick shook his head. "No sense of adventure." He set two glasses on the bar and poured a good three-finger drink. "That'll be a dollar."

Roth flipped a ten-dollar gold piece on the bar. "Leave the bottle."

Wootton scooped up the coin. "What brings you boys to New Mexico?"

Roth swirled the whiskey in his glass. "We're on the trail of a killer."

"Bounty hunters?"

"I am. Ty here is a deputy US marshal."

"Interesting partners."

"We're interested in different things." Roth took a swallow. "You see or hear anything of a half-breed with one eye passin' this way?"

"No, can't say I have. Who'd he kill?"

"Two women we know of so far. Tried another in Denver a couple of weeks back. That one shot him a little bit for his trouble. Uses a knife on 'em when he's had his sport."

Wootton paused, wiping a beer mug. "I may have heard something that might help after all. Give me a minute."

He came around from behind the bar and crossed the tavern to a table just finishing supper. He whispered something in the ear of a bearded man dressed in buckskins at the head of the table. The man glanced at Roth and Ledger, pushed his chair away and followed Wootton back to the bar. His lean rawboned frame, sun-hardened features and rough dress gave him the look of a mountain man.

"This here's Able Cross." Uncle Dick tossed his head at the man. "He's guiding the wagon train camped down below. Able, these men are on the trail of a man might have something to do with them two you lost." He returned to polishing glasses behind the bar.

"Mr. Cross, Ty Ledger. This here's Johnny Roth."

Cross shook Ledger's hand then Roth's.

Roth offered the bottle. "Care for a drink, Mr. Cross?"

"Don't mind if I do. Best call me Able, then."

Uncle Dick set a glass on the bar.

Roth poured.

"Mind tellin' us what happened?" Ledger said.

"We lost a young couple on the trail three days ago. They fell behind, like they done most every day on account a them oxen they was drivin'. We didn't think much of it. They usually caught up when we stopped for the night. Couple of nights ago, they never came in. Next morning I checked the back trail myself. That's when we found 'em. The husband had been shot. The wife . . ." His voice trailed off.

"Gutted," Roth said, his voice barely audible.

Cross arched an eyebrow. "How'd you know?"

"The man we're after leaves them that way."

Cross cut his eyes from Roth to Ledger. "We found her tied to the wagon wheel neked. I took it for Apaches the way she was cut until I saw sign."

Roth caught Ledger's eye. "Well, I guess we still got his trail."

Ledger nodded and turned to Cross. "What sign?"

"Lone rider on a shod horse."

"Which way did he go?"

"We followed the trail south a half mile or so before it turned southwest, tracking the Santa Fe Trail. He knew they were stragglers. He made sure he gave the main body a wide berth. I hope you boys get the son of a bitch. Animal like that deserves no better'n what he gives."

Ledger turned to the bar. He had the picture. A sour ball

gathered in his gut. He could feel the opportunity of a good meal about to go to waste. They needed to catch this hombre and soon. Every day he ran free innocent women were at risk to die. He gazed at his glass. What would make a man do such a thing? The worst killers in nature killed for food or survival. At least they had reasons. This animal seemed like he killed for the sport of it. He knocked back his drink and poured another.

Roth clapped Cross on the shoulder. "Much obliged, Able. You've been a big help." He turned back to the bar. Ty had that look. He'd seen it when they left the graveside. He'd never seen anything like it before. He could understand some. Not enough by the look of it. He wore vengeance like a scar. He wondered if the killer's blood could wash away that kind of rage. He doubted it.

Chapter Ten

South Spring Ranch
Rio Pecos Valley

Oppressive heat burned off some in early evening. Caneris's boots crunched the parched scrabble as he crossed the yard to the main house. He wondered what the boss had on his mind at this hour. If he had something to discuss, he usually let it wait until morning. He could make out Chisum's dark form seated in a rocking chair in the shadows on the porch. He sat silent as Caneris climbed the step.

"You wanted to see me, John?"

"I do, Wade. Pull up a chair. It's cooler out here."

Caneris scraped a heavy wooden chair across the rough-cut planks and set it across from Chisum. He sat heavily at the end of a long day. "What can I do for you?" The question hung in the air unanswered as though the boss were thinking it over. He sent for him for a reason. He must have something on his mind. Finally he spoke.

"You're right about Murphy and Dolan. They do hold all the cards. That bunch down on Seven Rivers fill their government contracts with my beef and the law won't lift a finger." He paused. Night sounds filled the silence. A horse whickered softly out toward the corral.

Caneris read serious purpose behind the observation. Things were about to take on some new direction. "What do you figure on doing about it?"

"We're going to hire some men."

The notion didn't surprise Caneris. Still he wanted to be sure he understood. "We've got our usual summer crew."

"I don't mean stockmen. I mean gunmen."

There's gonna be a war. "Plannin' on trouble's likely to bring it. What about going to the US marshal in Santa Fe?"

Chisum weighed the idea against the night sounds. "John Sherman is a fair-minded man, but Santa Fe is a long way from South Spring."

"Maybe he'd send a deputy down here."

"What good would one man do? Murphy and Dolan have the boys down on Seven Rivers. The sheriff and his deputies are in their back pocket. We're outgunned, Wade. A deputy US marshal wouldn't leave us any better off than we are now."

"He could deputize some boys."

"Rustlin', murder and such are local offenses. Not much call for federal jurisdiction. No it's up to us to teach them murderin' rustlers a lesson. They figure out that stealin' Long Rail stock is bad for their health, they'll stop soon enough. You put the word out up to Fort Sumner and down on the Tularosa. John Chisum's hirin' competent men."

Caneris set his jaw and pushed his chair back with a scrape. "We'll get to it first thing tomorrow, John." He had a bad feeling about this, a real bad feeling.

Santa Fe Trail

Lucy never considered there could be advantages to mules. Sitting atop the wagon box she watched harsh terrain pass through a forest of twitching ears. These ungainly-looking cousins to the horse had a reputation for being stubborn. What more could a body possibly need to know? She might have just as easily booked passage with a freighter driving a team of oxen. They were every bit as common on the trail south. Now as the long, hot, dusty miles rolled by in endless succession, the fluid strides of Captain Cory's mule team seemed brisk by comparison to the plodding, bawling teams of stinking oxen they passed. The team of matched bays, a Jack and three Jennies never entered her decision to book passage with Cory. That distinction belonged to the old muleskinner himself.

If Cory had another name Lucy didn't know it. Cory could be his given name or surname. It didn't matter. She doubted the crusty old gent in the dusty gray coat seated beside her ever captained anything more than this wagon. Likely he'd promoted himself from the Confederate ranks after the war. She booked passage to Santa Fe with him for two reasons. While he was in Denver, he'd bothered to bathe. That set him apart from most freighters including the bullwhackers who made their way driving oxen. A bath and the fact he called her a respectful *Miss Lucy.* She liked that. She doubted he'd be much protection on the trail. The old cap-and-ball, single-action army revolver he wore butt-forward in the scuffed military-style holster with the tarnished button stamped CSA probably wouldn't fire reliably, let alone hit anything. The single-shot rifle stuffed in the wagon boot at his foot still used paper cartridges. The notable security Captain Cory provided was the fact that he treated her like a lady. That suited certain personal resolutions she'd made as part of her decision to head south.

The wagon creaked and jolted down the rough-worn trail to the jangle of harness brass and Cory's colorful admonishments and encouragements to the team. After jostling for what seemed like an eternity of hot dust and bruises, the Santa Fe Trail swept out of the northeast toward the Raton Pass turnpike junction.

"Will you be taking the turnpike, Captain Cory?" Lucy figured she knew the answer, but she felt obliged to ask nonetheless.

Cory shook his head. A man of few words, he reserved most

of them for his mules.

"It's a good deal shorter and likely an easier passage."

"Ain't payin Wootton's toll."

"Oh, for heaven's sake, I'll pay the toll. The chance of a good meal and a proper bed are more than worth the fee."

"Gotta pay fer them too. My cookin's free."

"Not free, Captain, it's merely included in the fare I paid. I say we take the high road and enjoy the comforts of Mr. Wootton's hospitality."

"Suit yourself, Miss Lucy. It's highway robbery if you ask me."

South Spring Ranch

Chisum stood on the porch, squinting into the shimmer of late afternoon sun. Two shadows resolved out of the glare. Little more than dark specks at first they took shape as the riders drew closer. He measured the distance to the rifle rack beside the door. He didn't expect trouble, but in these times a man couldn't be too careful. Recollection flickered in his eye. Josiah "Doc" Scurlock might have been mistaken for a schoolteacher. Chisum remembered a sober young man with a prominent nose, mustache and chiseled cheekbones. He wore a dark frock coat pushed open behind the butts of his guns as was his habit. The pair drew rein in front of the porch.

"Doc, what brings you back to South Spring?"

"Afternoon, Mr. Chisum, me and Charlie here heard up to Fort Sumner you was hirin'. Business ain't been too good of late. I thought you might take us on. This here's Charlie Bowdre. Charlie, meet John Chisum."

"Pleased to meet you, Mr. Chisum."

Chisum nodded. He couldn't find anything special to recommend the man. Plain featured and average of appearance in every respect, he had questioning eyes and a mustache that drooped to a weak chin. He wore a double-breasted shirt, baggy canvas britches and a Colt .44 holstered butt-forward on his left hip. Chisum turned back to Scurlock.

"We're not punchin' cows this time, Doc. We're hirin' guns."

"So we heard. What's the play?"

"Jesse Evans and them Seven Rivers boys of his have become intolerable. The law's in Murphy and Dolan's pocket. The sheriff won't do nothin' to stop the rustlin.' They killed one of my hands the last time they hit our herds. I'm fixin' to do something about it myself."

"Evans still doin' Dolan's dirty work, is he?"

Chisum nodded.

"Some things don't change much." He let his gaze drift south in the general direction of Seven Rivers. "Well if you're lookin' for men, I got no love lost for Evans."

The rancher puckered his mustache around a nod. "If Bowdre here can use that gun near as good as you, the pay's fifty dollars a month and keep."

Scurlock leaned sidesaddle and spit. "I'll vouch for Charlie watchin' my back."

"Good enough for me. Head on over to the bunkhouse and look up Wade Caneris. Wade ramrods the cattle side of the outfit. Tell him I said he should find you boys a place to stow your gear."

Scurlock touched the brim of his hat, wheeled his horse and set off across the yard at a trot.

That's two. Chisum turned to the house to see about supper.

Chapter Eleven

Santa Fe

Santa Fe nestled in the foothills at the southern tip of the Sangre De Cristos on the banks of the Santa Fe River. Church spires and adobe architecture gleamed against faultless blue sky proclaiming the city's rich Hispanic and religious traditions. The center of governments past and present occupied the dusty corners of Lincoln and Palace Avenue. The single-story adobe-and-tile Mexican Palace held the northwest corner next to the quadrangle known as the Government Corral to the west. The more-recent two-story headquarters of the New Mexico territorial government stood on the opposite corner across Lincoln to the south.

Patch lounged in the shade of a covered boardwalk across Palace from Government House. After two days he felt caged by the civility of the territorial capital. So many men in suits made him restless for the lawless border territory further south. Santa Fe, however, had one attraction that held his interest. Brown-skinned Mexican and Navajo women ripe with promise walked the streets in brightly colored skirts. He savored the familiar anticipation coursing in his blood. He ambled south on Palace toward Grant, searching for a cantina.

He couldn't read the sign. The words *El Lobo* were painted over the picture of a wolf. He felt a brotherhood with the wolf. His brother called him to the cantina door. Inside, the thick adobe walls provided relief from the heat of the day. Dim light pooled on the hard packed dirt floor beneath the open windows and the door shaded by a covered boardwalk. The bartender polished a glass with a rag too stained for the work.

A lone vaquero dressed in black sat at a corner table. His chair tipped back against the wall, his boots propped on the tabletop. Window light played on silver spurs and conchos in his hatband. Ivory-handled revolvers slung at each hip. He smoked a cigarillo, his dark eyes hooded behind a cloud of smoke. A jagged scar, earned in a knife fight, sliced his left cheek. He had a thin black mustache, accenting the downward turn of a cruel mouth. A shock of black hair fell across his forehead beneath the brim of his sombrero.

Patch chose a table across the room where he could keep an eye on the pistolero. A rustle of skirt floated to his side. He cocked his good eye at the fine figure of a woman silhouetted in shadow and light. Dark hair hung in loose waves to her shoulders. The dim light revealed creamy copper swells veiled beneath a white cotton blouse. Shadow claimed the dark rise with each breath. Her eyes glittered. He felt her heat. His mouth went dry, his chest tight. "Taquila."

She turned to the bar with a flounce of skirt and a fluid sway in her hips. The pistolero followed her with his eyes. The bartender poured. The pistolero scraped his boots off the tabletop and rocked his chair forward. The dark-eyed woman turned to Patch his drink in hand. Her bare feet padded the dirt floor to the rhythm of those hips. She bent to place the glass before him. He felt her heat again. The scent of her filled him.

A silver dollar hit the table with a clatter, breaking the moment. The pistolero snaked an arm around the woman and pulled her to him possessively. "Maria, let me buy my compadre here his drink."

Patch sat back, his hand dropping to the hilt of his knife.

"I wouldn't try that if I were you, amigo." The pistolero smiled a crooked smile.

Patch reached for his glass and lifted it in toast. "Muchas gracias."

The woman scooped up the coin and twisted away in a pout.

"Hot tempered that one." The pistolero jerked his head after her. "She requires a strong hand. My hand." He let his words linger. "So, amigo, what brings you to Santa Fe?"

As a rule Patch avoided casual conversation. In this case he would make an exception. He had no desire to provoke this man's guns. If he needed to kill him, better to do it with a knife in his sleep. He also needed information. "I am traveling south in search of work."

"What kind of work?"

"Work that pays."

The pistolero laughed. In a blink he drew his pistol, spinning it to full cock. He leveled it at Patch's good eye. "You mean work like this?"

"If it pays."

The pistolero nodded. "Ride southeast to the Pecos. Follow the river south to Seven Rivers. Find Jesse Evans. Tell him Crystobal sends you. He will have work for you."

"Again, muchas gracias." Patch drained his glass.

Crystobal smiled. "Maria, more taquila."

The woman hurried to the table with two fresh glasses. She set them down quickly and scurried away.

The pistolero raised his glass, knocked back his drink and slammed the glass on the table with a crack. "One more thing, compadre, leave Santa Fe before Maria gives me reason to lose my generous humor with you." He flicked his cigarillo to the dirt floor, turned on his heel and stalked back to his corner table. He tipped his chair back, propped his boots on the table and pushed his sombrero over his eyes.

South Spring Ranch

Caneris fitted the split rail into a notch in the corral fence post. He paused to mop his brow with a bandanna. Fence-mending made for hard work on a hot day. He bent over the nearby water bucket and ladled himself a cool drink. He splashed the dregs over his face and wiped the wash away. His vision cleared. Down the road three riders turned into the gate and jogged toward him. You could see the cold ready edge on 'em at a hundred yards. The boss would have himself a small army at the rate they were signing on.

The trio drew rein. A tall, rough-shaved hombre with a double rig appeared to be the leader. "We're lookin' for John Chisum."

Caneris jerked a thumb toward the ranch house.

The man touched the brim of his hat with a nod. The trio rode on to the house and stepped down.

Frank McNab stretched his six-foot frame and handed his rein to Big Jim French. "You boys wait with the horses." He clumped up the porch step, squared his shoulders and rapped on the front door. Inside, boots scraped the plank floor. The door swung open.

"Mr. Chisum?"

"Yeah." The stranger had clear blue eyes and a square jaw.

"Frank McNab's the name. We heard you was hirin' good men."

Chisum glanced over McNab's shoulder. Two men stood in the yard holding horses. One looked to be mixed blood with dark features and black hair. A bull of a man he had powerful shoulders and a barrel chest. The other, younger man had a ruddy face splashed with freckles and an unruly shock of red hair. Altogether he gave the impression of a mischievous prankster.

"The big one's Jim French. We call him Big Jim. The other's Tom O'Folliard." O'Folliard flashed a crooked grin as if he knew he were the subject of the conversation. "If you need good men, you couldn't do no better than us."

"I'll be the judge of that, Mr. McNab."

"Mind if I ask what the job is?"

"Rustlers, Jesse Evans and his thievin' crowd of Seven Rivers boys."

"And Dolan's law won't do a lick to stop 'em."

Chisum raised an eyebrow. "You catch on pretty quick, Mr. McNab. You handle those guns half as fast?"

"Some folks say. Them as doubted it, mostly don't say so no more. Please call me Frank."

"Them two worth their wages, Frank?"

"They wouldn't be ridin' with me if they weren't. Since you brought it up, what's this job pay?"

"Fifty dollars a month and keep."

McNab met Chisum's eyes level. "You want three good men, then?"

Chisum nodded.

McNab extended his hand. "Much obliged, Mr. Chisum."

"Don't be." Chisum took his hand. "You'll earn your pay." *That makes five.*

Raton Pass
Santa Fe Trail

Uncle Dick's Inn and Tavern provided a welcome break from long days filled with trail dust and grit. The room was clean with a real bed. For fifty cents she'd purchased the luxury of a bath, a hot bath. She soaked away trail grime and the tangy scent of mule sweat. The tavern room served a hot meal seated at a table with a proper place setting and a real napkin. Good roast beef, potatoes fried crunchy and warm tortillas made a nice break from Captain Cory's hardtack, beans and assorted canned fare.

The dour-looking proprietor introduced himself as Uncle Dick. He looked more like a hanging judge than a welcoming innkeeper, until he revealed the jolly contradiction in his personality. She was the only guest in the inn that evening. Cory spared himself the cost of a room for the company of his mules. Uncle Dick saw no reason a woman shouldn't have a drink and certainly not alone. He cleared her supper dishes away and returned to the table with the whiskey bottle and a glass for himself.

He poured two glasses.

"Where you bound for?"

Lucy took a sip. "Santa Fe for a start."

"You have family there?"

She shook her head. "I lost my family some years ago crossing the Arkansas trying to get there. A friend of mine headed that way. It gave me the notion to finish the journey."

Wootton nodded. "What do you plan to do when you get there?"

Lucy shrugged. "I had a business up in Deadwood. I might start another or find some other line of work."

"Deadwood? Tough town from what I hear." He didn't pry at the line of business she might have been in. Pretty woman like that in a boomtown like Deadwood. The choices seemed limited. "You figure you'll catch up with your friend there?"

Lucy's gaze drifted off with the question. "Maybe."

"He must be something special."

She cut her eyes back to Uncle Dick. What made him say that? He knew. How did he know? His eyes read her thoughts. "He is."

He topped up their glasses. "Then I hope you find him. What's his name?"

"Ty Ledger. He came this way on the trail of a killer."

Wootton furrowed his brow. "He and his partner were here. We had a wagon train come in. They lost a straggler couple. Ledger said it sounded like the work of the man they was after. The woman . . ." Wootton cut his words.

"Was raped," Lucy finished.

"How'd you know?"

"He tried to attack me back in Denver. Got a bullet for his trouble. Too bad I'm not a better shot. If I was, this might all be over and that woman might still be alive."

"A body can't second-guess theirself on such things."

"I guess not. Any idea where Ty went?"

"The wagon master lost the killer's trail, but he was headed southwest. I'm guessin' you're headed for the right place to find your friend."

"I hope so."

Candlelight flickered over the blank page. She'd found it difficult to record her thoughts on the trail. Here she seemed able to catch up.

> *He'd been here. They'd both been here. The monster had taken another victim. Ty clung to his trail. Now it seems I too have joined in the hunt. Justice pursued evil. Or was it vengeance? Did it matter? The result would surely be the same. Or would it? Justice ended in vindication. Vengeance ended in something bitter, something less satisfying. What am I following here? Something good I hope. Good might come of justice. Of vengeance, who could say?*

She bit the tip of her pen in thought. Had she really undertaken this journey? Or might she awaken from some foolish dream. No she was awake all right. Perhaps addled in her thinking, but awake nonetheless. Little in life is certain. Nothing ventured the old saw went.

For good or ill, Ty Ledger, I'm coming.

Chapter Twelve

Santa Fe
July 1877

Ledger and Roth rode into Santa Fe at mid afternoon under a cloudless sky. Intense sunlight bleached the sky white and baked the adobe buildings lining the dusty street. Roth squinted against the shimmering glare as they jogged west on Washington Avenue toward the center of town. They drew rein at the corner of Washington and Palace.

Ty swept his gaze up one street and down another. "Be like lookin' for a needle in a haystack."

"Maybe not." Johnny tilted his chin down Palace. "We got help. You're a deputy US marshal. The territorial marshal's office should be down there somewhere around the government office. A little professional courtesy and we might find him or get some idea of where to look."

"You do think of everything don't you, Roth."

"Somebody's got to be the brains of this outfit." He wheeled south on Palace and squeezed up a trot.

They crossed Lincoln and drew rein in front of a two-story bleached adobe building. A tarnished brass plate beside the door proclaimed *Government House, New Mexico Territory.* They stepped down and dropped rein over a weathered rail, the whitewash cracked and peeled by harsh desert conditions. Ty led the way up the steps into a shaded lobby that afforded little relief from the heat. Signs pointed the way to the General Assembly chambers on the right, up the stairs to the governor's office, the US attorney's office and down the hall at the back of the first floor to the US marshal's office. Ty led the way.

The door to a small office stood open at the end of the hall. Inside a bored deputy dozed at a desk cluttered with wanted circulars and assorted court-related paperwork. A newly hung portrait of President Hayes hung on the wall beside the desk. Ty tapped the door frame, snapping the deputy awake.

He blinked and suppressed a yawn, smoothing his mustache in the web of his thumb and forefinger. He cocked an eye toward Ledger and Roth. "Ah, what can I do for you, boys?"

"Deputy Marshal Ty Ledger, I'd like to see the marshal."

"I'm marshal for New Mexico." A wiry little man with a red mustache appeared in a doorway at the opposite end of the office. He glanced from Ledger to Roth. "John Sherman, at your service." A nephew to the war hero General William Tecumseh Sherman, the family resemblance was noticeable. "What can I do for you?"

"Marshal, pleased to meet you. This here's my partner Johnny Roth. We're on the trail of a killer we believe may have come this way. We thought you might be able to help us."

"I'll do what I can. Come on in." Sherman led the way into his small office. He waved Ty and Johnny to two barrel-backed chairs. "Have a seat." He took his place at a rolltop desk cluttered with warrants and wanted posters. A single dusty window lighted the room. A map of New Mexico Territory hung on the wall opposite his desk. "What can you tell me about the man you're after?"

"One-eyed half-breed goes by the name Patch," Ty began. "He gets his women at knifepoint. Cuts them up when he's done."

Sherman shook his head dismissively sweeping his hand over the pile of paper on his desk. "I'd like to help you boys get an animal like that, but I'm afraid there's nothing here that fits what you're tellin' me. What makes you think he hit Santa Fe?"

Roth shifted in his chair. "We don't know for sure that he did. I've been followin' him south from Deadwood. His last victim was found up on the Santa Fe Trail. His trail headed this way until it petered out."

"Lots of people come down that trail. Unless he crossed the law here, we'd never know. Any idea why he'd come to Santa Fe?"

Roth shook his head. "Mostly he finds his victims in towns, Deadwood, Laramie, Cheyenne then Denver. He was headed this way when he caught up with the last one. Not much to go on other than the pattern, I'm afraid. Can you think of any suggestions?"

Sherman knit bushy eyebrows in thought. "He's half-breed you say."

Ty nodded.

"He'd probably pass for Mexican. You might ask around the cantinas. Someone might remember a man with one eye." Sherman lifted his chin in resignation. "I don't know what else to tell you boys. Sorry I couldn't be more help."

Ty rose to shake Sherman's hand. "It's a good thought, Marshal. A couple of his victims were working girls." For some reason he didn't want to think of Lucy Sample in more common terms than that.

Three days later they found their way back to Government House on Palace and Lincoln. They'd crossed Santa Fe from east to west, north to south with nothing to show for the effort. Ty tipped his hat to the back of his head, letting the hot early evening breeze dry his forehead. "What town needs this many saloons?"

Roth chuckled. "A man could lose himself here beyond bein' found."

"It seems like our boy might have done just that." Ty looked off to the west. "Lincoln here looks pretty respectable. I guess that makes it Grant Avenue tonight."

"What are the chances you'll find a saloon on a street named after Grant?"

Ty chuckled at the reference to the former president's fondness for liquor. He led the way across Lincoln to the boardwalk headed south on Palace. He spotted the sign from the corner of Palace and Grant. "El Lobo, sounds like him don't it?"

"It does. I'm almost over last night's thirst, must be time for another."

A small crowd of vaqueros stood at the bar or clustered around tables toward the back. A corner table at the front of the bar stood empty. Roth led the way to it. He pulled up a chair putting his back to the wall.

Ty took the chair across from him with his back to the door. He didn't see her cross the cantina to their table. The look in Roth's eyes announced her approach.

"This is Crystobal's table." She held her voice soft and low, heavy with warning.

Roth made a show of looking around. He shrugged. "Doesn't seem to be anyone here now. We'll just sit a spell. Besides Ol' Crys is a friend. After I saved his life he told me many times, 'Amigo, anything I have is yours.' " Roth's smile said *anything.*

"You saved Crystobal's life?"

"Sí."

She visibly relaxed. "He never told me. What will you have, señor?"

"Taquila, one for my friend too. You can call me Johnny. What's your name?"

"Maria."

"Maria, that's a pretty name, almost as pretty as you. Ol' Crys has good taste." She favored him with a smile that radiated heat. Her skirts swirled as she started for the bar. Roth watched the fluid sway of her hips. "Fine-lookin' woman."

"You didn't tell me you knew anybody in Santa Fe."

"I don't."

"But you just said you saved this Crystobal's life."

"I did."

"Roth, you don't make any sense."

"Sure I do. She thinks I know him so I'm safe."

"But you just said you saved his life."

"Haven't killed him yet, have I?"

Maria returned with their drinks. She set them on the table and prepared to return to the bar. Roth caught her by the hand. She slid beside him. He could feel the heat of her hip against his arm.

"My friend and I are looking for a man."

"We see many men here."

"Not like this one. He's half-breed, got one eye." Recognition flickered in her expression. "You know him?"

"Why are you looking for him?"

"He kills women."

Maria drew her free hand up to her throat. "He was here last week. He said he was looking for work. I think he is a pistolero."

Roth cut his eyes to Ty.

He set his jaw, his eyes pinched at the corners his breath taught. "He does his best work with a knife."

Roth turned back to Maria. "Do you know where he went?"

"Crystobal sent him to the Seven Rivers country. He said he might find work with a man there."

"Do you remember the man's name?"

Maria thought for a moment. "Crystobal called him Evans, I think. Yes, I remember, Jesse Evans."

"Good girl." Roth lifted his glass and drank. He favored her with his most fetching smile. "Now, bring us a bottle and a glass for yourself. You've been a big help. I'd like to show you how much I appreciate it."

Ty tossed off his drink. "I need some air. I'll see you back at the hotel, Johnny."

Outside evening shadows faded to deep blue and purple. The hot breeze felt fresh after the stale smoky air in the cantina. Ty walked back toward Palace, his boots beating a hollow tattoo on the boardwalk. He turned north on Palace for the two-block walk to Washington.

Long days on the trail with no end in sight dulled his rage. Now with some idea of where they would find Victoria's killer, his thirst for vengeance flared again like an ember stirred to light fueled by fresh air. He'd formed a picture of the killer, a greasy stinking brute. He imagined confronting him. What to say? The man had to know fear. He had to know death came for him at the hand of Victoria's avenger. How to kill him? The man had to know pain, Victoria's pain. Ty had no answers for these questions. He had only the burning need to answer them. He'd have time to think on the trail. He had time to plan. Make him fear. Make him remember. Inflict slow pain. Exact vengeance, he turned the words over beside his rage. Would it be enough? Could there ever be enough?

He turned west on Washington. The stately, three-story Palace Hotel dominated the north side of the street in the middle of the block. He climbed the steps to a broad veranda fronting the hotel and stepped into the richly appointed candlelit lobby. The hotel dining room beyond the registration desk on the left quieted after the busy dinner hour. A curved stairway ascended to the guest rooms past a dark wood paneled salon. Settees and easy chairs upholstered in brocades of blue and green invited guests to the comforts of the salon for refreshments and quiet conversation. Ty crossed the lobby toward the stairway his boot heels clicking the polished wooden floor.

"Why, Ty Ledger, imagine finding you here."

The soft throaty tones of a familiar voice halted Ty mid-step. He glanced over his shoulder toward the sound. She stood in the arched entry to the salon. He scarcely recognized her. She wore a simple gray dress fitted to her petite curves. A matching hat with a splash of feathers perched atop a pile of sable curls completed an elegant effect. Dim candlelight gave her features the soft glow of light cream. Her childlike dark eyes turned liquid as she measured him with a mischievous hint of amusement.

"Lucy, is that you?" For some reason the words seemed to catch in his throat.

She finished her smile. "Surprised to see me, handsome?"

"Why, yes, yes, I suppose I am." He turned back to the salon. She held out her hands and he took them. Small and delicate, they disappeared in his. Their quiet strength did not. "What brings you to Santa Fe?"

A wistful flicker danced at the corner of her eye. "I got bored in Denver. Have you caught your killer yet?"

"Not yet, but we're closin' in on him."

"Good. I wouldn't want you to waste too much time chasin' the past."

"Have you had supper yet?"

"I have, but if a gentleman were to offer a lady a sherry, I'd welcome the company."

"I think I'd like that." He offered his arm. She took it, her touch as light as a feather. He led her to a settee in the corner of the salon. She took a seat on one end. He took the wing chair at her elbow.

A black man in a starched white jacket appeared. "May I take your order, sir?"

"A sherry for the lady, I'll have whiskey."

"A lady," Lucy mocked. "You say it as though you mean it."

Ty held her eyes, filling the moment. "I do."

"I like that."

The waiter returned with a silver tray and set the drinks on the low table in front of them.

Lucy lifted her glass. "To New Mexico and new beginnings."

Ty lifted his glass and met her eyes, drawn to them in the way he remembered the first time they met back in Dodge. "To New Mexico." He touched his glass to hers and took a swallow.

"So, what makes you think you're closing in on your killer?"

"He was here about a week ago. He's on his way south to the Seven Rivers country. We think he's got a job down there with an outfit run by a man named Jesse Evans."

"South, toward Lincoln?"

"I expect we'll pass through Lincoln on the way."

Lucy smiled. "What a wonderful coincidence. I was thinking of going to Lincoln myself, but I had no notion of how I would get there. Mind if I ride along?"

"Ride along? How? We don't have a carriage."

"On a horse, silly. You put one foot in one stirrup and the other foot in the other stirrup. Sit your butt down and off you go."

"I don't know Lucy, Lincoln's a long ride. It's more than a hundred and fifty miles. Surely you can find a more comfortable ride."

Lucy straightened her back. Candlelight flashed in the determined dark center of her eyes. "Now hold on just a minute, Ty Ledger, let's don't go carryin' this lady thing too far. I'm quite comfortable on the back of a horse."

Ty raised his hands in mock surrender.

"Besides," she softened with that hint of a smile. "I much

prefer present company to the dusty, smelly mule skinner who brought me here from Denver."

"Thanks." He frowned. "I think. Have you got a horse?"

"I will by tomorrow morning."

He took her hand and drew her around the table. She stood beside his chair, her smoky eyes locked in his. She removed his hat, tossed it on the table and settled her hips in his lap. Heat radiated from the swell of bodice, warming his cheeks as she bent her lips to his, drawing a curtain of black tresses over his eyes. The moist tip of her tongue parted his lips. Musk assaulted his senses. Breath caught in his throat. She moved against him, ripe with promise.

"Maria! Get off him!"

The black-clad vaquero grabbed her by the hair and threw her to the floor against the bar. Her head hit with a smack.

"I will deal with you later, puta bitch!" He turned to Roth, black with rage. The veins in his neck throbbed, the scar on his cheek burned crimson. "So, amigo, you take Crystobal's table. You steal kisses from his woman. Have you so little respect for your life?"

"I don't know seems like she didn't mind givin' them kisses away. As for bein' your woman, who'd want to be woman to a man treats her like you just done?"

"Insolent pig, Crystobal shall take great pleasure in killing you."

Maria whimpered from the floor. "He said he was your friend. He said he saved your life."

"Shut up, slut! Crystobal has never seen this pig before."

"That don't mean I haven't saved your worthless life."

"Crystobal remembers his amigos. He would remember an amigo who saved his life. You, pig, are a liar. The only thing Crystobal hates worse than a pig is a liar."

"Liar? I ain't no liar. Hell, I ain't killed you yet, have I?"

Crystobal's hand snaked to his holster.

Roth's Colt flashed. The muzzle exploded in a burst of powder smoke. The heavy .44 bullet opened a dark hole in the pistolero's chest, narrowly missing his heart.

He staggered back, eyes wide in disbelief. Powder charge hung in the air. His pistol hit the floor with a dull thud. He toppled backward and lay still. Maria threw herself on his body, keening and wailing in loud sobs.

"I guess she was his woman after all. Sure had a strange way of showin' it." He holstered his gun and stood. He cocked his head to the bartender. "Send for the sheriff. Nobody leaves until he gets here."

The lamp wick trimmed to a mellow glow. Her gray traveling dress and hat hung on a peg beside the small dresser. Her riding clothes were carefully laid on the side chair. She sat on the bed at the night stand converted to a writing table. She opened her journal to a new entry. She half closed her eyes. A hundred fifty miles of rough country stretched out in her mind, five maybe six days of possibilities on the trail. The prospect filled her with excitement. She was going with him, but with him to where? Lincoln? Who knew what that meant? She was going with him. Who knew where that might lead? It wasn't the where so much as the going. She caressed the blank page with her finger composing her thoughts.

I found him in Santa Fe. He seemed glad to see me. We talked. I felt it again. I think he may have too. Tomorrow we are leaving for Lincoln. I'm riding with him. This page feels like the beginning of a new story. I don't know where it leads. Who knows how it might end? All I know is it feels new. This is why I left Denver. It was the right thing to do . . .

Chapter Thirteen

South Spring Ranch

The rambling adobe hacienda with its tiled roof said this rancher must be very rich. The bunkhouse, stables and corrals sprawled across a broad yard on the road to a gateway arch further to the south. Patch approached the ranch from the northwest. He would strike the Pecos River further to the east and follow it south to Seven Rivers. Such a fine hacienda must hold much treasure, how many valuable prizes he could only wonder. It might also be heavily guarded, though the yard seemed quiet in the distance. He could not pass the possibility of such plunder without taking a closer look. He circled south keeping to the low places out of sight of the ranch until he found an arroyo to hide his pony. He melted into the rocks and sage, working his way through the hills for a closer look. He moved cautiously. As he neared the rear of the house he paused to listen. A soft gurgle told him water must be nearby. He found a low rise from which he could observe the back of the house through a thicket of tall waving grass.

A woman in the brightly colored skirt and plain white blouse of a peon tended a small garden behind the hacienda. As Patch crept closer he could see the dark copper skin of an Indio or Mexican. Long black hair covered her face catching the sun as she bent to her weeding. The vision stirred his medicine. She straightened from her picking. She was young by the alert turn of her breasts, a fine prize even if there were no riches inside the hacienda. Treasure there must be. Gold, some silver, maybe jewels, who could say? His chest filled with anticipation. His breathing grew shallow. He felt her struggle. She is strong. He sensed no fear in her. She would fight like a lioness. Such fighting pleased him. He savored the conquest in his mind's eye.

Dawn Sky felt it. A disturbing presence she could not explain. It was strong and sour, like some great predator. She stood and turned toward it. She saw nothing. Evil washed over her. She sensed hungry eyes hidden in the heat shimmers on the hillside. Something must be there. She straightened her lean frame. She shaded her eyes with a hand to her forehead. She searched the rocks and sage for a shape, something that didn't belong there. Nothing moved beyond the gentle caress of the wind. She heard nothing save the sound of the creek and the buzzing of bees sampling the fare in her garden. What accounted for the evil disturbance in the quiet of her spirit?

Patch put his vision aside. Something disturbed her. She could not have seen or heard him, yet suddenly she became watchful. She looked for something. She stood in the shimmering heat, searching the rocks and scrub where he lay hidden. Someone may be coming. Someone he could not see, someone coming behind him. He listened, afraid to move. He heard nothing. Someone coming from the west might discover his pony. A fly buzzed near his ear. It settled on his cheek below his good eye. He fought the urge to wave it away.

The woman turned toward the corral and bunkhouse. Patch chanced a look behind him, chasing the fly from his cheek as he did. He saw nothing. He released the breath he'd been holding. He turned back to the woman. A large black man walked toward her from the bunkhouse. He dressed like a cowboy. He carried a gun. Patch took advantage of the distraction. He backed away, before both of them could begin looking for him. He reached the safety of a dry wash and hurried back to the arroyo and his pony.

Swain sensed something was wrong. The way she stood, still as a post staring into the hills. He let his eyes follow hers. Nothing. He stretched his stride coming to her side.

"What is it, Miss Dawn?"

Her breath eased. The big black man made her feel safe. She liked him. "Dawn Sky felt something out there, something evil." She lifted her chin to the northwest.

"You think a varmint maybe?"

She shook her head and shrugged. "It is gone now."

"Don't you fret none, Miss Dawn. Ol' Deac'll go have a look." He touched the brim of his hat, hefted the Henry rifle to his shoulder and set off to the west.

An hour later, a quarter mile northwest of the hacienda he found fresh horse droppings in a shallow arroyo. A boot print broken in the cracked dry wash pointed back to the house. Someone had been there. Nearby he found a hoofprint headed south.

Palace Hotel
Santa Fe

A man had to enjoy a good steak. The potatoes were fried crisp in the drippings, the biscuits fresh baked. The wine presented a decent vintage. He folded the white napkin and eased his chair back from the table. You had to enjoy a meal like that, but eating alone left a man time to ponder his troubles. By rights Alexander McSween shouldn't have had many. A lawyer with the reputation for an aggressive advocate, McSween specialized in other people's problems. He had a beautiful wife and an established frontier practice in Lincoln. In truth, Lincoln was the problem. It was the county seat and that promised a bright future for an ambitious lawyer when he arrived. The problem was growth, or more properly the lack of it. Lincoln, he soon learned, was a one-client town and so it remained today.

The partnership of Lawrence Murphy and James "Jimmy" Dolan controlled most of the commercial interests in Lincoln. Murphy's failing health resulted in Dolan buying him out this past spring, but that hadn't changed anything. The House, as its substantial mercantile establishment was known, controlled everything. If he didn't work for Dolan all that remained of his practice were small land dealings. He'd gotten on fine with Murphy. Recently relations with Dolan had become strained over the matter of an insurance claim that hadn't settled to Dolan's satisfaction. The insurance dispute illustrated Dolan's problem. He and Murphy were smart businessmen, to a point. They reasoned rightly that selling to local landholders and businesses on credit would yield economic and political power. What they hadn't reckoned completely was the amount of cash it took to sustain such an enterprise. McSween had a way to solve that problem, but he couldn't see wasting it on the arrogant likes of Jimmy Dolan. He hated the thought of pulling up stakes, but unless something changed for the better, the situation in Lincoln would likely come to that.

He rose from the table. Not quite six feet tall, he wore a dark frock coat with matching trousers. An unruly shock of thick brown hair fell over his forehead. The quiet hum of conversation coming from the salon invited a drink before turning in. He crossed the polished lobby, his heels tatting staccato echoes. He eyed the dimly lit crowd, searching for a table or a lounge chair. All appeared occupied. He was about to give up when a young man at a table near the door stood.

"I say, I've an empty chair here if you care to join me."

The British accent sounded plainly out of place. The notion

of a foreigner in the territory capital piqued his curiosity. "That's very kind of you." He extended his hand. "Alexander McSween. May I buy you a drink?"

"John Tunstall. I've just ordered, but kind of you to offer." He signaled the waiter.

McSween appraised the young man as he drew back a chair. He affected a serious demeanor with the dignified bearing of British breeding. He had a refined manner, alert brown eyes and a prominent nose that gave his mouth the appearance of being small. He wore his wavy brown hair barbered about his collar and ears. He had a thin mustache with a patch of chin whiskers that might never rise to the stature of a beard.

A waiter in a starched white jacket appeared.

"Sir?"

"Whiskey."

"Very good, sir."

"So, Mr. Tunstall, you're British I take it."

"I am and please, call me John."

"Then you must call me Alex. You're a long way from home. What brings you to Santa Fe?"

"A bit of business I hope." The waiter arrived with the drinks. Tunstall lifted his glass. "Cheers."

"Cheers." McSween took a swallow. "May I ask what sort of business you're in?"

"You may. Just now I'm looking for a business to invest in. What do you do Alex?"

"I have a law practice."

"Ah, a barrister. Here in Santa Fe?"

"No, in Lincoln, about a hundred fifty miles south."

"Then you, sir, are also a long way from home."

"I suppose I am. Have you found a business that interests you?"

"Not really. I've some thoughts on land speculation, but I've yet to encounter the right piece of property. Santa Fe may be a bit too well established for the sort of opportunity I envision. Tell me about your Lincoln. I've not heard of it before."

"Lincoln is the largest county in New Mexico. The Pecos River valley makes it prime ranch land. Lincoln is the county seat."

"Those are all ingredients to opportunity."

"You would think they would be. Unfortunately the business community is dominated by a small group that controls everything."

Curiosity pecked at Tunstall. "How do they do that?"

"It starts with the mercantile. They operate the only store in the county. If you need something, you buy from The House at whatever price they think you should pay."

"The House?"

"Dolan operates a rather large mercantile. Locals call it The House."

"I see. Well that problem seems easily remedied. All you need is another mercantile and a bit of old-fashioned competition."

"Easier said than done. It takes money to do that."

"Yes, well that is where I might step in. I have capital to invest. I hadn't thought about a mercantile, but this House you describe sounds like an opportunity ripe for the picking. The ranch land in the area may also suit some of my other ideas."

"You're serious, aren't you?"

"Of course I'm serious. I told you I'm looking for a business opportunity."

McSween drained his glass. "In that case I have another thought for you, if you have the time." Tunstall nodded. "Then let me buy that drink I promised." He signaled the waiter. "It will take more than a mercantile to beat Dolan. He sells at exorbitant prices to be sure, but he gets his real power by selling on credit. Everybody owes him money. His problem is that he doesn't take in enough cash to finance all the credit he extends. It takes cash to keep the enterprise going."

"Yes, I can see that." The waiter arrived with the drinks.

McSween leaned across the table with a conspiratorial glint in his eye. "I know how to fix that."

Tunstall couldn't disguise his skepticism. "I have substantial resources, but there is a limit to my funds just as there is to this ah . . ."

"Jimmy Dolan."

"Yes, quite so."

"I can fix that."

Tunstall knit his brow. "Now, it's you who strike me as serious."

"I am."

"Just how, then, would you do that?"

He glanced about to assure himself no one was listening. "With a bank."

Tunstall sat back, letting the notion sink in. He broke into a broad grin. "By jove that's brilliant! A mercantile and a bank, capital idea!"

"Capital in more ways than one." McSween smiled.

"Yes, I believe I shall have to pay your Lincoln a visit. Of course I shall need legal services for anything I might do."

"When it comes to chartering a bank, you'll need more than legal services."

"Oh, how so?"

McSween sat back. "You'll need a partner."

Tunstall pursed his lips and nodded. "I see. Something of a head for business yourself, is it? You colonials are so quaint. Shall we drink to it, then?"

Chapter Fourteen

Seven Rivers

Patch scouted Jesse Evans's ramshackle ranch from the hills northeast of the valley. A broken-down split-rail fence set off a hardscrabble yard. The rambling house, thrown together from adobe and rough-cut timber had a shingled roof in need of repair. A run-down barn and corral in worse repair than the house clung to the south end of the yard. A long clapboard outbuilding between the barn and the house served as a bunkhouse. A covered porch ran the length of the bunkhouse north wall to a cook-shack at the back of the yard. Caution warned him against simply riding in without knowing what he was riding into. Men who hired men for work such as he sought were often as dangerous as the men they employed. For all he knew the man called Crystobal could be an enemy of this Jesse Evans. The mere mention of the name might sign his death warrant.

He waited and watched throughout the long afternoon. No one stirred at the ranch, save a few scrawny chickens pecking in the dirt yard. Even they disappeared by early afternoon, taking shelter from the afternoon sun. Toward evening four men rode in from the west returning from the day's labor. They unsaddled their horses and turned them out in the broken-down corral for water and graze. Soon evening cook-fire smoke rose from the shack chimney. It was time to ride in before darkness made his approach seem threatening. Patch stepped into his saddle and eased down the gentle slope to the ranch yard below.

Billy "Buck" Morton squinted east from the cookshack porch. "Rider comin'." Morton had a moon face, heavy jowls and small blue eyes lost in fat folds. He had the appearance of an overstuffed scarecrow. His belly rolled over his gun belt on narrow hips and spindly bowed legs. Stringy blond hair hung below an old derby hat that looked one size too small for the way it perched on his head, cocked at an odd angle.

Jesse Evans appeared on the porch fronting the house. Short and solidly built he had cropped dark hair, a square jaw, a generous mouth and a slightly crooked nose courtesy of a saloon brawl over a whore. Ladies found him fetching in that dangerous bad-boy way. He stared off to the north, sizing up the rider with a humorless expression. He wore a bibbed shirt, bracers and woolen britches. A .44 Colt rode butt-forward on his left hip.

"Frank, Buckshot, out the back and cover us." Boots inside the house followed the order. The backdoor slammed as the men spread out.

The rider drew rein at the gate. "Hello the house. I'm lookin' for Jesse Evans."

"You found him. State your business."

"Man up to Santa Fe said I might find work here."

"What man?"

"Called himself Crystobal."

Evans glanced at Morton. Morton shrugged. "Boys, show our visitor the little reception we made for him." Frank Baker and Buckshot Roberts stepped out from behind opposite sides of the house and barn. Baker leveled a Winchester at Patch. Roberts held a sawed-off shotgun. "Now ride in with your hands where we can see them."

Patch urged his pony forward at a walk, holding his hands plainly visible. He drew rein in front of the porch.

Morton eyed him up. "None too pretty, is he?"

Evans grunted. "Crystobal sent you?"

"He said you might have work for me."

"What kind of work you do?"

Patch paused. "I don't keep my hands in plain sight."

Evans laughed. "Never know when that might come in handy."

"We know Chisum's hirin'," Roberts said. Buckshot Roberts earned his nickname courtesy of a shotgun wound to his right shoulder. Lean and gnarled as a hickory stick, he wore a wide brimmed slouch hat with a round crown over a shaggy mop of gray hair. He had lean chiseled features, weathered and lined, with a heavy drooping mustache. Thick eyebrows shading watery blue eyes met over the bridge of a hawk-like nose.

"So they say." Evans pursed his lips. Crystobal might be an arrogant bastard, but he was a competent arrogant bastard. An extra gun might indeed come in handy. "What's your name?"

"Patch."

"Patch. That's it?"

"Don't need no more."

"All right, we'll give you a try. If you earn your keep, you can stay. Buck, show Patch here the bunkhouse."

White Oaks
New Mexico Territory

Sun flared on the western peaks, turning the clouds crimson and pink. Purple and blue shadow spilled into sandstone hills and draws sculpted by the centuries, cloaking them in the muted onset of evening. Ty signaled a halt on the bank of a creek. The creek bottom provided graze for the horses where it passed through a stand of white oak and juniper. The stream gurgled with the last ripples of spring runoff slowly flowing into summer.

He watched Lucy step down from the buckskin mare she called Buttercup. They bought the horse for her the morning they left for the ride down to Lincoln. She sat her horse well and offered no complaint for the heat or long days in the saddle. The girl who looked out of place in the paint and frilled finery of her saloon-girl life seemed comfortable in the plain spun blouse and long skirt she wore on the trail.

He stepped down from the steel dust and took Buttercup's rein. "I'll look after the horses, while you get a start on gatherin' wood for a fire."

By the time Ty and Johnny had the horses watered and picketed for the night Lucy had a fire built, coffee brewing and a skillet of fatback sizzling beside it.

Roth spread his saddle and blanket beside the fire and poured a cup of coffee. He settled down with his cup. "Just like home."

Ty paused, spreading Lucy's blanket. "You ain't had much home if fatback and hardtack on the trail fill the bill."

"That may be so, Ty, but what's missing is more than made up by your pleasant and amusing company."

Lucy heard the lonely echo in Ty's comment. "Johnny just appreciates what he's got here and now."

"Right you are, girl. It makes for a more pleasurable evening than turnin' sour over what you don't have."

Ty let it pass. Roth might be right, but that didn't do anything to lift his spirits.

Lucy served the boys plates of fatback and hardtack, poured herself a cup of coffee and sat down on her blanket with her plate.

Roth eyed her across the fire. "So what are you plannin' to do once we hit Lincoln?"

She shrugged. "I don't rightly know. I've got time. I'll figure something out."

"Hell, I bet Lincoln's got a saloon."

She shot him a sharp glance. "Not for me, Johnny. I'm finished with that."

A fire crackle or the occasional scrape of hardtack on a plate passed for conversation the rest of the meal. When they finished Ty gathered up the plates and went off to rinse them in the creek. Lucy stoked the fire. Johnny propped his head on his saddle and settled down for the night.

Ty washed the plates and set them aside. He sat on the grassy bank with the gurgle of the creek and night sounds for company. The barest sliver of a moon rose in the east. Stars came out, glittering brightly like a field of diamonds strewn across a black velvet blanket. How many times had he and Victoria sat on their porch and admired such a sky? He felt alone, lost in the quiet beauty of the night. Times like this the loss confronted him. You couldn't put it aside for the promise of vengeance. The time he'd spent with Victoria seemed so full of promise with the baby coming and all. Bright life one morning turned to ashes by nightfall. So sudden, so cruel, he tamped his grief in a quest for vengeance. It gave him purpose to get past the moment. It drove him through the days that followed. Now they had a destination. He'd find his man at a place called Seven Rivers. He tried to picture the scene. He wanted to feel the relief that would come from killing the monster. He couldn't. Times like these anger and vengeance did not fill the void. Times like these neither one was enough.

"You miss her a great deal don't you?" Lucy's buttery tone made it more statement than question.

Ty glanced up. He'd been so lost in his thoughts, he hadn't heard her approach. Starlight caught liquid in his eye. He nodded.

She sat beside him, smoothed her skirt and folded her hands in her lap. Night sounds surrounded them. The creek gurgled. Crickets chirped. A coyote sang a distant song. "You know killing him won't bring her back."

He cut his eyes to her profile shaded in starlight and shadow. It was as though she read his thoughts. "It's something I've got to do."

"I know that. Just don't expect that killing him will make things right for you." She folded her legs up under her skirt. "Grief has to run its course. You have to let it."

He looked into her eyes. "Lucy, I . . ."

She put her finger to his lips. "Hush now. There's nothing you need to say to me. I've got time. Just make sure you leave some for yourself."

His chin dropped, his eyes averted. His shoulders sagged.

She knelt beside him, wrapped her arms around him and hugged him to her breast. He shuddered racked by a silent sob. She held him. *It's a start.* She ran her fingers through his hair. *Men, the good ones at least, are just little boys who get big.*

Lincoln

J. J. Dolan & Company

The bell over the door clanged, announcing the arrival of a customer. The shriveled little clerk behind the counter turned to the door, his feather duster paused over a shelf facing of canned tomatoes. The new arrival stood silhouetted in bright sunlight, his shadow cast across the dimly lit plank floor. The clerk blinked owlishly behind smudged spectacles and adjusted the garter holding up one sleeve. Dust mites floated in the muted splashes of sunlight pouring through the streaked front windows, testimony to the futility of dusting the shelves. The customer closed the door and crossed to the counter.

"Afternoon, Mr. Evans, what can I do for you today?"

"Got a list of supplies, Jasper." Evans pushed the penciled list across the counter. "Dolan around?"

"I am." Jimmy Dolan emerged from his office at the back of

the store. "Come in. I've got a matter to discuss while Jasper fills your order. Your visit saves me sending word down to Seven Rivers."

Evans followed Dolan into his comfortably appointed office. "Have a seat. Care for a cigar?"

Evans took one from the box Dolan offered. He bit the tip and flicked a lucifer to light on his thumbnail. He lit Dolan's cigar, then puffed his own, billowing a cloud of blue smoke.

Dolan settled into his desk chair. Bright sunshine poured through the window at his back shielding his expression in shadow. "We've got a little job for you, Jesse. I've got an order for a hundred fifty head of cattle for Fort Stanton. It's worth five dollars a head if you supply them."

"Your price is twenty dollars a head delivered. We know where the money goes Dolan."

"Yes, well, Jesse, you must understand we have business expenses to cover."

"And the army hasn't got an alternative supplier to feed the Mescaleros. My price is going up. Chisum's hiring guns. Filling your orders just got more expensive. I need eight dollars a head to cover my expenses."

"Eight dollars! Why that's highway robbery."

"You get what you pay for, Dolan. You can take it out of your little arrangement with Sheriff Brady for all the good it does me."

"You found our . . . shall we say, influence . . . useful enough when Baker got himself arrested."

"Yeah, well nobody's shootin' at your political cronies. My price is eight dollars a head, four now and four when the order is filled."

Dolan's jaw tightened. He opened his desk drawer and took a stack of bills out of the cash box inside. "I need those beeves delivered to Fort Stanton by the fifteenth." He counted out six hundred dollars and pushed the stack across the desk.

Evans scooped up the bills. "Pleasure doin' business with you, Jimmy."

A soft knock sounded at the door. Jasper stood in the doorway blinking behind his smudged spectacles. "Your order's ready, Mr. Evans. That'll be eighty dollars."

Evans eyed his stack of bills.

Dolan's anger eased some.

Chapter Fifteen

Pecos River Valley
July 1877

Evans and his Seven Rivers boys rode north along the west bank of the Pecos. They mounted a rise less than two days' ride out of Seven Rivers and drew rein. Several hundred head of Long Rail cattle grazed the grassy river bottom in the valley below. Evans stood in his stirrups and searched the horizon for any sign of Chisum men. He saw none.

"There they are boys, prime for the taking. We'll make camp here. In the morning we'll cut out our pick and drive 'em up to Rio Hondo. We'll hold 'em there while we change them Long Rails to Seven-R's for the drive up to Fort Stanton."

Evans led the way off the crest of the valley wall to the southwest. They pitched camp, picketed the horses and set themselves down to a supper of beans, biscuits and coffee.

Frank Baker broke out a bottle to flavor the coffee and passed it around. Buckshot Roberts refused with a dismissive wave. The crusty old gunfighter's dour disposition seemed particularly prickly at the moment.

"What's eatin' you?" Evans said.

"I don't like it."

"Don't like whiskey? Since when?"

Roberts shook his head and scowled. "Not the whiskey. It's too damn quiet. We know Chisum's been hirin'. Where are them guns? Why are them cattle down there unguarded?"

Baker poured whiskey in his cup. "Buckshot, you'd doubt your luck if a gold double eagle was to fall outta your ass. The cattle ain't guarded. That'd be our luck."

"Frank's right," Evans said. "No sense borrowin' trouble. For whatever reason, them cattle is there for the takin'."

Jose Chavez let his horse pick its way along the riverbank in lengthening blue shadows. The south river herd spread out along the river bottom as peaceful as could be. The gentle lowing of the herd and the lapping of the river sang a lullaby to day's end. Chavez figured to bed down for the night and head back to South Spring in the morning. As he looked for a place to spread his blanket, he spotted a wisp of smoke rising against the blue-gray southwestern sky beyond the valley wall. Someone was camped close to the herd, someone who didn't belong there.

He squeezed up a lope across the grassy river bottom. He urged his horse up the valley wall and drew rein in a shallow draw without breaking the skyline. He stepped down and ground tied his horse. He drew the Winchester from his saddle boot, shifted the .44 on his hip and set off up the draw on foot. As he neared the crest of the ridge he pushed his sombrero off the back of his head to tug on the stampede string. He dropped to his belly and crawled to the top of the crest. A rocky outcropping concealed him as he looked over. A small campfire crackled a quarter of a mile to the south and west. Four or five men circled the fire, their horses picketed nearby. Chavez had seen enough. This bunch needed watching. He crept back down the draw, collected his horse and stepped into the saddle. He let the horse pick his way north along the valley wall in the gathering gloom. He found a sheltered spot overlooking the valley where he picketed his horse and settled into a cold camp.

He awoke to bawling cattle as the eastern horizon turned pink and blue. Something had disturbed the herd. He scrambled up the rock outcropping that hid his position. He could make out little in the shadowy darkness below. As the first rays of sunrise lit the morning sky, Chavez made out blue shadows. Riders moved among the cattle, cutting out a small herd.

By the time the sun cleared the horizon the rustlers had cut a herd of around a hundred fifty head. The point rider headed them up the valley wall to the west. Chavez watched them clear the valley and push the herd off to the northwest. He saddled his horse and mounted up. He wheeled away to the north, keeping out of sight below the valley wall. He dropped down to the river bottom and squeezed up a lope for the ranch.

South Spring Ranch

Late afternoon sun hung low in the western sky when a rider appeared, pushing his mount at a steady lope up the river trail south of the ranch. Caneris recognized Chavez as he reached the gate and galloped up the road to the ranch house. The fact he didn't pull up at the corral told Caneris something must be wrong. He followed the wrangler at a gangly gaited run up the road to the main house. Chavez stepped down from his blown mount as Chisum appeared on the porch drawn by the sound of a galloping horse.

"What's wrong, Jose?" Chisum knew an experienced vaquero would never push his horse that hard unless it meant trouble. Caneris skidded to a stop beside Chavez, near as winded as the man's horse.

"Rustlers, Mr. Chisum. They hit the south river herd this morning. They took about a hundred fifty head and drove 'em northwest."

Chisum set his jaw. He'd expected this. "That herd is headed for Fort Stanton sure as we're standin' here."

Caneris scratched his chin. "Not with Long Rail brands and no bill of sale."

"They'll take care of that problem before they get there. Wade, tell the boys to get ready. We'll head out at first light. With luck we can cross their trail at the river and catch 'em red-handed."

"Should we send for Sheriff Brady?"

"What for? He'd as likely take the rustlers' side as ours. No, this is a job we need to look after ourselves."

Chisum led them out at dawn. Frank McNab, Doc Scurlock, Charlie Bowdre and Tom O'Folliard followed close behind. The cowhands, Caneris, Swain and Chavez brought up the rear. Chisum pushed hard, taking advantage of the early morning hours before the heat of the day forced a slower pace to save the horses. They rode with grim determination. The boss had made it clear. This incident would end in gunplay and likely a hanging bee.

The sun rode high at mid afternoon when the boss drew rein on the south bank of the Rio Hondo southeast of Lincoln. Caneris drew up next to Chisum.

"What do you make of it, boss?"

Chisum squinted off to the west. "I figure they'll cross west of here. Where they are now depends on where they stop to fix them brands, south of the river or after they cross."

Caneris eased back in his stirrups. "If they're headed for Fort Stanton, that sure makes sense."

"They're headed for Fort Stanton sure as I'm sittin' here." He nodded in agreement with himself. "All right, Jose, scout for sign southwest. The rest of us will cross the river and ride west to see if they've crossed. My gut says we're ahead of 'em. We got a good two hours of daylight left before we make camp. You can circle back along the river to find us. I'm guessin' we'll cross their trail somewhere on the south fork of the river tomorrow or the day after."

Chavez wheeled his horse and rode off into hills thatched green gold and dotted in prickly pear. Chisum led the rest of the men across the river. Two hours further west with no sign of a crossing, he called a halt for the night. A short time later, Chavez rode out of the purple shadows spreading south of the river. He splashed across and stepped down.

"No sign of 'em Mr. Chisum. I expect you're right about bein' ahead of them."

Chisum nodded. "All right then, boys, build us a campfire. They ain't no one around to notice."

The next morning Chisum sent Chavez southwest again. He led the rest of the men west along the north bank of the Rio Hondo. Puffball white clouds streamed out of the northwest on a hot wind. At mid morning they reached the main fork in the river. Chisum took the south fork. The wind picked up toward midday, lashing riders and horses with stinging sheets of sand. The men covered their noses and mouths with bandannas and pulled hats down to shade their eyes under the brim. The sun rode high overhead when Chisum spotted the mouth of a dry wash cutting away from the riverbank to the north.

McNab saw it too.

"John, what say we hole up there for a spell? Get the men out of this damn wind and sand. We're blind out here till Chavez picks up their sign."

Chisum clenched his jaw in resignation. He wheeled his big buckskin up the riverbank to the mouth of the wash.

Chavez tracked his way south and west below the south fork of the river. He weathered the heat of the day and the wind-driven sand searching for sign. A hundred fifty head of cattle didn't go up in smoke. They had to be out here somewhere. Then he spotted a dust cloud too big to be explained by the wind. He squeezed up a lope, hugging a ridgeline between himself and the cloud. A half mile further on, he heard the first faint sounds of bawling cattle sweep by on the wind. He drew rein to listen, making sure his ears hadn't played tricks on him. He eased his horse up a rocky ridge through mesquite and creosote bush, clinging to the ridge wall. He drew rein below the crest and stepped down. He ground tied his horse and climbed the rest of the way on foot. As he reached the crest of the ridge he heard whistles and drover calls join the bellows of the herd. He ducked his head around the base of a boulder. The Long Rail herd lined out along the valley floor below, pushing northwest toward the river. It'd be another few hours before the herd picked up the scent of water and quickened its pace. *Bien,* Chavez thought. He had a lot of ground to cover.

The wind died some by late afternoon. Chisum had about decided to resume their trek west when Bowdre called out a rider from his lookout at the rim of the wash. Chisum, McNab and Caneris scrambled down the wash to the mouth.

Caneris was the first to recognize the approaching rider. "It's Chavez, ridin' like a man on a mission." The three men stepped into open view. Caneris waved his hat and shouted, "Jose, over here." Chavez drew up, recognized his boss, eased his horse across the river and climbed the bank to the wash.

"I found 'em, Señor John. They're about a half day south of the river."

"Good work, Jose." Chisum rubbed his chin considering his next move.

McNab spoke up. "I say we stay put, John. Camp here for the night. They'll likely get to the river sometime tomorrow morning. Once them cattle get the scent of water, they'll likely hold 'em there to change them brands. We can take 'em by surprise then. If we cross their trail now and they spot us, they might run. Sooner or later we'd have to do this all over again."

Chisum chewed on McNab's reasoning. Waiting went against his nature, more so when he was mad. Still the man made sense. "All right, Frank, you're the professional. Wade, tell the boys we'll camp here for the night."

Morning arrived with a thick blanket of low gray cloud, running out of the mountains to the west. It might have signaled rain if there'd been any moisture to the high desert air. Caneris roused the crew. Swain stirred the fire to light and brewed coffee while the men saddled their horses. They gathered around the fire for a breakfast of hardtack and coffee.

McNab picked up the planning where he left off the afternoon before. "I'm thinkin' we ride west until we see some sign of 'em. We can swing south around 'em and take 'em by surprise. We should have 'em pinned against the river."

Chisum nodded. "OK, boys, you heard Frank. Mount up and let's go get us some rustlers."

Four hours later the morning clouds cleared. Caneris made out the sign first. "There." He pointed to a thin wisp of smoke rising against the blue sky beyond a low ridge south of the river. "Somebody's heatin' a branding iron, I reckon."

McNab ran a gloved hand over the rough stubble on his chin. "Head south from here 'til we find a place to skirt that ridgeline without breakin' the horizon."

Chisum let McNab take the lead. An hour later they circled through a narrow gap in the ridge south of the smoke sign. McNab signaled a halt. "Hold the men here, John. I'm gonna ride ahead and have a look at what we're up against."

The men stepped down to rest their horses. McNab picked his way up the trail through the gap in the ridge. As luck would have it, the gap emptied into a long draw that followed the ridgeline back north toward the river. He let his horse pick the way down the draw out of sight of the rustlers up ahead. He kept his pace slow so as not to kick up any sign that might give away his presence. The draw played out less than a half mile from the riverbank. The sound of the cattle lowing and squealing under the sear of the branding iron told him he'd come about as close as he could without showing himself. He drew rein and stepped down. He dropped his rein and climbed to the rim of the draw.

The herd spread out along the grassy river bottom grazing and watering. Two rustlers worked the branding fire half a mile beyond the draw at the riverbank. Three mounted rustlers held the herd on the west, cutting the steers for branding as needed. He liked the lay of the land. A plan unfolded over the scene. He slipped back to collect his horse and stepped into the saddle. He squeezed up a trot back down the draw, confident the rustlers were too busy and too far away to notice they were about to come in for a very bad day.

Chisum and Caneris stood up expectantly when McNab's horse danced around the notch into view. Chisum tipped his hat to the back of his head as McNab stepped down.

"Gather the boys, John, and we'll go through this once." Chisum waved the men around. McNab dropped to his knees and traced a line in the dirt. "The river runs here. Two of 'em are doing the branding here. The other three are holding and cutting here, here and here." McNab stabbed the sand with his finger. "This cut here empties into a draw that runs along the ridgeline to about here. We should be able to get close, without them knowin' we're comin'. We'll hit 'em from there. When we break cover, Tom, Charlie, swing west and take out the drovers. Wade, you, Deacon and Jose follow along with them. Hold the herd as best you can. John, you, Doc and me will ride straight in on the two at the branding fire." McNab looked to Chisum for any final words.

"All right, boys, you heard Frank. Any questions?" None followed. "One last thing, don't waste good lead on any sons a bitches we can hang."

Chapter Sixteen

Rio Hondo Crossing

Evans held the smoking-hot running iron, waiting for the half-breed to steady the steer. They'd put in a hot dusty day's work with at least one more yet to come. When the breed had him, Evans stepped in and fitted the 7R over the Long Rail. The steer bellowed. Evans stepped back. The half-breed jumped clear as the steer lunged to its feet and trotted off to the river. Evans replaced the iron in the fire and waved Buck Morton over with the next steer on the end of his loop.

Nearby, Patch's pony whickered, flaring his nostrils to the wind. The half-breed followed the horse's lead with his good eye. A whisper of dust rose along the ridgeline a half mile south. "Riders come." He pointed to the sign.

Evans turned to the warning. *Damn,* he'd been afraid of this. It had to be Chisum men and they had them dead to rights. "Frank!" He pointed to the crack in the ridgeline where the first couple of riders appeared. "Stampede 'em!"

He pulled the running iron out of the fire and ran for his horse. Roberts, Baker and Morton opened fire, spooking the herd back down the valley toward the ridgeline. Patch leaped to the back of his pony and joined the shooters driving the cattle at their attackers.

The spooked herd trumpeted alarm and bolted in wide-eyed flight. They pounded down the valley toward the Chisum men. Great clouds of dust rose over a bawling band of bobbing brown backs. Dust drew a curtain over the Seven Rivers boys.

"Scatter," Evans yelled over the thundering stampede.

The boys wheeled their horses and raced back to the river. They splashed across and split to the north, east and west, leaving the Chisum men to confront terrorized cattle confusion.

"Son of a bitch!" Chisum exploded at the sight of the charging herd. "Wade, get your boys out front and turn 'em."

Caneris, Swain and Chavez galloped back along the ridgeline, whistling, calling and shooting in the air to turn the herd west. Faced with the frenzied herd, Chisum and his gun hands had all they could do to hold their spooked horses in the choking dust. By the time the herd swept past and they found their way to clear air the rustlers had disappeared across the river.

Lincoln

Luck, good luck, bad luck, damn luck, Evans cursed his fortunes as he laid down a torturous trail northeast toward Lincoln. If it hadn't been for the half-breed's Injun sense they might have caught us flat-footed. So much for good luck. Bad luck was they'd lost the herd. Worse yet they'd left behind a herd mixed of 7R and Long Rail brands. He'd take care of that business quick as he got to Lincoln. Then he'd have to deal with Dolan. He'd be mad as hell. He'd paid for a herd they couldn't deliver. Without it Dolan had no beef to fill his contract.

He rode into town and pulled up in front of the jail. He stepped down, looped a rein over the rail and headed for Brady's office.

"Afternoon, Sheriff."

"Afternoon, Jesse. What can I do for you?"

"I need to report some stolen cattle."

Brady's eyebrows lifted in disbelief. "Kind a careless of you, Jesse, that kind of trouble usually falls on other folks."

"Yeah, well my beeves was rustled just the same. I figure it might a been some of Chisum's men. You be on the lookout for any Seven-R brands mixed in with the Long Rail herds."

Brady fixed Evans with a knowing look. "I see. Sure I'll be on the lookout for that. Count on it."

"Much obliged, Sheriff. Now if you'll excuse me, I need to find Jimmy."

"I expect you do."

The doorbell clanged. Jasper paused mid sentence in his praise of the bolt of fabric he held for a woman in a simple gray bonnet and plain spun dress. He blinked behind his spectacles as Evans appeared in the dim light behind the closing door.

"Dolan in?"

He didn't wait for an answer. Boot heels punctuated his path across the plank floor. His rap on the office door frame brought Dolan up from his ledger. He stepped in and closed the door without waiting for an invitation.

"Chisum men caught us changin' brands down on the Rio Hondo. We had to stampede the herd to get away."

"You lost the herd?"

"I told you Chisum was hirin' guns. Well he used 'em. We was damn lucky to get away."

"You lost the herd? How the hell am I supposed to deliver my contract?"

"You might try buyin' the beeves for a change."

"Shut up, Jesse! I paid you good money for that herd."

Evans bit his tongue.

"You say you were changing brands, so that means you had Seven-R brands mixed in with the Long Rails. You might just as well have pinned a confession on the tail of one of those steers."

"I took care of that. I told Brady the Seven-R cattle was

stolen. If Chisum brings any charges in, it'll be my word against his."

"I'm pleased to see you find my little arrangement with the sheriff so convenient. Now get out of here. I need to figure out where to get a hundred fifty head of cattle by the fifteenth."

Lincoln

The trail spilled out of the hills northwest of town. Ty drew rein on a sun-drenched rise overlooking Lincoln in the distance. Lucy and Johnny drew up on either side of him. A strong northwest breeze ruffled sage and hat brims in swirls of dust. The town sprawled along a gently curving main street shimmering in the heat on the north fork of the Rio Hondo.

"Home sweet home." Johnny lifted his hat and wiped his sweat-slicked forehead on a sleeve.

The steel dust shifted hip shot under Ledger. "Sure don't look like much. You sure about this, Lucy?"

"Seemed like a good idea at the time. Besides, a girl's got to have someplace the man of her dreams can take her away from."

Roth chuckled. "Now there's a thought for you, Ty."

Ty shot his friend a *that'll be about enough out of you* look and eased the steel dust down the hill toward the river and the west end of town beyond. They picked up a lope to the riverbank and splashed across. Beyond the far bank they jogged into town. A weathered sign on a rambling clapboard building across from the imposing J. J. Dolan & Company store proclaimed the Wortley Hotel. Ty drew a halt. "Will this do; or do you want to look for something else?"

"This'll do for now. I don't imagine this town has much more to offer unless I find a room somewhere."

They stepped down at the rail, pulled their saddlebags off the horses and climbed the steps to the boardwalk. The sparsely appointed, dusty lobby glowed in dim sunlight. A balding sleepy-eyed scarecrow stood behind the registration counter. Garters pinned up thread-thin sleeves of a soiled shirt damp with sweat. He wiped the shine off his pate with a blue bandanna. "Welcome to the Wortley, folks. What can I do for you?"

Ty stepped up to the counter. "We need a couple of rooms. One for the night, the lady will be staying a bit longer."

The clerk pushed the register across the counter. "That'll be two dollars for the night, a dollar a night for as long as the lady stays."

Ty fished in his pocket for a dollar. Lucy took a five-dollar gold piece from her handbag and placed it on the counter.

"Any chance a girl might find a bath around here?"

The clerk took two keys down from their hooks behind the counter. From the look of the board they'd be the Wortley's only guests. "I can have the stable boy bring the tub to your room and fill it for you."

"That would be very nice, thank you."

"That'll be six bits." He handed the keys to Ty. "Rooms are down the hall." He jerked a thumb over his shoulder. "Stable's out back, that'll be another six bits."

"Johnny and me'll take care of the horses, Lucy. You go on and get settled. Come get us when you're ready to go find some supper." He turned back to the clerk. "My partner and I need some supplies. Where can we get them?"

"J. J. Dolan & Company across the street," he motioned toward the large, two-story building known as The House. "Ain't no other source of supply in Lincoln."

"We'll see you when we get back, Lucy. Come on, Johnny, let's get us some supplies and put up the horses."

They left the horses at the Wortley hitch rack and crossed the street to the store. Ty climbed the step to the boardwalk fronting the store. "You mind doin' the shoppin' Johnny? I aim to take a look around. See if maybe I can turn up some sign of our boy."

Johnny nodded. The door to the Murphy & Dolan General Store clanged open. Inside his eyes adjusted to the dim light.

"Afternoon, young feller, what can I do for you?"

Johnny crossed the store to the clerk behind the counter. "I need some supplies."

"Well, we got 'em. What'll it be?"

"Let me see, five pounds of flour, two pounds of coffee, a pound of sugar, sack of beans, a side of fatback, half dozen cans of tomatoes, half dozen cans of peaches and three boxes of forty-four rimfires." He selected a handful of cheroots from a humidor while the old clerk filled his order.

The old codger bent over a scrap of paper, licked the tip of a stubby pencil, noting the prices as he divided the items between two flour sacks. "You can tie these sacks off for easy packin'." He totaled his ciphers. "There, that'll be fifty-three dollars."

"Fifty-three dollars! Why we filled an order like this in Santa Fe for half that."

"That's Santa Fe, this here's Lincoln."

Johnny turned to a dark suited figure standing in the office doorway behind him. "And who might you be?"

"James Dolan, proprietor at your service." Dolan's deep voice filled the store.

"Well, Mr. Dolan, I got to tell you your prices are just this side of highway robbery."

"If you don't like my prices, get your supplies somewhere else."

"There ain't no place else."

He shrugged. "Then I guess you like my prices."

Chapter Seventeen

Silas, the stable boy, poured the last bucket of water in the big copper tub set in the middle of the small room. He fetched it from a cistern in the stable yard where it warmed in the sun. She handed him a quarter. His dark eyes widened white against the sweat sheen on his black skin.

"Jes' let me know when you's finished, ma'am, and I'll clean that right up for you."

"Thank you, Silas, it'll be a while. I plan to enjoy this." The boy let himself out.

Lucy unbuttoned her shirt, wriggled out of it and laid it on the bed. By the time you added a tub to the bed, dresser, side chair and a small wardrobe she barely had room for herself. It didn't matter. She unfastened her long skirt and added it to her shirt pile. She pulled her muslin camisole over her head and slipped out of her pantaloons.

She stared at her naked reflection in the looking glass over the dresser. The question came unbidden. *What would Ty think of her in the altogether?* It was a shameless thought for a woman of genteel sensibilities. She'd long since discarded such sentiment. She raised an eyebrow in critical appraisal. She'd taken as much care as a girl could in the trade. She'd weathered her years in the sportin' life without much of the damage suffered by other girls. She started young and stayed away from tobacco, whiskey and laudanum, all vices common in the trade. She still had creamy skin and a petite figure with delicate curves. She flushed at the thought of the dark, rough-shaved Texan and stepped into the tub.

She settled into the warm, soothing water and stretched her legs, resting her head on a towel folded across the rim for a makeshift cushion. She let the waters caress her body. Her mind drifted to the foolish gamble that brought her to a godforsaken trail's end like Lincoln. All for the sake of a man too grieved to notice. Well not quite. She thought back to that night on the creek bank. He'd begun to grieve. He needed to get by that. Vengeance wouldn't do it. Vengeance only put off the grieving. He needed to get by that too. He'd cried some that night. She'd been there for him too. He'd turned to her in that moment. She needed to write that in her journal. It was a start, small maybe, but a start nonetheless. The feeling of their first meeting was still there. He noticed it all right. She felt it. And when she did, it warmed her. *In time,* she thought, *all in good time.*

Morning sun streamed through yellowed lace curtains. Lucy rolled on her back and stretched. Clean sheets felt luxurious after weeks on the trail. A hollow in the pit of her stomach told her she'd slept late into the morning. Ty and Johnny would be well on their way down to Seven Rivers by now.

Ty. She turned the memory of the previous evening over in her mind. They'd had a pleasant supper in the hotel dining room. After dinner they walked into town as far as the first saloon that caught Johnny's eye. He excused himself and headed off after some fun. Ty gave her his arm and they strolled to the other end of town and back again. They talked a little. Small talk mostly about this or that little thing Lincoln might have to offer. They didn't talk about the shadow hanging over the trail to Seven Rivers. The man with one eye had no part in a pleasant evening stroll. When they got back to the hotel they sat on a bench out front, listening to the raucous saloon sounds up the street mingle with the night sounds at the quiet end of town. They had little more to say, though neither of them seemed to want to confront that awkward moment, saying good night and good-bye.

When Ty said he'd best get some shut-eye, he walked her to her door. She remembered the look in his eye as he held hers. She saw something there, something real, something hidden. She wished she could put her finger on the meaning of it. "You be careful," she'd said. "I will," he'd said. She took his hands in hers and squeezed them. They were warm and strong. "You come back, now." He paused. "I will." "Good then." She opened the door and left him to his search and the demons that drove it. She left something of herself with him, something unfinished. Something that might bring him back, she hoped.

She rolled out of bed, surrendering to the day. She poured water from the pitcher on the dresser into the bowl beside it. She splashed her face and dressed in a simple blue gingham dress, the only one she'd brought with her besides the gray traveling dress. She went down to the dining room for a bite of breakfast. Afterward she wandered across the street to the J. J. Dolan & Company mercantile. She'd surely need another dress or two.

She stepped inside to the clang of the visitor's bell. The old clerk behind the counter smiled. She smelled coffee and smoked meat with a musty hint of sacking beneath it all. She wandered among the shelves until she found the bolts of cloth. She selected two fabrics she liked, though she puzzled over the problem of making them into dresses. She knew enough of sewing to replace a button or mend a torn hem.

She felt a presence, watching her. She turned thinking it must be the clerk. He was average height and dark, quite handsome really, with wavy black hair and dark eyes. He wore an elegant black frock coat and a brocade vest of soft gray.

"May I help you?"

He had a voice to turn a girl's knees to water and a come-hither look in his eye that might make you want to. "I'm interested in these two fabrics. Is there a seamstress in town who might make a dress or two for me?"

"You're new here. I thought so." He bowed stiffly. "James Dolan at your service."

"Lucy Sample." She mocked his formality with a curtsey. "Now, about these fabrics, Mr. Dolan, is there someone who might make me a couple of dresses?"

"Please, my friends call me Jimmy. I believe the widow O'Hara does a fine job as a seamstress, though I've had no personal experience with her work."

Lucy giggled at the suggestion the man might own a dress. Dolan smiled at his own wit. "Where might I find Mrs. O'Hara?"

"She owns the white house with the green door on the east end of town. If you like I'd be happy to escort you there myself."

"That's very generous of you, Mr. Dolan, but given your most excellent directions I'm sure that won't be necessary. Now if you would be good enough to hold these fabrics for me, I'll have the widow take measurements so I know how much to buy."

"We'd be delighted to do that, Miss Sample. It is *Miss* Sample isn't it?"

"It is, Mr. Dolan."

"Please call me Jimmy. If I can't show you to Mrs. O'Hara's perhaps you would consider having dinner with me?"

"That's also very kind of you, sir. Perhaps another time."

"Ah, I see. It must be that you are seeing someone."

"No, not really."

"I find that hard to believe. I mean a woman as lovely as you must have plenty of suitors."

She smiled. "You're too kind, Mr. Dolan. But as you correctly surmised, I am new in town. I'll return for these fabrics." She turned on her heel and started for the door. *He really is quite the charming devil.*

James Dolan's description of Mrs. O'Hara's place made finding it easy. The green door on the whitewashed, two-story clapboard was quite distinctive. A small front yard separated the house from the street behind a neat white picket fence. The gate opened with a welcoming squeal. She crunched up the walk to the front porch and rapped on the door with a lace curtained window. Footfalls beyond announced that the widow was home. A rather stout, pleasant-looking woman with steel-gray hair opened the door. She took Lucy in with a lively appraising glance.

"Yes?"

"Mrs. O'Hara?"

"I am."

"My name is Lucy Sample. Mr. Dolan over at the mercantile said you might make a couple of dresses for me."

She smiled at the prospect. "You're new in town."

"Yes, I am."

"Well then, my dear, welcome to Lincoln. Come in, come in. Would you care for some tea?"

"Why, yes, that would be lovely."

She led the way to a small neatly appointed parlor just off the front hall. "Have a seat, dear. I've just brewed a fresh pot. I won't be but a minute." She disappeared down the front hall to the kitchen at the back of the house.

Lucy took a seat on a settee near the front window. She could hear faint sounds of cups and saucers bustling about the kitchen. Moments later the widow returned with a tray bearing a china tea service and a plate of molasses cookies. Lucy smiled to herself. She hadn't felt so at home since before her family left Missouri.

Mrs. O'Hara set the tray on a low table beside the settee and poured. She handed Lucy a cup. "Please have a cookie." She took a seat beside the settee. "What brings you to Lincoln, if you don't mind my asking?"

She thought. What to say? Simple truth might be the best start for a new life. "I'm finishing a journey my family started. I lost them crossing the Arkansas. I thought at least one Sample should make it here."

"Oh my, I'm so sorry, dear. Well I'm pleased you've completed the journey. Now let's see about those dresses."

Pepin Ranch
Rio Hondo South Fork

George Pepin watched the dark rider on the black horse jog up the trail to his ranch. A slope-shouldered man of paunchy build. He wore a rough spun shirt and well-worn vest with a battered derby hat perched on a head full of shoulder-length white hair. He had cherry cheeks where his hat brim failed to shade his fair skin from the effects of the sun. An explosion of eyebrows gave his watery blue eyes a look of perpetual surprise. A bushy drooping mustache sobered a countenance that might otherwise be taken for a jovial Father Christmas. He'd carved his ranch out of the Pecos River valley when he had to fight both Indians and rustlers to do it. The years had given him a grit most men in the territory respected, even Jimmy Dolan, the visitor drawing rein in his yard.

"Jimmy, what the hell brings you all the way out here?" Pepin didn't bother to get out of the rocking chair on the porch for his greeting.

"Now there's a welcome if I ever heard one, nice to see you too, George." Dolan stepped down and looped a rein over the split-rail rack.

"Aw, you know what I mean. Pull up a chair and sit a spell. Care for a drink?"

"George, after that ride I believe I will."

Pepin disappeared into the small ranch house. He returned moments later with a whiskey bottle and two glasses. He set the glasses on an overturned nail keg that served as a table. He poured two drinks, handed one to Dolan and returned to his seat in the rocker. He lifted his glass to Dolan and took a swallow. "All right, Jimmy, to what do I owe the unexpected pleasure of your company?"

"I need a hundred fifty head of cattle to fill a contract at Fort Stanton by the fifteenth. My regular supplier defaulted on me."

Pepin eyed the man suspiciously. He had a pretty good idea who the regular supplier was. Jesse Evans wasn't known for defaulting. This ought to be good. "I don't run that big a herd anymore Jimmy. The only one I know in these parts who does is Chisum."

"I know, George, that's why I'm here. I need you to buy them from Chisum for me. I'll pay you a dollar a head for your trouble."

Pepin rocked forward at the mention of money. "Seems like a goodly sum to pay for a job you could do yourself."

"Chisum wouldn't sell cattle to me. He wants the government contracts I hold. If he knew the herd was for me, he'd know I can't fill my contract. If I default, he has a chance to take the contracts for himself."

"You have got yourself in a box, Jimmy." Pepin knocked back his drink and poured another. Dolan held out his glass for a refill. "How much you willin' to pay for this herd?"

"Counting your dollar I could go up to sixteen. I don't make much of a profit at that figure, but it buys me time to find another supplier. If you do better, I'll split the difference with you."

He smiled at the opportunity to better his share and winked. "I'll see what I can do."

"Just get me that herd by the fifteenth, George."

Seven Rivers
Rio Pecos Valley
Roth pulled up on a low rise. A broken-down ranch sprawled across the shallow valley below. Nothing moved other than a wind-driven tumbleweed rolling across the yard. He pointed his chin. "Not much to look at is it."

"Don't look too prosperous from here." The steel dust pawed the parched scrabble, catching scent of the Seven Rivers remuda. "How you want to play this?"

Roth shrugged. "If our man's there, he doesn't know we're after him. I say we play it friendly until we know what we're up against. If we find him, try to follow my lead. I know you want to kill the son of a bitch, but let's don't go gettin' ourselves killed in the bargain."

Ty nodded. He wiped sweat from his palm on a pant leg, adjusting the Colt on his hip. *Kill the son of a bitch.* He might actually be down there. He set his jaw and eased the steel dust forward.

They rode in, slow and easy, alert to any sign of movement. It bothered Roth that he didn't see any. "I got a strong feelin' we're bein' watched," he said under his breath.

At about fifty yards a voice called out from the house. "That'll be far enough. Keep your hands where we can see 'em and state your business."

"We're lookin' for Jesse Evans. Crystobal said he might be hirin'."

"Keep 'em covered boys." A solidly built man in a bib front shirt stepped out of the house. "I'm Evans. Ease on up here." He waited. Johnny and Ty rode forward.

"Mr. Evans, my name's Johnny Roth. This here's Ty Ledger."

"Did you hear that boys? I'm Mr. Evans." He laughed. "Crystobal didn't call me that. He's got the manners of a rattlesnake. You might be too genteel to work for this outfit."

"Crystobal had the manners of a snake. Now he knows Johnny Roth backs his play."

Evans furrowed his brow. "What do you mean?"

"I had to put a bullet in him."

"You shot Crystobal? Why?"

"Maria took a little shine to me." Roth eased back, ready to draw if Evans made a move.

Evans shook his head and burst into laughter. "It would be a woman that got him in trouble. Guess he won't be sending me any more men. I best take what I can get. Step down and I'll introduce you to the boys."

Chapter Eighteen

South Spring Ranch

"Rider comin," Bowdre shouted from the west rim of a shallow draw where Swain, Caneris and Chisum worked river herd strays. Doc Scurlock snapped alert from his lookout on the east slope. Chisum had taken to having his gunman guard his work crews. He eased the Winchester free of his saddle boot. One rider didn't pose much of a threat. Then again a man never got hurt by being too careful. The rider looked little more than a dark speck heading their way from the northwest. A thin trail of dust drifted behind his easy lope, before vanishing in the dun green and rust hills.

Chisum settled the buckskin, his attention riveted on the approaching rider. As he drew near recognition grew out of the black vest, fluttering in the breeze and the battered hat that required a helping hand to stay perched on his head. *George Pepin, now what do you suppose brings him down here?*

"It's all right, boys." He returned his rifle to the saddle boot.

Bowdre and Scurlock eased off their weapons.

Pepin jogged the last yards into the draw.

"Mornin', John. I didn't expect to run in to you out here like this."

"Mornin', George. I might say the same. What brings you to South Spring?"

"I got a bit of business to discuss if you're of a mind."

"I've always got time for business. Let's ride up to the house, if you've got the time."

"That suits me fine. A cool drink of water would go pretty good right now."

Chisum turned in his saddle. "Take these bad boys home, Wade. Doc, you and Charlie stay with 'em."

The orders drew Pepin's attention to the two armed lookouts. "You got professional guns watchin' your herds, John?"

Chisum fixed Pepin with a serious expression. He had no reason to distrust the man, but every cattleman in the territory knew the rustler problem. "Let's just say I've had enough of Evans and his Seven Rivers scum. Next time they try me, we're gonna give 'em a hot helping of hell." Chisum wheeled his horse and squeezed up a lope.

Next time, Pepin thought. They must have come up short enough the last time to cause a *default.*

Twenty minutes later they rode into the yard at South Spring and stepped down in front of the house. Chisum led the way up the step to the shaded porch. "Have a seat, George." He pulled up a heavy log framed chair. "Dawn."

She appeared in the doorway almost as soon as he finished her name.

"Have you got a glass or two of that lemonade for our guest?"

She disappeared with a nod.

They settled into the shaded comfort of the porch. Chisum took the chair across from his guest. "So, George, what's on your mind?"

"I'm lookin' to buy a small herd, John."

Chisum furrowed his brow in suspicion. "I thought you cut back on your operation."

"I did." Pepin expected Chisum would be skeptical. He'd decided the best lie should be one close to the truth. "One of my old customers up in Denver lost a herd bound for the UP crews working the Denver spur. He asked if I could help him out. I figured it was worth a ride over here."

"Anybody I might know?" Chisum smelled Dolan's hand in this unexpected and entirely too coincidental turn of events.

Dawn padded barefoot across the porch carrying glasses and a pitcher of lemonade. She poured a glass for Pepin and one for Chisum.

"Leave the pitcher, Dawn. We'll take care of ourselves." She returned to the house.

"Fine-lookin' woman you got there, John."

"She's a good girl, takes good care of me. A man gets to be our age, George, that's about all you can ask."

Pepin chuckled in agreement.

"Now where were we? Oh yes, you were about to tell me who your customer is."

"John Carmody, though I don't suppose that'd mean anything to you."

"You're right. I don't know that name, though I do know of a James or two." Chisum didn't want Pepin to go off thinkin' him stupid. "So how many head you lookin' to buy?"

"I'm lookin' for a hundred fifty head or so."

"Hmm." Chisum fixed Pepin with hard stare. "I almost lost a herd about that size not so long ago."

Pepin took a swallow of lemonade. He guessed Chisum was on to him, might as well get to the point. "I can offer fifteen dollars a head, John."

Chisum sat back in his chair. A small smile spread under his mustache. "Twenty-five dollars a head."

Pepin choked on a swallow of lemonade. "That's right close to robbery, John."

"Dolan set the floor on cattle prices in these parts with his Fort Stanton contracts. Twenty dollars a head I believe is what he gets. If you want a price like that, you best talk to Dolan."

"But I got to drive 'em to Denver, John."

"Where they'll be worth thirty, maybe thirty-five dollars. Twenty-five dollars a head, George, that's my final offer."

Pepin lifted his glass. Dolan would pitch a righteous fit. Chisum had him over a barrel and he knew it. "This is mighty good lemonade, John. I'll check with my buyer, but I expect you've got a deal."

Seven Rivers

Buck Morton rang the bell, calling the boys to supper. The lean-to that passed for a cookshack stood in back of the bunkhouse next to the main house. The boys ambled around from the front of the bunkhouse in slanting rays of setting sun. One by one they shuffled past the pots, filling their plates with fatback, beans and biscuits. Pots of coffee and cups were set on the long, rough-cut table on the bunkhouse side porch.

Ty and Johnny took their seats on the benches at the far end of the table. They'd mostly kept to themselves since arriving at the ranch. Aware that Evans and his men would keep an eye on the newcomers, they waited, watched and listened. One thing was certain. They'd seen no sign of Patch.

Evans was the last to arrive, taking his place at the far end of the table. Little was said around mouthfuls of fatback and beans until Frank Baker broke the silence.

"Hey, Jess, what ever happened to the breed?"

Roth cut his eyes to Ty and got charged interest in return.

Evans shrugged. "He scattered at the river with the rest of us. He may be takin' his time comin' back, or maybe he just drifted on. I doubt he got caught."

Baker tore a biscuit. "Saved our asses, spottin' Chisum and his men the way he done."

"Who's the breed?" Roth kept the question casual.

"One-eyed half-breed called himself Patch," Evans said. "Crystobal sent him too. Smelled out a trap on the last job we run. He should have come back by now."

Morton scraped his plate over the side of the porch. "Maybe you can pick up some word of him in Lincoln, Jess. We're about due to make a run up there for supplies."

Evans sopped his plate with a biscuit. "I ain't goin' into town for a spell. Dolan's still pissed over that herd." He looked down the table. "Give Ledger the list. He can go."

Lincoln

"Twenty-five dollars a head! That's the best you can do?" Dolan fair near burst the vein bulging at his temple. "Why that's more than the contract pays, not countin' expenses." He pressed the bridge of his nose between thumb and forefinger. Adding the four dollars he'd paid Evans for nothing and the one he'd owe Pepin he calculated thirty dollars a head. At a contract price of twenty dollars he'd lose ten dollars a head! He ground his teeth in frustration unable to come up with another option.

Pepin shrugged. "Chisum knows."

"You told him?"

"Hell, no. I ain't stupid. Neither is he. He knows what the army pays. He figured you're my buyer. He said you set the floor on prices around here with your army contracts. He suspects Evans tried to rustle a herd that size for you. He's got you over a barrel. He knows it. He might not be able to make his suspicions stick; but he's gonna stick it to you good."

"I need the damn herd. Without it, I default on my contract. The army will throw it out to bid again."

"So? What's to stop you from winning it again?"

"Chisum will meet my price, just to cut his losses."

"Underbid him."

"I got expenses. I need the cash."

"So what are you going to do, Jimmy?"

"Buy the herd. The bank will cover your draft. You'll get your commission when the herd's delivered to Fort Stanton."

Pepin nodded and left.

Dolan stood, clasped his hands behind his back and turned to the office window. "He got me this time, but I'll get the son of a bitch. I swear I'll get the son of a bitch." *There's got to be a way.*

He turned to his desk, rubbing his chin in thought. He drew his chair up and sat drumming his fingers. *Chisum and his hired guns can't get away with taking the law into their own hands.* He pursed his lips and removed a sheet of stationery from the desk drawer. He took pen in hand and wrote.

The Honorable Samuel Axtell
Governor, New Mexico Territory
Santa Fe, New Mexico
Dear Sam,

Chapter Nineteen

Fort Stanton
New Mexico Territory

Fort Stanton sprawled alongside a creek bottom in a mountain valley west of Lincoln. The post proper consisted of neat adobe and clapboard buildings arranged along the sides of a long central parade ground. Patch lounged in the shade of an adobe wall south of the parade ground in the poor section inhabited by Indians. Here he became lost among the people, distinguished only by his eye patch.

He watched the shapely Navajo girl approach in her brightly colored skirt as he had each day for the past few. Setting sun fired her simple white blouse with the promises of her womanhood. Each evening she went to the officers' quarters at the fort. She licked the army's boot with her favors. She shamed her people. Something about the way she carried herself struck a match to the old rage. She looked past him as though he were not there. The look reminded him of his mother, stroking her medicine bag as she watched him driven from the village like an animal. He hated that look. His medicine stirred. Tonight when she returned from the fort she would see him. She would know fear. She would know his power and feel his blade.

Hours later her dark figure came toward him in the moonlight. He eased back in the shadow of the adobe wall. He'd chosen this place carefully. A breach in the wall led to cover beyond.

His paint waited there. He felt the hilt of his knife. He heard her bare feet pad softly on the sandy path. His mouth went dry. His breath grew short and tight. His blood quickened. He stilled his breathing.

She passed the breach in the wall, her dark copper skin silvered in moonlight. He struck with the silent swiftness of a mountain puma. He clamped a hand over her mouth. His arm circled her waist in a vice-like grip. He pulled her through the crumbled breach in the wall to the shadows beyond. She struggled against him, twisting this way and that. Struggle fanned the flames of rage and demand. She bared her teeth, trying to bite him. He dropped his hand to her throat and squeezed. A choked cry fighting for voice faded. She went limp against him.

He dragged her away from the wall into the shadows of scrub oak beyond. He laid her on the cracked parched earth. He tore her blouse from her back and stuffed it in her mouth. He tied her hands behind her with a rawhide thong. He rolled her over and drew his knife. The blade flashed in the moonlight as he slit the waistband of her skirt. The cloth gave up a soft ripping sound.

He planted his feet and admired his prey. Her eyelids fluttered. His shadow fell over her. Her eyes blinked open round and white. She tried to struggle. Her eyes fell on the blade. She went still, accepting what would be.

Patch staggered deeper into the scrub oak. His paint browsed quietly in the moon glow. His hands felt wet and sticky. He tugged at his britches. Blood mingled with sweat smeared his belly. He remembered the moment she realized, the moment she saw him. He saw his blade touch her. Now he felt only the echoes of rage, heavy and drained. Hot blood had run its course. Instinctively he checked the paint's cinch. He stepped into the saddle without looking back at the body, lying in moonlit gore. A shallow creek east of the fort would cover his tracks. He splashed into the silvered stream and eased the paint south with the current.

Santa Fe

"You sent for me, Marshal?" Deputy US Marshal Robert Widenmann stepped into Sherman's small office. The marshal looked up from the file on his desk.

"I did, Rob, come in."

"Thank you, sir." Widenmann took a seat. He had a pleasant round face and blue eyes that belied the timber of the man. He had thick sandy hair thatched with unruly cowlicks that added to the appearance of youth. He fought off his boyish appearance with a mustache and serious demeanor. He wore a black cutaway coat and britches with .44 pistols rigged butt-forward on each hip.

"Rob, we've got a situation developing down in Lincoln between the big ranchers and the small ranchers. Prominent citizens claim it's getting bigger than local law enforcement can handle. They've appealed to the governor for help. Axtell is all over my ass to do something about it."

"What's the problem?"

"Small ranchers claim the big operators monopolize free range grazing."

"By big operators you mean Chisum."

Sherman nodded. "They've had a couple of scrapes over it. Now Chisum is hiring guns and taking the law in his own hands. I want you to go down there. Find out what's going on."

"How do we fit in, John? It sounds like local jurisdiction to me."

"It is. The locals are saying they can't handle it."

"So the governor calls on us? Isn't that where he might turn to the army?"

"He might, but he didn't. I expect he'd prefer to keep it low-key. Calm things down if he can."

"So where do I start?"

"The governor suggested talking to James Dolan."

"Dolan's no rancher. What's he got to do with it?"

"Concerned citizen, he spoke up for the little guys. He's got influence with the governor. Axtell is listening to their side of the story."

Widenmann scowled, rubbing his chin. "Chisum's got a big operation, but big don't make it wrong."

"I'm not sayin' it is. The small ranchers are the ones complainin'. No way of tellin' from here who's in the wrong."

"The governor won't like a range war down there, either."

"I know. That's why it'd be best if you can settle the problem before it comes to that."

"John Chisum's a big man. If he's got his back up, he won't be easy to stop."

"Chisum's also a reasonable man. If you can talk the situation down, do it. If not, deputize whatever men you need to keep the peace."

"Seems like that puts us right in the middle of a matter outside our jurisdiction don't it?"

"I didn't say it was going to be easy, Rob."

Widenmann rose. "I'll head down there in the morning."

Lincoln

The steel dust jogged into the east end of town tailing a horse with an empty packsaddle. Ty's thoughts turned to Lucy. He hadn't thought much about her since he left Lincoln. Suddenly he found himself wondering how she'd made out. Strangely he hoped she hadn't gone back to the trade. He wondered why such a thing should matter. Somehow it did. And then as if she read his mind she stepped out of a neat white house with a green door. He drew rein in front of the house, waiting for her to notice him. She looked pretty as a picture in a yellow dress that set off her sable hair.

She started down the path from the porch to the street when she noticed him. "Ty!" Her eyes smiled.

He stepped down. She rushed through a creaky gate to greet him. Without thinking, he swept her up in a hug that just felt like the right thing to do. He liked the way she hugged him back, until she caught herself and pulled back.

"Well look at you, handsome, aren't you a sight for sore eyes."

She favored him with a sunny smile that said she was purely happy to see him.

"You look mighty good yourself, Lucy. Lincoln seems to agree with you."

"Lincoln's all right. It's better now that you're back."

She said it like she meant it. "I'm afraid I can't stay long. I just came in for supplies."

Her smile faded.

"Well at least you're here for a visit. You didn't get him yet did you?"

He shook his head. "We're on his trail. He joined up with an outfit down to Seven Rivers. He wasn't there when we got there. It feels like we're getting close. The Seven Rivers boys think he's comin' back, but nobody knows for sure."

"Well he's still in the area. They found a young Navajo woman over at Fort Stanton a couple of days ago. It sounds like some of his work."

Ty looked off up the street. "How many more before we get him?"

"You'll get him. Now let's have some lunch and talk about more pleasant things."

He smiled, gave her his arm and let her lead him up the

street to the hotel as he led the steel dust and the packhorse. He tied the horses at the hotel hitch rack and followed Lucy into the café.

The burly owner, waiter, cook, wearing a stained apron showed them to a table. "What'll it be?"

"Biscuits and gravy," Lucy said.

"I'll have a steak. All I've eaten since we left is fatback and beans."

Lucy laughed. "At least you're not wasting away, cowboy."

"So what have you found to keep you busy since we left?"

"I moved into a room at Mrs. O'Hara's place. She made a couple of dresses for me. When I asked her where I might find a room she said she had one. It's cheaper than the hotel and it includes board, so I've got some time to figure out what I'm going to do."

The café man lumbered out of the kitchen carrying two steaming plates. He set biscuits and gravy in front of Lucy. Ty's steak sizzled on the plate with a generous helping of browned potatoes.

He picked up his knife and fork. "That looks like a fine way to save a man from his own humble cookin'."

Lucy cut into a biscuit. "The biscuits are nice and light too. I'm not sufferin', though. Mrs. O'Hara's a fine cook."

"Sounds like you've got it pretty good over there."

"I do, until I have to go to work."

"Any ideas on what you might do?"

"Not yet."

"You could always go back to workin' in a saloon."

Lucy lifted an eyebrow. "Yes, I suppose I could." Her voice trailed off. He lifted a forkful of steak. She caught his eyes in hers. "I thought, maybe, you wouldn't want me to do that."

He thought a moment. "I guess that's right. I wish you wouldn't."

She brightened. "Good." She pushed a bite of biscuit around a puddle of gravy with her fork. "You plan to ride over to Fort Stanton?"

He nodded around a mouthful of steak. "I expect he's long gone, but maybe I can pick up something of his whereabouts."

"What about your supplies?"

"I'll have Dolan fill my order while I'm gone."

"Then you'll be back tonight."

"Should be."

"Maybe we could have supper then?"

"I'd like that."

Lunch finished, Ty paid the bill. He took a room and stabling for the packhorse at the hotel. Lucy followed along as he led the steel dust across the street to the J. J. Dolan & Company store. The visitor bell roused old Jasper to a cheery "Hello, Miss Lucy."

"Hello, Jasper."

"What can I do for you?"

"Nothing for me, Ty here has an order for you to fill."

Ty pushed the list across the counter. Jasper gave it a quick look.

"This'll take a little while."

"No trouble. I've got to ride over to Fort Stanton this afternoon. I'll pick it up in the morning."

"Good afternoon, Miss Sample." Dolan appeared in the doorway to his office, dapper in his black suit. "What a pleasant surprise." He crossed the store to take her hand. "And who might this be?" He looked Ty up and down.

"Ty here's an old friend. Ty Ledger, meet Mr. Dolan."

"Jimmy," he corrected, extending his hand with a forced smile. "I can't seem to get her to call me Jimmy, but you may. Any friend of Miss Sample's is welcome here."

Ty doubted it, but took the man's hand anyway. He didn't occupy Dolan's attention any longer than a perfunctory shake.

That distinction went to Lucy and no mistaking the look in his eye when he did.

"You are a most persistent man, Mr. Dolan, Jimmy if you like, but you must call me Lucy." She smiled up at him.

"There, that's better. Now, Lucy, may I remind you of that invitation to dinner?"

Dolan didn't waste any time. His attentions to Lucy didn't improve Ty's impression of the man.

"I'm sorry, Jimmy, I'm to have supper with Ty this evening, perhaps another time."

Dolan cocked an eye at Ty. "Will you be in town long?"

"Just long enough to fill this supply order and pay a visit to Fort Stanton."

"Good then, I'm sure Jasper here can take care of your supply needs in short order. Good day, sir. And Lucy, I'll hold you to that invitation."

She smiled again. Dolan turned to his office. Ty gave her his arm. "I'll be back to pick up those supplies in the morning."

Outside he paused on the boardwalk. "Nice fella. He'd probably make real interesting supper company."

"Oh, I don't know. Strikes me as being kind of full of himself."

"Well he sure seems to take a shine to you."

She arched a brow with a wry smile. "Why, Ty Ledger, I do believe you're jealous."

"Who, me?"

"Yes, you."

"I believe I best be on my way over to Fort Stanton if I'm to be back in time to save you from supping with Jimmy Dolan."

She laughed. "If you hurry, you should make it just fine."

The mischievous twinkle in her eye made him feel like an open book.

Chapter Twenty

Early evening purple shadow crept out of the west as Ty approached the picket fence in front of the house with the green door. He'd spent the ride back from Fort Stanton mulling what little he'd learned from the post commander. There could be little doubt Patch killed the girl. Army scouts lost the trail of the suspected murderer in a nearby stream. He must have followed the stream for some distance. They found no sign of him leaving the stream to the north or the south. His gut told him the killer headed south. The question he couldn't answer was if the killer would return to Seven Rivers.

He cleaned up at the hotel after returning to town and hurried off to meet Lucy still absorbed in thought. As he reached the gate, a sudden realization took him by surprise. He was about to call on a woman. The thought stopped him. His mind raced back to the wisp of a girl who didn't belong in that saloon back in Dodge. He'd found that woman again in a saloon in Denver. He remembered the sound of her voice in the hotel lobby in Santa Fe. He remembered sitting beside her on a creek bank somewhere on the back trail north. She held him. It was a comfort. He remembered the awkward pause saying good night that first night in Lincoln. He'd felt something riding into town that morning and then again the way Dolan looked at her. He was about to call on the woman, waiting behind that green door. Waiting for what? She seemed to feel something for him. He'd thought his capacity of feeling such things died with Victoria, or did it? Did he have feelings left to give? He didn't know. He guessed he'd find out soon enough.

He crossed the yard. His boot sounded a hollow announcement as he mounted the porch step and rapped on the door. Muffled footsteps sounded lightly beyond. He felt an odd mixture of anticipation and apprehension. The door swung open. She stood silhouetted in the soft glow of lamplight. She wore a pale blue dress that gave her girlish figure the delicate line of fine porcelain. Dark hair piled high in curls lit red gold in the dim light. Her eyes glittered, innocent and wise all at once. She smiled that smile that seemed to say she could see right through him and what she saw amused her.

"Hi, handsome."

He looked down, suddenly conscious that his hotel cleanup hadn't gotten all the trail dust. "I guess I'm no Jimmy Dolan."

"I know." She closed the door softly and took his arm.

They walked up the quiet street arm in arm. Night breeze soothed the heat of the day, fluttering tendrils of hair in the arch at her neck.

"What did you find out at Fort Stanton?"

"Not much. He killed a Navajo girl this time. He caught her returning home from the fort. Seems she was a . . . regular visitor there."

"Ty, this is Lucy. She was one of the camp belles."

"They found her outside the wall in the morning in pretty much the same condition as the others. They found sign of a horse and moccasin prints. The commandant sent out a patrol to track him, but they lost the trail. The commandant didn't know much beyond that. Turns out I knew more than he did. I asked around some. A couple of people remembered seeing a man with a patch. He must've kept to himself. No one had any idea where he came from or where he went."

"So where does that leave you?"

He shrugged. "Headed back to Seven Rivers, I reckon. Maybe he'll show up back there. For right now, though"—he squeezed her arm—"I'm plannin' to have supper with the prettiest girl in Lincoln."

She gave him an amused smirk. "Slim pickin's in a town full of Indians, mamacitas and widows."

"I ain't complainin'."

The café served roast beef, biscuits and green chilies with fresh-baked apple pie and coffee. After dinner they strolled back down the moonlit street to the widow O'Hara's. They walked slowly under a star-dazzled sky in no hurry to bring the evening to an end. Inevitably they reached the gate and crossed the yard to the shadowed porch.

Lucy paused at the door. Starlight reflected in the dark pools of her eyes. "I had a lovely evening, Ty."

"I did too."

She tilted her chin. "I know you mean to catch that killer, but don't stay away too long. I kind of like having you around."

He bent to the upturned bow of her lips so close he could taste the sweetness of her breath. He touched his lips to hers, so soft, so light, the barest brush of a feather. She slipped her arms around his neck, her lips soft and moist. The kiss exploded in a flash of summer lightning. She flooded his senses. Breath caught in his throat somewhere behind the hammer in his chest. Time stood still. She filled his arms small, tender, urgent. Hungers awakened. She gasped for breath against his neck.

"I didn't know if you'd ever get around to that, cowboy."

"I didn't know I had it left to give."

"Oh, you do. You surely do." She rose up on her tiptoes and lightly touched her lips to his lips. He held her tight. She teased his lip with the tip of her tongue and they dissolved in another kiss. When they parted she rested her head on his chest listening to his heart. She trembled.

"That'd like to undo a girl, cowboy."

"Not just any girl. I know the feelin'."

"I hope so." She stepped back and dropped her eyes. "Now you go catch your killer if you must, but hurry back. Don't do either of us any good to let all that go to waste." She touched her fingers to his lips and disappeared behind the green door

Seven Rivers

The ride down to Seven Rivers gave a man considerable time to ponder things. He had a strong feeling they were closing in on the killer. He expected they'd get him. The man needed to be stopped. He'd surely be the one to do it. He'd have his vengeance. Then what? Lucy was right plain enough. It wouldn't bring Victoria back. It wouldn't make her rest any easier. He might flush some of his anger, but how much? He'd still be at a loss without his vengeful purpose. Lucy understood that. She understood him, maybe better than he understood himself. Could she help him find some new purpose? Could she be that purpose? After last night, he couldn't deny they felt something for each other. It wasn't the same as Victoria. It couldn't be, could it? No. His feelings for Victoria had come slow and shy. He'd been younger then. Time had a way of changing things.

He'd never have thought about such things so soon if it weren't Lucy. There was something there all right. A little something from the first time they met. Something they remembered in Denver. Something brought her to Santa Fe. Something they touched last night. Something he guessed could grow strong, if he let it. Could he let it? He didn't know. No point fretting over it until the killing was done. The memory wasn't fretful. It was downright pleasant. It made for pleasant company on a long ride.

He rode into the yard, leading the laden packhorse to the

cookshack behind the bunkhouse. He stepped down and ground tied the steel dust. If it weren't for broken fencing, Seven Rivers pretty nearly wouldn't have any. He looked around for sign of Evans and the boys. The place looked deserted. He shrugged. Nothing to do but unload the supplies. He untied the canvas panniers hung on the packsaddle and began unloading the bundles Jasper wrapped for the ride down from Lincoln. Boots clumped the plank porch behind him. He looked over his shoulder. Roth ambled around the corner at the front of the bunkhouse, stretching out a wide yawn.

"About time you made it back. I was beginnin' to think you'd give up and run off with Lucy."

"Where's Evans and the boys?"

"They rode out this mornin' lookin' for stray cattle. Left me to watch the place."

"You mean stray Long Rail cattle."

"I expect so. Any sign of our boy?"

"He killed a Navajo girl up to Fort Stanton four days ago. I take it he ain't been back here."

Roth shook his head and spit. "No sign of him. I'm beginnin' to wonder if he will come back. Sure as hell wouldn't be for the food. Not a lot of women in these parts either I've noticed."

Ty thought of Lucy. He didn't fancy her having another run-in with the son of a bitch. He didn't even know if she still carried her gun. "Give me a hand unloading these supplies."

Roth stepped off the porch. He hefted a bundle up on his shoulder and followed Ty to the cookhouse. "Chisum's hirin.' Maybe our boy decided to switch sides. He'd be closer to his favored form of entertainment."

"We're guessin'. He could be anywhere."

"He could be, but he ain't here. We wouldn't even know about the Navajo girl if you hadn't gone to Lincoln. You want to kill a wolf, you guard your flock. Our best chance is to catch him on the prowl or pick up his trail after a kill."

"I rode over to Fort Stanton and talked to the commandant. They sent out patrols, but they couldn't stay on his trail."

"That leaves prowlin', I reckon."

Ty set his bundle on a rickety table in the dusty cookhouse. "What are you suggestin'?"

Roth dropped his bundle beside Ty's. "I think he's as likely to turn up in Lincoln lookin' for a victim as he is to come back here. I say we check the Chisum outfit to make sure he hasn't switched sides. We tell Chisum to be on the lookout for a man who may be ridin' with the Seven Rivers bunch. Then we head back to Lincoln and keep our eyes and ears open."

"You think he'll show up there?"

"He showed up in Deadwood, Cheyenne, Denver, Santa Fe and Fort Stanton. The man's got a powerful urge he needs to scratch sooner rather than later. Even if he comes back here, he won't stay long."

Johnny made a strong case, even if it had set him to worrying over Lucy. "What about Evans?"

"What about him? If we get gone now, he can't stop us. He might be pissed off some, but I doubt it'd be enough to come after us. Let's put some trail dust between us and this outfit before nightfall."

CHAPTER TWENTY-ONE

South Spring

High summer sun beat the Pecos River valley like a hammer striking an anvil. Roth and Ledger followed the river on the ride north, taking advantage of grass, water and shade from the occasional copse of trees along the river bottom. Late on the afternoon of the second day they swung west toward the Chisum ranch. Dusk closed in as the gate came into view. Roth squeezed up a short lope along the dusty road to the main house. They passed the corral and bunkhouse, drawing rein at the residence. Roth stepped down and looped a rein over the hitch rail. He led Ty up the porch step to the front door.

The dark-eyed girl who answered his knock was definitely not John Chisum. The usually-ready-for-anything Roth forgot his purpose in a moment of awkward confusion.

"Yes?"

She had a low timbered voice, soft and unexpected, coming from someone so—so unexpected. Roth recovered. "Ah, is Mr. Chisum in?"

At that boots sounded on the plank floor behind her. "Who is it, Dawn?" Chisum appeared at her shoulder before she could answer. "I'm John Chisum, what can I do for you?"

"Mr. Chisum." Roth extended his hand. "Johnny Roth, this here's my partner Ty Ledger. We heard you're hirin.' We're lookin' for a man. We thought you might know something of his whereabouts."

"You the law?"

"Ty here's a deputy US marshal. I'm a bounty hunter."

"Kinda odd partners. Who are you after?"

"One-eyed half-breed, goes by the name Patch."

Chisum shook his head. "I've hired a few new men, but he ain't one of 'em. Sorry you chased all the way out here for nothing. I was just about to have a drink, come in if you care to join me."

"That'd go real good after a long ride, Mr. Chisum." Roth brightened, now fully recovered.

"Dawn Sky, we'll take our whiskey in the parlor."

Roth's gaze followed the girl as she floated away on a swirl of colorful skirt.

"Please call me John." Chisum smiled leading the way to a spacious parlor appointed in leather-covered chairs and a settee drawn up before a massive stone fireplace. Lamplight gave the adobe walls and plank floors a warm glow.

"Sit down boys." Chisum settled himself in a comfortable chair beside the silent fireplace. "Now tell me about this man you're lookin' for."

Roth picked up the story. "You hear about the Navajo girl that was murdered over at Fort Stanton?"

Chisum nodded gravely. "Terrible thing that was, cut up and all the way I heard."

"Since early spring, I've been on the trail of the man who did it. He's killed four women we know about. One of 'em was Ty's wife."

Chisum cut his eyes to Ledger. "I'm sorry, son, real sorry. I guess that explains the partnership. I take it your part in this ain't exactly official business."

Ty shook his head.

Dawn Sky came into the room with glasses and a bottle of whiskey on a tray. She set the tray on a low table in front of the settee where Roth sat. She poured three glasses of whiskey. The scooped neck of her cotton blouse revealed soft copper woman's swells. She smelled of cinnamon. The effect hit harder than a whiskey buzz. She served Chisum his glass and handed another to Ty. Roth caught her eye for an instant as she handed him his glass, a small smile softly turned the corners of her pretty mouth. Roth felt the air sucked out of the room as she withdrew. He couldn't recall having been so affected by the mere presence of a woman.

Chisum called Roth back from her siren song. "Well for justice or money I'd sure 'nuf like to help you catch a skunk like that. Don't know that I can, though. What makes you think he's still around here?"

Ty took over the conversation for the obviously distracted Roth. "He came this way to sign on with the boys down at Seven Rivers."

"Now you got my interest. I know some about them sons a bitches."

"The way we pieced it out, the gang scattered after some raid they were on. Patch never came back to the ranch. Next thing we knew he killed the girl at Fort Stanton. We thought he might have decided to sign on with you."

Chisum shook his head. "I like to think I'm more particular than that. The raid they was on hit my river valley herd. Me and my boys caught 'em on the Rio Hondo. We run 'em off and recovered our cattle, but the rustlers saw us comin' and got away. Evans claimed he had cattle stolen too, accounting for the Seven Rivers brands mixed in with my Long Rail steers. The rustlers took the running iron with them so I had no way to prove they was changin' the brands. Probably wouldn't have made a difference anyway. The two-bit sheriff up to Lincoln is in Dolan's pocket. The House buys the beef Evans and his boys run off and sells it to the army and the reservation cheap. We've caught 'em red-handed and had the charges dropped. I'm hirin' guns to make my own law." He turned to Ty. "Say, you're a US marshal."

Ty nodded.

"While you're lookin' for your wife's killer, maybe you could help us prove Dolan and Evans are behind the trouble we're havin' around here."

Ty scratched the dark stubble on his chin. "I don't know about my jurisdiction here, John. I was deputized up in Wyoming. I'm happy to help if I can, but officially I'd have to clear it with Marshal Sherman in Santa Fe."

Chisum knit his brows. "I don't know about Sherman. He seems honest enough, but the politics in Santa Fe ain't no better than they are in Lincoln, just more of it."

"Johnny and me met Marshal Sherman on our way through Santa Fe. I expect he'd remember me if I was to wire him and ask for authority to look into your complaints."

"I'd be much obliged if you would, Marshal. I'm not in favor of takin' the law into my own hands, but I'm damn sure gonna protect what's mine if the law won't."

"I'll see what I can do, John. I can't promise anything. That one-eyed killer's my first order of business."

"Sounds like that needs doin' too. We'll keep an eye on things and let you know if we come across anything. Now I expect you boys could use a bite to eat and a place to bed down. I'll take you down to the bunkhouse and introduce you to my foreman, Wade Caneris. He'll have Cookie put on a couple of extra plates. The bunkhouse is full, but Wade will find you a place you can bed down in the barn."

As they walked to the front door Roth glanced into the dining room opposite the parlor. She stood in the shadow of the kitchen door, her dark eyes following him. He smiled. She dropped her eyes. A faint scent of cinnamon quickened his pulse.

Roth clasped his hands behind his head and stared into the black barn loft. The sweet smell of straw mingled with the familiar tang of horse sweat. The occasional hoof stomp thumped through the hard packed dirt floor. Ty breathed quietly out of sight in the shadows nearby. The air felt thick and warm. Roth got up. He shook a bit of straw out of his hair and walked to the pool of moonlight at the barn door. The night stillness hung in the air, with only the barest whisper of a breeze to freshen it.

She stood like a statue across the yard beside the house. She stared off to the west, the point of her chin tilted to the night sky. He felt drawn to her. He set off across the white lit yard his boots crunching the parched dirt. She seemed not to notice as he drew near. The planes of her cheeks and the bow of her lips made delicate carvings touched in moonlight. Her presence radiated a mysterious strength.

"I knew you would come."

Her voice sounded soft and low like the night breeze. A curtain of unbound hair fanned in black wisps.

"How did you know?" His throat cracked dry on the question.

"I felt your spirit call to me. You are the one they call Johnny."

"I am." She turned to him, her eyes hooded in shadow. They touched him across the span of an outstretched arm that separated them.

She tilted her chin up at him. "The evil one you search for was here."

"How do you know?"

"I felt the evil. He is a very bad man. He frightens Dawn Sky."

"Don't be afraid. We'll get him. Besides, I'm sure you're safe enough here with Mr. Chisum. Is he, is he your husband?" The question felt clumsy, awkward for the asking. Where had that come from? She lifted her eyes to his and shook her head. He liked the answer before he heard it.

"My mother was his slave. She died when I was a child. Mr. Chisum raised me like a daughter. I serve him now. Dawn Sky knows no other life."

"Have you always been able to feel people's spirits?"

She nodded. "It is a gift and a curse. Dawn Sky cannot explain it."

"What did my spirit say when it called to you?"

She lowered her eyes into shadow.

He could feel the warmth of her blush.

"It made Dawn Sky's heart sing."

"I'll take that for something good."

She lifted her eyes to his. Work-hardened fingers touched his lips with the light brush of fine silk. She turned and disappeared around the back of the house. Roth stood stone still in the moonlight, transfixed by a vanished apparition and the faint scent of cinnamon.

Chapter Twenty-Two

Lincoln

Deputy Marshal Rob Widenmann rode into Lincoln under a cloudless sky bleached blue white by a blazing mid-afternoon sun. He jogged his horse through the sleepy west end of town and drew rein at the sheriff's office. He stepped down and looped a rein over the hitch rail. His tired mount shifted hip shot as a tumbleweed bounced down the street running east through town. He clumped up the step and let himself into the dimly lit office. The sheriff sat at his desk.

"Sheriff Brady, Rob Widenmann, US marshal's office, Santa Fe." Widenmann stuck out his hand.

Brady rose and shook the offered hand. "Marshal, what can I do for you?"

"Marshal Sherman sent me down to look into the trouble you've been havin' with some of the ranchers around here. What can you tell me about what's goin' on."

Brady's eyes narrowed. *Federal law from Santa Fe, what the hell was that about?* He shrugged. "We've had some complaints of rustlin'. Lots of finger-pointin' between big operators like Chisum and the small ranchers, but nobody's been able to prove anything."

"You've looked into the allegations of course."

"I got a small office here, Marshal, just me and a couple of deputies. We can't cover the whole county. None of it strikes me as a concern for federal jurisdiction."

"Marshal Sherman's concerned about a report that Chisum may be takin' matters into his own hands."

"He's hired some men. They run a bunch of rustlers off a herd stolen from the Seven Rivers boys. Chisum claimed the cattle was his. Ended up one man's word against another. Likely hurt Mr. Dolan worse than either of 'em."

"Dolan?"

"James Dolan, owns the mercantile here in town. He's got contracts to supply beef to Fort Stanton and the Mescalero reservation. When the Seven Rivers boys couldn't fill his order he had to find another source of supply. Likely more expensive, I reckon."

"Sounds like Chisum had cattle."

Brady shook his head. "Chisum'd rather have Dolan's contracts than a fair price for his stock."

"Hmm." Widenmann smoothed his mustaches. "Where might I find Mr. Dolan?"

Brady jerked his head. "Big building on the right where you came into town."

Back outside Widenmann woke his sleeping horse and led him up the street. A hand-lettered sign over the door proclaimed, *J. J. Dolan & Company.* He wrapped a rein around the side yard fence and ambled over to the front door. The visitor bell clanged over protesting hinges. A sleepy-eyed clerk poked his head out from behind a dusty shelf.

"Where might I find Mr. Dolan?"

The clerk jerked an unruly fringe of white hair toward an office door at the back of the store. Widenmann's boots clipped the worn plank floor as he crossed the store to the office. Dolan sat at his desk, puzzling over a ledger scratched with figures in neat rows and columns.

He rapped the door frame. "Mr. Dolan? Rob Widenmann, sir, US marshal's office. May I have a moment of your time?"

Dolan gestured to the chairs drawn up in front of his desk. "Have a seat, Marshal. What can I do for you?"

"Marshal Sherman sent me down from Santa Fe to look into the trouble between the ranchers around here. I understand you brought the matter to Governor Axtell's attention."

"I did. I rely on the small ranchers for the beef I supply the army and the reservation. I've been concerned for some time that they're bein' pushed out of business by Chisum monopolizing the free range. Now he's turnin' the Pecos valley into an armed camp with hired guns. It's a bigger problem than local law enforcement can handle."

"So the sheriff says. He also says rustlin' charges have been brought on both sides."

"That's just Chisum's excuse for bullyin' the small ranchers. He don't like the competition. He'd be just as happy if he could ruin them and me. Then he'd have those government beef contracts all to himself. Pretty penny they'd fetch that day with no competition."

"What would you have me do about it?"

"Stop Chisum from takin' the law into his own hands for a start. Most if not all of those guns he's hired has got to be wanted. Find out who they are. Arrest them that's wanted and Chisum won't be able to muscle the small ranchers around the way he does. If he leaves 'em alone, I'll have a fair chance of meetin' my contract obligations to the army. I lost good money and a lot of it over the last herd Chisum stole. My man had to buy replacements from him to keep me from defaultin' on my contracts. The son of a bitch knew he had me over a barrel. Stuck it to me real good he did."

Widenmann bunched his lips under his mustache. "I'll ride down to South Spring and give Chisum's crew the once-over to see if we've got dodgers on any of 'em." *Chisum just might have another side to the story.*

"Best not listen to anything that lying sidewinder says, Marshal. He's a land-grabbin' cattle thief. That's how the governor sees it. So will you, if you get it right."

Widenmann narrowed his gaze. He didn't appreciate Dolan's threatening tone. The man seemed cocksure of the governor's opinion on the matter, damn cocksure. "I'll keep that in mind, Mr. Dolan."

"See that you do, Marshal. I'm sure you'll get on just fine."

Widenmann collected his horse and led him across the street to the Wortley Hotel. He didn't notice the two riders down the street headed his way. He looped a rein over a cracked split rail and climbed the step to the dusty lobby. A fat black fly buzzed to a stop on the counter. A thin balding clerk, better suited to scaring crows, rewarded the fly with a halfhearted swat.

"What can I do for you?"

"I'll be needin' a room for a few days."

The clerk spun the register around to his guest. "That'll be a dollar a night." He took a key from the board behind the counter as Widenmann signed.

Outside, Roth and Ledger stepped down at the rail and climbed the step to the Wortley lobby.

The clerk glanced at the register. "Room two, Marshal Widenmann, down the hall there."

Roth glanced at Ty.

"Excuse me, are you a US marshal?"

He glanced over his shoulder at two young men behind him. The tall one with the dark shave asked the question. The one with the double rig looked on for the answer.

"Deputy Marshal Rob Widenmann at your service."

"My name's Ty Ledger, deputy marshal out of the Wyoming Territory. This here's my partner Johnny Roth."

"You're a long way from home, Marshal. What brings you

down here?"

"Please, call me Ty. We came after a murderer, but one of the local ranchers asked me to look into a problem he's havin' with rustlers. I was plannin' to contact Marshal Sherman up in Santa Fe to see if he might give me the authority."

"Marshal Sherman sent me down here to investigate similar complaints. I may need the help. Let's talk."

"Let us get checked in."

"Meet me in the saloon and I'll buy you a beer."

"Best offer I had all day." Roth smiled.

The bartender set three frosty mugs on the table and returned to his other job in the kitchen. Widenmann lifted his glass and took a long pull. He wiped foam from his mustache on the back of his hand. "So what sort of trouble have you been asked to look into, Ty?"

"John Chisum says the Seven Rivers boys are rustlin' his cattle and sellin' em to Jimmy Dolan for his government contracts."

Widenmann arched a brow. "Funny, Dolan and the sheriff told me Chisum was tryin' to run the small ranchers out of business by turnin' the Pecos valley into an armed camp."

"Chisum's hired some men. Says he has to protect what's his since the sheriff won't lift a finger to enforce the law. He claims the sheriff is in Dolan's pocket."

"The sheriff says he doesn't have enough men to look after the whole county. Dolan complained to Governor Axtell. He says Chisum is tryin' to run the small ranchers out of business. That's what got Marshal Sherman up to sendin' me down here."

Roth paused, his glass halfway to his mouth. "We know some about them small ranchers down on Seven Rivers. The outfit's headed up by Jesse Evans. The killer we're after spent some time workin' for him. We went down there lookin' for him. He wasn't there. We signed on with Evans for a time, hopin' our boy would show up. Turned out he never came back after some cattle raid Chisum and his men busted up. We picked up enough talk to know it was Evans and his men Chisum run off. Evans covered his tracks by claimin' he had cattle stolen too."

"So you say Chisum's got the right of all this."

"Sure looks that way to me," Ty said.

"Tell me about this killer you're after."

Roth took the question. "One-eyed half-breed, gets his enjoyment out of forcin' his way with women and killin' 'em for sport. Four we know of so far. One of 'em was Ty's wife."

Widenmann glanced at Ledger. "I'm sorry."

Ty nodded to his beer.

Roth let it pass. "I picked up his trail in Deadwood. Ty signed on in Cheyenne. Last we know he killed a Navajo girl over to Fort Stanton a couple of weeks ago."

"One-eyed half-breed makes for a pretty recognizable description."

"You'd think so." Ty's voice barely rose above a whisper. "So far the son of a bitch has been smart enough to stay one step ahead of us."

"You think he's still around these parts."

"Dawn Sky thinks so." Roth drained his glass.

"Dawn Sky?"

"Chisum's housekeeper."

"How would she know?"

"Long story."

"Well I expect I need to ride down to South Spring and have a talk with Chisum myself in a couple of days."

Roth signaled the bartender for another round. "Mind if I ride along?"

"I wouldn't mind the company a bit. What about Ty here?"

"I expect Ty would rather keep an eye on things here in Lincoln." A knowing twinkle crossed Roth's eye.

Ty fixed him with a hard set to his jaw.

Chapter Twenty-Three

Ty climbed the porch steps and rapped on the green door. He removed his hat, absently turning the brim in his hands. The door creaked open. A portly older woman, with strands of gray hair trailing from a bun piled high on her head, looked him up and down with warm gray eyes.

"Yes?"

"You must be Mrs. O'Hara, Ty Ledger's my name. Is Lucy here?"

Mrs. O'Hara smiled. "Why, yes she is. Won't you come in? I'm sure she'll be pleased to see you." She stepped back from the door and called up the stairs. "Lucy dear, you've a gentleman caller."

A light step sounded at the top of the stairs. Ty looked up. A cloud of blue gingham floated down. Lucy smiled. Her eyes twinkled.

"Ty, what a pleasant surprise, what brings you back to Lincoln?"

He shuffled his boots. "A hunch, sort of, I guess."

Lucy made a low throaty chuckle at his tongue-tied answer.

"What's funny about that?"

"A girl could hope for more reason than that." She watched the color rise under the coarse dark stubble on his cheeks. She smiled again.

Mrs. O'Hara pursed her lips and turned her ample bosom down the hall toward the kitchen at the back of the house.

He recovered himself. "I, I thought I'd drop by to see if you had supper plans for this evening."

"As a matter of fact, I don't. Say, I've got an idea. Buttercup needs some exercise. I'll fix us a picnic supper while you fetch her up from the livery."

"Best idea I've heard all day. I'll be back right quick." He put on his hat, stepped off the porch and hurried down the walk.

Lucy closed the door and made her way to the kitchen where she found Mrs. O'Hara lining a picnic hamper with a clean checked napkin. Lucy busied herself slicing a loaf of fresh bread.

"He seems like a nice young man."

"He is."

"He likes you well enough to get schoolboyish around you."

Lucy smiled. "I hope he likes me."

"Here, take some of these pickles."

Lucy took a smoked ham from the pantry and set it on the table. Mrs. O'Hara handed her a sharp knife.

"You like him too, then."

Lucy met her eyes in admission. "Yes, I do."

"That sounds like the makin's of a good beginning."

"It's not that easy. Ty's wife was murdered this spring. He's here looking for the killer."

"Is that why you're here?"

Lucy blushed. "Maybe." She cut two thick slices of ham and returned the ham to the pantry.

"You take it from my widowed years, dear. You want him, don't let him get away."

Lucy put the knife on the washstand. "You can't take what's not ready to be given. He needs to settle his accounts. Then we'll see what happens. In the meantime all I can do is keep him comin' back."

Mrs. O'Hara nodded. "Like I said, don't let him get away."

A knock sounded at the front door as Lucy finished packing

the basket. "That'll be Ty, give me a minute to change into my riding clothes."

Lucy ran off to the front hall and hurried up the stairs, leaving Mrs. O'Hara to follow with the basket and a knowing smile.

The widow opened the door. "Come in, Mr. Ledger. Lucy's just gone up to change."

"Thank you, ma'am." Ty removed his hat and stepped in. The door clicked closed behind him.

"Come have a seat in the parlor. I've heard quite a lot about you."

Ty followed the portly widow into a neatly appointed if somewhat threadbare parlor. He took a stiff wooden chair beside the settee that seemed too small to hold his frame. "Mostly good I hope."

Mrs. O'Hara seated herself on the settee. She appraised the length of him over the rim of her glasses. "Of course it's mostly good, but then I must consider the source. Such judgments I find are best left up to me."

He shifted uncomfortably in the chair, unable to shake the feeling of a stallion led out at auction.

"Tell me, Mr. Ledger, how long do you plan to pursue this desperado you're after?"

"Till I get him, ma'am, and please, call me Ty. Desperado might be too kind a term for the animal we're after, but I won't disturb your sensibilities with the particulars of what he's done."

Her eyes softened in wrinkled folds at the corners. "I've heard some of it. I thank you for that. Will you be staying in town long?"

"For a spell I reckon. Johnny and me think he's still in the area and Lincoln's the biggest town around. He has a habit of lookin' for his victims in town."

"Oh my, there's a dreadful thought. About the man you're looking for I mean, not you staying in town. I suspect there's a young lady upstairs who might like that idea."

The chair became intolerably uncomfortable. His ears burned telltale red. A stair creaked beyond the parlor. He turned to the promise of a rescue.

"Now, Mrs. O'Hara, I hope you haven't been too hard on Ty here." Lucy smiled from the hallway at the bottom of the stairs. "We wouldn't want to scare him off, would we?"

Ty rose, grateful for the chance to escape all this feminine attention. He crossed the parlor. Lucy picked up the hamper from the side table in the entry and took his arm.

"You two enjoy your ride and don't be too late with that killer skulking about."

Outside the slanting rays of setting sun began to paint the street in long shadows. Lucy ran down the porch steps to the fence gate. Buttercup greeted her with a soft whicker and a warm nuzzle. Ty followed carrying the hamper. He tied it on the back of his saddle. He gave Lucy a leg up, untied Buttercup and handed her the reins. He swung up on the steel dust and wheeled west out of town.

They splashed across the river, sun lighting the surface a golden fire. The horses surged up the west bank. Lucy glanced over her shoulder at Ty with a mischievous grin and put her heels to Buttercup. The little buckskin broke fast. He answered the challenge, putting the steel dust into his gallop without need of much encouragement.

Buttercup stretched her gallop. Wind whipped Lucy's sable hair, streaming burnt red in the fire claiming the western peaks. Ty pulled alongside, flashing a determined grin as they climbed into the hills. She gave a low throaty laugh and bent to the buckskin's neck. Buttercup's black mane flicked her cheek. She could feel Ty's smile merge with the power of Buttercup's stride beneath her. She thrilled to the rhythm of the little mare's stride. She swept up a grassy knoll and reined in near the top.

"This looks like a perfect place to have a picnic and watch the sunset."

Ty nodded and stepped down. He ground tied the steel dust and untied the hamper and his blanket. He handed the hamper to Lucy and spread his blanket. She dropped to her knees and opened the basket. He tossed his hat on the blanket and sat beside her. They ate in silence, watching the orange red sky sink into purple behind ragged mountain peaks.

"That was pretty," she sighed. Her eyes shown with reflected last light. He smiled. As if announcing the second act of the evening's entertainment, crickets struck up their night song. Lucy looked over her shoulder. "Oh my, look at that." A full moon hung low and bright on the eastern horizon.

They turned to watch it rise. She inched closer to him. He wrapped an arm around her and drew her head to his shoulder. She felt light and comfortable resting against him. The moon rose, growing smaller as it climbed higher. A glittering blanket of stars spread across the night sky. Reflected light lit the fine features of her face. She tilted her chin and caught him staring at her.

"See anything you like, cowboy?"

He gave her a squeeze, drawing her to him. She lifted her chin, the bow of her lips touched in moonlight and shadow. She felt small and delicate. Her eyes drifted half closed as he bent to her. A small pulse beat in her throat. Her breath tasted soft and sweet. He touched her lips with his. Her arms reached for him. The kiss exploded in white light. Breathing stopped. Hungers ignited. He lost his balance feeling himself floating, falling. The coarse wool blanket brought her to him. Somewhere deep at the back of her throat, she made a small sound. He remembered to breathe. Her heart hammered against him. He held her close. She yielded to him, passion bound in calico and denim. Desire etched in granite.

She broke the kiss with a small gasp and rolled on her back. He hovered over her. A single crystal tear trickled down her cheek in the moonlight.

"Lucy, what's wrong?" His voice felt rough and thick.

"Oh, Ty, it's me. It's the old me. I've never felt for a man the way I feel for you. You're someone special. I want to be special for you. I don't want to be that saloon girl anymore."

"You are special." He kissed the tear away.

"You really mean that?"

"I do. And I understand what you mean. There's no shame in want. We both want, but we've time to wait till it's right."

She turned her eyes to his, soft and smoky. "Ty Ledger, I could kiss you."

"I believe you already did. In fact, parts of me are damn sure you did."

She blushed in the moonlight. "I'm sorry."

"Don't be. Feelin's like that give a feller reason to keep comin' around."

She smiled misty-eyed and melted into his arms with a kiss sweet and clean as new spring grass.

Chapter Twenty-Four

Widenmann and Roth rode out of Lincoln in the gray light before dawn. They trailed southeast toward South Spring. The sun rose hot in a clear blue sky. A stiff breeze blew out of the northwest at their backs.

"Not that I mind the company, but what makes you think you might find your killer around Chisum's place?"

"He's ridden with Jesse Evans's Seven Rivers boys against Chisum. Dawn Sky says he's been around South Spring."

"Chisum's housekeeper?"

"Right."

"She's seen him?"

"Not exactly, more like she felt him. If he's been back, she'll know. If not, I'll probably ride down to Seven Rivers to have another look around."

"What's the connection between Dolan and the Seven Rivers boys?"

"Dolan provides a ready buyer for cheap beef. His army contracts sell below market. He needs a cheap supply. What could be cheaper than stolen cattle? He pays Evans and his boys enough to make it worth their while and he keeps the difference."

"You're pretty sure Dolan is buyin' rustled stock."

"I'm sure of it. We heard it out of Evans's own mouth."

"They got a boy down there by the name of Frank Baker?"

"They do. Why?"

"Chisum brought him in to Sheriff Brady back in the spring. He filed rustlin' charges on him. Had a witness too. I looked at the records before I left Santa Fe. Baker claimed he didn't do it. Said he caught Chisum's man tryin' to run off Seven Rivers cattle. The charges were dropped. One man's word against another. Course it didn't help none that Chisum's man was black."

"Yeah. That story strikes me as convenient if you're buyin' cattle cheap from those small ranchers and sellin' it to the government. I can promise you Dolan ain't askin' for a bill of sale on the stock he buys."

"Word around the courthouse was the district attorney got pressure from the governor's office to let Baker off. Seems like a lot of influence for a small-time ranch hand."

"More like the kind of influence that gets a man government cattle contracts."

"That's what I thought when you and Ty told me Chisum had the right of the Seven Rivers boys stealin' his cattle. Might make settlin' this case a bit awkward."

"What do you mean awkward?"

"Politics up to Santa Fe is a little one-sided. Some folks call it the Santa Fe Ring. Marshal Sherman don't hold with it, but there's folks up there with a lot of power. It don't look like Chisum's got many friends among 'em."

Roth shook his head. "Give me a nice simple bounty to collect every time. I know who I'm after and which end of the gun to grab."

Widenmann chuckled. "Times like this, I envy you that."

"Let's pick it up. If we push some we'll make South Spring by tomorrow evening."

Patch drifted south from Fort Stanton in the general direction of returning to Seven Rivers. He struck the Rio Hondo and paused to water his horse. He let his thoughts drift with the current. They led him to the rich hacienda. The girl filled his mind's eye. He might have had her had the big black man not come to her bidding. The hacienda too promised riches untold. The possibilities tugged at his medicine mingled with greed. His pony lifted its nose from the stream. His nostrils flared to the breeze with a soft whicker.

Patch swung east along the riverbank. The day wore into slanting light. Purple haze bloomed foreshadowing an end to the day. He drew rein in a copse of cottonwood along the river bottom. A deep ravine spilled out of the hills to the riverbank. The ravine would shelter a campsite with graze and water for his pony among the trees. He gathered wood for a small fire in spite of the evening heat and built it on the floor of the ravine near the riverbank. He stripped to breechclout and moccasins in the way of his Comanche blood and sat cross-legged before the fire. He ate a simple meal on the roasted haunch of a rabbit he'd taken along the trail at midday. Night sounds surrounded him. The river gurgled. Crickets chirped. A mournful coyote wailed in the distance. His eye became heavy. He drifted into a troubled vision.

She appeared in the flames beyond the circle of firelight. The witch mocked him. She stroked the medicine bag at her belt. His mouth went dry. Her taunt stirred his need to hunt. The vision blurred. The witch tormented him. She drew him to this place. She smiled wickedly. She meant to strip him of his medicine with her witchcraft and kill him. He must kill her first. *Yes, he would take his vengeance from her. He would feed his power with her blood.* He gripped the hilt of his blade. He felt the heat of the fire. He took it for her fear. Blood and hate fed pain and power. Vengeance gripped his hand. The blade flashed, plunged, slashed and thrust. The vision exploded in gouts of red mist and flame. He fell beside the embers, his rage spent for a time.

Darkness closed around him. The hacienda and the girl appeared in his dreams. The witch could wait for another day. Tomorrow he would hunt.

South Spring

Caneris led his horse and the big buckskin Chisum favored across the yard to the house. He looped the reins over the rail, ducked underneath and clumped up the steps. Dawn Sky answered his knock followed moments later by Chisum.

"The boys are ready, John."

Chisum took his hat down from the peg beside the door and lifted his Henry rifle from the gun rack. "We're gonna move the river valley herd further north where we can keep an eye on 'em with a bigger crew, Dawn. Don't wait supper. It'll likely be late by the time we get back."

She nodded. Caneris followed Chisum down the steps to the horses. She watched them gather their reins and step into the saddle. Chisum wheeled the buckskin and squeezed up a trot across the yard to the bunkhouse where a half dozen mounted men waited beside the road to the main gate. The riders fell in behind as they loped down the road to the gate. They swung southeast, raising a cloud of yellow dust against the clear blue sky and soon disappeared into the hills. *Don't wait supper* meant she had only to prepare for her own needs. The bright sun promised a fine day. She could do her chores for the day in the morning and treat herself to a bath in the creek beyond the garden.

The land shimmered in golden waves under late afternoon sun. Dawn Sky walked barefoot along the garden path down to the creek. The barest hint of breeze stirred plant leaves and ruffled tendrils of unbound hair. She paused at the creek bank, absorbing the warmth of the sun. The creek ran slowly now, its banks withdrawn from the spring runoff. A gentle gurgle where it touched the rocks made soft music. She wriggled her toes in the hot sand and lifted her blouse over her head. Light breeze licked a trickle of sweat between her breasts. She untied the thong at her waist and let her skirt pool at her ankles. She stepped out of the skirt and waded into the stream. She settled into the gentle flow, warm yet refreshingly cool against the heat of the sun. She rested her head on a flat stone and gave her body to the current. Sunlight glittered on rippled surfaces where the stream burnished the rich copper hues of her skin to a sparkling sheen.

She let her thoughts drift. The current caressed her, soft and pleasant. She imagined ice-blue eyes as she had that night in the garden. She felt no shame for her nakedness. A small ripple of desire stirred, strangely drawn to the vision of a white man. Sun and sensation mingled. Her eyes drifted half closed. She let herself become one with the stream.

Patch drew rein in the hills, overlooking the hacienda. He saw no sign of movement beyond a lazy dust devil, circling the deserted corral. He waited and watched. The sun warmed his back. Nothing moved. He eased his pony forward, picking his way down the rocky slope. He approached the hacienda cautiously, searching for any sign of movement. He reached the bank of a shallow creek. Something splashed nearby, up the stream. He slipped down and crept up a small rise along the bank. A slow smile creased a tight cruel line. Hot blood quickened. The prize to slake his thirst lay in wait up the stream.

An evil presence intruded on the pleasant song, chanting her reflections. She sensed it, sudden, close. Alarm caught bitter in her throat. No time to think. She scrambled up the bank, grabbed her clothes and ran toward the house. Her heart pounded. Exertion and fear pumped her legs.

★ ★ ★ ★ ★

Patch watched her bolt from the creek gleaming wet. He laughed. He ran to his pony and leaped into the saddle. He put his heels to the pony's flanks, galloping up the creek bed in a spray of glittering light. He bore down on the fleeing figure. Terror filled the wide dark eyes that glanced back over her shoulder. She bounded up the step to the back door as he slid his pony to a stop. He leaped from the saddle little more than steps behind her. His moccasins touched the ground as the door slammed. He mounted the steps to the porch in two long strides. He put his shoulder to the door as a heavy bar dropped into place on the other side. He heard heavy breathing close. He beat the door with his fist in frustration. Bare feet slapped the floor beyond his reach. There must be another way in.

Dawn Sky ran through the kitchen to the front of the house. She bolted the front door and pulled a Winchester from the gun rack beside it. Her breath came in tight gasps.

He circled the house, pausing to look in each window. At the second near the front of the house he saw her across the dimly lit room. A dark shadow, she fumbled with her skirt. She bent to step into it. A blood vision enflamed him. She managed to pull the stubborn skirt over her damp hips and disappeared from sight. He ran to the front porch.

A board creaked on the porch beyond the door. Soft moccasins lapped hollow, coming closer, closer. The door latch clicked. The bolt jarred. A muffled grunt strained on the other side. Would it hold? Instinct told her it would not. Not for long, not for this crazed evil spirit.

★ ★ ★ ★ ★

Muffled metallic rifle action sounded alarm behind the door. He twisted away from the door frame as the shot exploded. Wood splinters burst from the hole where he'd stood an instant before. Armed she might deny him his prize. He drew his pistol, angered. He eyed the door hinges. Two shots might defeat the bolted door. Beyond the door the rifle jacked another round.

Chapter Twenty-Five

Roth drew rein. "You hear that?"

"Sounded like a gunshot."

"South Spring's just yonder. That could mean trouble." He spurred the black into a gallop. Widenmann broke hard on his heels. He crested a rise overlooking the ranch. A paint horse stood at the back of the house, no sign of a rider. *Dawn Sky,* her name exploded in his brain. Fear turned his gut to an icy ball. A second shot cracked the stillness beyond the house. Roth cut his eyes to Widenmann and filled his right hand with a gun. He pounded down the gentle slope to the back of the house.

Patch heard them. *Riders come fast.* He ran down the porch away from the approaching hoofbeats. He ducked around the side of the house and circled back toward his pony. Two men galloped toward the house from the northwest. They splashed across the creek and galloped toward the front of the house. He let them pass around the house to the south and ran to his pony. He swung into the saddle. He heard boots on the front porch. Someone called her name. He kicked up a gallop around the hacienda, coming at the riders from behind. Their horses stood at the side of the porch. He rolled over on his pony's neck in position to fire under the horse's head. He shot the bay horse in the hindquarter. The black bolted. They would not be quick to pursue him. A pistolero dressed in black on the porch spun toward him. His gun flashed on a firing line, spitting fire and powder burn.

The shot whined over the empty saddle. Patch fired. The bullet pitched the gunman back against the hacienda door where he slowly slid to the floorboards. The second man in a black coat fired wildly as he galloped away.

He pulled himself back into the saddle and ground his teeth in frustration. Twice he'd been denied this girl. *What magic protected her?*

Roth sat up holding his left arm. Widenmann turned to him.

"How bad he get you?"

"No more'n a scratch. Ruin't a damn fine shirt, though."

Inside the door bolt scraped. The latch clicked open. Dawn Sky looked from Widenmann to Roth, holding a Winchester. She set the rifle beside the door and dropped to her knees beside Roth. Wide-eyed fear softened to concern. "You're hurt."

"Just a scratch, I'll be fine."

"Come into the kitchen. We must clean and bandage that." She helped him to his feet. He held the bloody sleeve to staunch the bleeding.

"I'll see if I can track down those horses. I think he may have shot mine." Widenmann set off after the horses, standing nervously at a safe distance in the fields north of the house.

Dawn Sky led Johnny into the kitchen. She pulled up a chair, sat him down and placed his hat on the table. She unfastened the buttons of his shirt and gently peeled it off his shoulders, exposing the wound. She bent to examine it. The bullet tore through his upper arm without striking bone. She went to the washstand and took a clean towel from the shelf below. She pressed the towel to the wound. "Hold this."

Roth did as he was told. He followed her with his eyes as she filled a kettle with water from a cistern and set it on top of the stove. Her light cotton blouse clung to her wet copper skin. She bent to stir the fire to light. Her hair dripped black diamonds onto her shoulders and the tile floor. It occurred to him he should avert his eyes. He couldn't. He guessed she'd been in the creek for a swim when he came on her.

"Did he hurt you?"

She paused at the stove, her back to him. "No. He meant to, but I felt him watch me. I ran to the house." Satisfied the water would heat, she turned to his injured arm. His eyes followed her. She seemed unconcerned by the immodesty of her circumstances. Roth forgot his wound. She lifted the towel.

Her hand brushed his. He felt something pass between them. He closed his eyes. Cinnamon sweetened iron blood smell. He reminded himself to breathe. "How did you know he was watching you?"

She shrugged. "Sometimes I know things."

"Like the night I found you in the garden?" He caught the corner of one dark eye through the curtain of her hair.

"Yes." Her voice came soft and low. She hesitated. "I was thinking of that before, before he came."

"Did you know I was coming then?"

She replaced the towel and turned to him. "No, I only hoped." She turned away as though she might have said too much. She busied herself checking the kettle.

Roth smiled. "You know they say a watched pot never boils."

She ignored him. "We will need bandages." She said it as if to herself and left the kitchen.

She moved with a quiet strength Roth had never noticed in a woman before. She was all woman for sure, all that and something more. He found himself waiting impatiently for her to come back when she'd been gone mere moments. She returned with a small bundle of muslin strips. She set them on the table and went to the stove. She took a fresh towel and soaked it in the kettle. She picked the kettle off the stove and set it beside his chair. She knelt beside him.

She removed his hand and the bloodstained towel from the wound. He felt quiet strength in her touch. She took the clean towel from the kettle and began washing the wound. It hurt. He eased the pain, inhaling cinnamon. She leaned close, her attention concentrated on cleaning the wound. So close, he could feel soft warmth. Sunset streaming through the kitchen window bathed her in red golden light. Dark copper skin came alive to the light. Breathing slowed, caught tight in his chest.

"I'm glad he didn't hurt you."

She lifted her eyes to his, locked, unspoken. "I should be more careful when I go to the creek."

"Go to the creek?" He'd guessed that part, why bother prying?

She pursed the delicate bow of her lips as she considered her words. "To bathe." She returned her attention to his wound.

He could see it all then, as clear to him as a vision to her. She'd given him something of herself in that moment, something that tasted sweet. She'd been thinking of the night he found her in the garden *before, before he came.* Suddenly capturing or killing the one-eyed bastard wasn't as much about money. It was about protecting this girl. He understood something more of Ty's loss.

"Promise me you'll be more careful."

She lifted her eyes to his and held them for a breath or two, considering the request and the man who asked it. She nodded and placed the blood-soaked towel in the kettle. The water turned pinkish. Strong fingers bound his arm with clean muslin strips.

Sundown deepened to early evening purple shadows. Roth and Widenmann sat at a long lamp-lit dining table eating the supper Dawn Sky prepared for them.

"Cain't remember havin' a fried steak taste this good." Roth munched a juicy forkful. Widenmann only nodded, filling his mouth with fresh-baked hot buttered biscuit. The arm hurt. Roth put his best face on it. Dawn sat in the corner across from the kitchen. Her eyes full of concern. He smiled as though nothing mattered except her cooking.

As they pushed back from the table, Dawn cocked an ear toward the front door. "Mr. Chisum comes." She left her chair and went to the door. Roth and Widenmann followed. They stood on the porch silhouetted in lamplight spilling out the open door. A pale moon lit the dust cloud following the blue-black riders up the road to the corral. Two riders separated from the group at the corral. They rode on to the house and the two men waiting on the porch with Dawn Sky.

Chisum drew rein and stepped down. He handed his horse's lead to Caneris. He recognized Roth as he stepped up on the porch. He took in Roth's bandaged arm as he extended his hand. "Looks like we might have had some trouble here."

"Afraid so, John." Roth took the rancher's hand in his good one. "Our killer paid a call on Dawn this afternoon."

Chisum cut his eyes to the girl. "You all right, honey?" She nodded.

"Marshal Widenmann and I showed up in time to run him off, though she'd been givin' a good account of herself before we did."

"Marshal?" Chisum turned to the dark stranger.

"Rob Widenmann, Mr. Chisum." He offered his hand. "Pleased to meet you."

"I'm in your debt, sir. Please call me John." Chisum put a protective arm around the girl. "You sure you're all right?"

She nodded again. "I shot two holes in the door."

"A door we can fix. The important thing is that you weren't hurt."

"The bad man shot Joh . . . Mr. Roth."

Chisum arched an eyebrow at her familiar reference to the handsome bounty hunter.

"It's no more than a scratch. Dawn patched me up. I'll be good as new in no time."

"Come on in and let's have a drink. It's been a long day all around."

The men settled in the parlor while Dawn went to fetch the whiskey bottle and glasses.

"I'm grateful you came by when you did, Johnny." Chisum glanced at Widenmann. "I don't suppose it was a social call."

"Johnny rode down here with me, John. Marshal Sherman sent me down from Santa Fe to look into the rustling complaints and reports that the disputes may turn violent."

"Well you come to the right place. I got plenty of rustlin' complaints, not that they do me any good with that two-bit tin star they got sittin' on his ass up in Lincoln. As for disputes turnin' violent, I expect the sons a bitches been stealin' my cattle think they already have."

"Johnny and Ty filled me in on some of that."

Dawn returned carrying a whiskey bottle and glasses. She set them on the table beside Chisum's chair. Chisum poured three glasses and passed one to each of his guests. He lifted his glass. "Here's thanks to the two of you. Dawn's like a daughter to me. I'd sure as hell be broke up if she was to get hurt or worse."

Roth lifted his glass. "We'll get him, John. I got a pretty good idea where he went."

"You best take care of that arm first."

"Time you get some rest," Dawn said. She left no room for disagreement.

Chisum pointed his chin at Roth. "You're on notice now, boy."

"I'm fine."

"You can have my room. Dawn Sky sleep on a mat nearby."

Roth raised his good hand in protest. "You'll do no such thing."

"Dawn Sky will do such thing. First change your bandage then put you to bed."

Chisum chuckled. "She's made up her mind, Johnny. You'd best go along peaceably, or I'll not be responsible for what happens next."

He drained his glass and stood. She really didn't have to ask him twice to go with her. "I guess this is good night, then."

"Get some sleep, son."

Roth followed Dawn out of the room.

"Care for another, Marshal?"

"Don't mind if I do. So who's behind the rustlin', John?"

Chisum refilled their glasses. "Jesse Evans and his Seven Rivers boys do the dirty work. Dolan's the money and brains behind the outfit, though I can't prove that part. We've caught Evans and his boys red-handed, but it don't come to nothin' with the law up in Lincoln. Brady's in Dolan's pocket. End of story."

"How do they get away with it?"

"The politics is all stacked on the side of the thieves. Frank Baker and some of Evans's men murdered a man on my night watch this spring. Baker denied it. Brady let him walk. One man's word against another he said. My witness was a freedman. You figure it from there."

Widenmann nodded. "I know about that one."

"Now it's up to me and my boys to protect what's mine. I'm surprised they sent for you. Seems like takin' a chance honest law might show up around here."

"Maybe you and your boys are doin' too good a job."

"Dolan lost money on his last army delivery. He actually had to buy the stock at market prices instead of at rustlers' prices."

"Well they may have made a mistake by callin' us in. You catch any more of 'em, you let me know. I'll lock 'em up over at Fort Stanton. Maybe we can get somebody to talk."

"You figure you've got jurisdiction to do that?"

"They're sellin' to the army. Those are federal contracts. I admit it's a stretch, but it might hold up long enough to get us some proof."

"I'd be much obliged for your help, Marshal. Now if you don't mind, I'd like to turn in myself. It's been a long day. You're more'n welcome to the guest room. It's right this way." Chisum led the way down a dark passage toward the back of the house. A single lamp lighted the guest room with a comfortable bed turned down for the night.

"Much obliged for the hospitality, John."

"Not much by way of thanks for your help. Best I can do just now."

She led him to a small room at the back of the house. She struck a match and lit an oil lamp on the table beside the bed. The room was clean and simply furnished. She turned down the coverlet. "You sit. I get bandages." She disappeared in the dark passage they'd come through.

Roth sat on the bed, suddenly tired. He worked the heel of one boot with the toe of the other, trying to remove it without straining his arm. Dawn returned with the bandages. She set them on the table beside the lamp and knelt beside him. She pulled off one stubborn boot and then the other. She unbuttoned his shirt and slipped it off his shoulders. The bandages crusted brown with dried blood.

"Bleeding stopped. That good." She untied the bandages one strip at a time. A small amount of fresh blood seeped from the deepest part of the wound. She reached across him, plucking a fresh bandage off the table. She felt close and warm against his chest. She re-bandaged the arm, tying it snug, her fingers strong yet light on his skin. He felt something in her touch. She must have noticed it too. She looked up, he caught her eyes and held them. Everything slowed in that moment. A small pulse beat in her pretty throat. She reached for another bandage. He fought the urge to take her in his good arm. She applied the bandage quickly, sensing the tension. She reached for the last bandage, wrapped and tied it in a moment. He caught her hand as she began to rise. She looked up at him, soft dark pools a man might drown in.

"Thank you." It seemed silly, but they were the only words he could force through the tightness in his chest. He cupped her chin in his hand. She did not pull away. Her eyes drifted half closed, riding the crosscurrents charging the moment.

"He'll never hurt you. I promise." He leaned forward. She rose to him. Her lips met his. Time stood still, soft and warm and cinnamon.

Heat flushed her cheeks. Her breath caught. "Dawn Sky nearby if . . ." Her words trailed off, the thought unfinished. She hurried from the room, closing the door behind her.

He felt strangely alone. He'd turned in alone every night for as long as he could remember without so much as a second thought. Not this night. Something had changed, something that smelled of cinnamon.

Chapter Twenty-Six

Johnny woke to the smell of coffee and bacon. He'd slept longer than usual. The pain in his arm reminded him why. He struggled into his pants, boots and shirt. He followed the sound of sizzling fatback to the kitchen. She stood at the stove. He remembered the kiss. He told himself he should feel a little sheepish. He didn't. The memory of her warm touch flooded him.

She looked over her shoulder. Morning sun touched her smile. "Did you sleep well?"

He nodded and crossed the kitchen, drawn to her side. She turned to him and tilted her chin, her expression one of quiet amusement. He held her eyes. Something had indeed changed, something unspoken, something good. He kissed her gently. She shuddered. He felt the echo.

"You make me burn bacon," she breathed.

He chuckled.

"They are in the dining room."

Chisum looked up when Roth came in. "How's the arm."

"It'll be good as new in a couple of days."

"Good, sit down. Help yourself to a cup of coffee. Dawn's got breakfast on."

Johnny poured a tin cup of steaming coffee and took a chair at the table.

"Marshal Widenmann here is fixin' to head back to Lincoln this morning."

"Don't s'pose you'll be ridin' back with me."

Roth shook his head. "I'm goin' after Patch."

"Not before arm heals." Dawn set a steaming bowl of scrambled eggs on the table for emphasis along with a platter of bacon and a basket of biscuits.

Chisum chuckled. "See what I mean?"

Roth didn't protest. He helped himself to some eggs and passed the bowl to Chisum. If he had to take it easy for a day or two, she'd be nearby. He turned to Widenmann. "Do me a favor then, Rob."

"Name it."

"Tell Ty I've picked up our boy's trail. He'll want to be in on this."

"Sure, glad to. Hope you get him."

"We will." His eyes cut to Dawn.

She lowered her eyes and returned to the kitchen.

Seven Rivers
August 1877

Patch settled in at Seven Rivers with little more than a "Where the hell have you been?" from Evans. To which he made no reply. Two days later things changed. Frank Baker returned from Lincoln with a load of supplies and a bit of news.

The boys gathered around the long table on the bunkhouse porch eating supper. Jesse held his fork up at the head of the table. "Beef steak sure beats the hell out of fatback, Buck."

Morton's moon face gave him a sloe-eyed half smile. "Never can tell when one of them Long Rail steers gets itself lost down this way."

"Son of a bitch Chisum won't never miss 'em," Buckshot Roberts drawled. "We ought a have beef more regular than we do. It'd aid the digestion of William's beans." Morton hated his proper given name. Roberts mocked him with it at every opportunity.

"There ain't nothin' wrong with my beans."

Evans had enough bean talk. "What's news up to Lincoln, Frank?"

"Not much. The news out of Fort Stanton might bother us some, though."

"What news?"

"Chero and his band jumped the reservation up in Oklahoma." All around the table eyes turned to Baker. "Word is they's headed for their ol' stompin' grounds in Texas."

Roberts looked to Evans. "We'd best keep an eye out all the same. That's a might too close for comfort where C'manch is concerned."

"You said Chero?" All eyes turned to the usually silent half-breed.

"I did. Why, is that snake somethin' to you?"

"Chero owes Patch a debt."

Evans laughed. "That's a good one. Fat chance you'll collect anything from him. Reservation Injuns ain't known for bein' wealthy."

"Blood is a debt."

Evans sobered. The half-breed glared pure venom. "You go after that bunch you'll wind up staked out under a skinnin' knife."

Patch met Evans's gaze in one blazing black pit. He rose slowly and left the table. Next morning he was gone.

Texas

Texas stretched out before him, vast and harsh. Wind-driven sage and sand rolling in an endless sea. He rode southeast. Hot wind drove him toward the old lands of his mother's people. He searched for sign. He knew this trail. He would find them near the place they drove him away so many summers past. Memory pictured the place he would find her.

The urge to hunt grew with each passing mile. It did not stir the familiar blood lust. The vision of the witch taunted him, hard and cold like her namesake winter moon. She mocked him as though he were a stranger. Her blood fired his rage. He savored the hate. She married the white man. She made him an outcast. Those he killed were taken in her place. Now she would fall before his blade. She would take his pain in a way the others could not. He would free his spirit of the ghost that haunted him.

Day drifted to night, night to day. Hot grew cold. Dark faded to dawn. He searched. He rode through endlessly rough country whipped by harsh wind. Sand stung his skin. Mile after mile the trail wandered over parched dry land patched in scrub sage. Sun scorched his good eye. Clouds of biting flies followed him like the witch's curse he carried.

She watched his passing, always just beyond reach, never leaving him. The presence fed his need to hunt, the demand to kill. She led him. She mocked him. She called him to his death. She did not hear her own death song in the calling. She did not see her death. Only he had that vision. Only he tasted vengeance. She cursed him with the uncontrollable urge. A curse he would return in her death.

Days later he crossed a trail. The sign said forty, maybe fifty ponies, some trailing travois. They traveled south. He stepped from his pony and knelt to study the trail. Pony sign said they passed this way some days ago. The hoofprints said they rode at an easy pace. He had time to catch them, time to find the witch who sent her vision to torment him. He looked off to the south. Blood and hate shimmered in the heat and dust on the trail to one final hunt. He swung up on his pony and squeezed up a lope.

★ ★ ★ ★ ★

South Spring

He found her in the kitchen as he had each morning. He took a brief moment with her before joining Chisum for coffee. She turned from the stove to greet him. Her eyes took in the double rig slung low on his hips. They clouded in question then saddened with knowing. He went to her with his soft morning kiss. She rested her head on his chest. Her arms flew around his waist, holding him in fierce silent protest.

"I have to." He whispered into hair scented cinnamon. She looked into his eyes and refused to let go. "I won't be long."

"Oh, I, ah." Chisum stood gape jawed at the kitchen entry. Dawn turned back to the stove.

"Mornin', John," Roth fumbled. "We was just sayin', ah, good-bye."

Chisum studied his empty coffee cup, reminding himself why he'd come to the kitchen. He'd seen the way Dawn looked at Roth. He'd taken it for concern. No fool like an old fool. "You plan on leavin', then?"

"I got a killer to catch."

Chisum poured himself another cup of coffee, glancing sidelong at Dawn. She stood stone-faced, poking a fresh-baked biscuit with a fork. "Coffee?" Roth nodded. Chisum poured a fresh cup. "That trail's plenty cold by now." He broke the tension in the kitchen by leading the way to the dining room.

"Don't need no trail. I figure he's gone back to Seven Rivers." They drew up chairs at the dining table.

"If you're fixin' to go down there, maybe me and a few of the boys ought to tag along. I'd hate for you to run into an unwelcome reception from Evans and his gang of cutthroats. We'd be more'n pleased to back your play with that bunch."

"Thanks for the offer, John. That would even things up some."

Chisum changed the subject with an awkward silence and an

appraising eye.

"John, about what you saw in there . . ." His words trailed off.

Chisum's brows knit, his eyes fit to bore holes in Roth's soul.

"I, we've found some feelin's for each other."

"She's like a daughter to me, Johnny. I'll not have her hurt."

"I wouldn't hurt her for the world, John. My case on that killer got personal when he come so close to hurtin' her."

Chisum sat back, pressing a thumb and forefinger to the bridge of his nose. "She's a grown woman. I have to remind myself of that. We've been together so long I don't want to admit it might not always be that way. You plannin' on comin' back after you get him?"

"I am."

In the hall beyond the dining-room door, Dawn Sky's heart took flight. She nearly dropped their breakfast plates.

Chisum nodded. "We'll speak more of it then."

Chapter Twenty-Seven

Lincoln

Widenmann jogged through town headed for the Wortley. Late afternoon sun trailed long shadows over windblown dust puffs kicked up by his horse. Not much moved in the heat of the day. Most folks took shelter in quiet chores. The few who went about some errand or other did so in brief appearances, giving as little of themselves to the heat as possible. Three horses stood hip shot at the cantina rail. Two more were tied out front of Dolan's store. Widenmann had the street to himself when he stepped down at the Wortley.

His boots scraped the plank floor, announcing his arrival. The scarecrow clerk dozed on a stool behind the registration counter. He swayed unsteadily, keeping his perch by some long practiced inner sense. He remained undisturbed by the new arrival. Widenmann tapped the counter bell. The scarecrow jerked awake, blinking owl-eyed.

"Oh, ah, welcome to the Wortley. What can I do for you, Marshal?"

"I need a room for a couple of days."

The clerk slid the registration book across the counter and turned to the board behind the counter to select a key. Widenmann scanned the page. Ty Ledger was registered.

"Is Mr. Ledger in?"

"No sir, I don't believe he is. That'll be a dollar a night."

Widenmann slid a five-dollar gold piece across the counter.

"Any idea where I might find him?"

"Try the widow O'Hara's place. The young lady he's been seein' stays there. If he ain't there she'll likely know where to find him. Mrs. O'Hara's is the white house with the green door on the east end of town. You cain't miss it." He handed Widenmann a key. "Room five is in back."

He stowed his gear in the cramped stuffy room and opened the window in hopes a night breeze might freshen things up. Back out at the hitch rack he stepped into the saddle and trotted back to the east end of town. He stepped down in front of the house with the green door and looped a rein over the picket fence. He sauntered up the walk to the front porch. Lace curtains hung in the windows gave the place a homey feminine touch. He rapped on the door. Footsteps sounded near the door. An older woman with graying hair piled high on her head greeted him. Widenmann tipped his hat.

"Mrs. O'Hara, Robert Widenmann, US marshal."

"What can I do for you, Marshal?"

"I'm looking for Ty Ledger."

"Well you've come to the right place. He and Lucy is fixin' a picnic supper to take for an evenin' ride." She smiled conspiratorially and whispered, "Sparkin's better in the hills." She called over her shoulder to the kitchen. "Ty, there's a US marshal here to see you."

Ty appeared at the end of the hall to the back of the house followed by Lucy. "Rob, I see you made it back from South Spring. Is Johnny with you?"

The marshal took Ty's hand. "No he's not. That's why I'm here. We had a run-in with your boy four days ago."

Ty tensed. "Anybody hurt?"

"We caught him tryin' to get at Chisum's housekeeper. Johnny caught one in the arm. Just a flesh wound, nothing serious. Anyway, he wanted me to let you know. Best we figure he headed south. I expect Johnny will be going after him as soon as he feels fit to ride. He took him attackin' that girl kind a personal. I think he might be sweet on her."

"Roth sweet on a girl? Why, it wouldn't be Johnny if he weren't. Thanks for bringin' word, Rob. Looks like I'll be headed to South Spring in the morning."

Behind him, Lucy grimaced. Just when she thought she might find a place in his life she felt a ghost again for a rival. The need to avenge her murder overshadowed everything for him. Would he free himself this time? Would she lose him to a killer's bullet? What if avenging her death didn't free him? A bittersweet mixture of fear, love and longing gathered in her heart. The marshal brought her back to the moment.

"Well, I'll be on my way. I don't want to spoil your ride," he said with a wink at Ty. "Good day, Mrs. O'Hara. Miss." He tipped his hat back on and left.

"Well, then." Lucy put her best face on. "Let's finish packing that saddlebag and go have a picnic. Looks like it may have to last a while."

They splashed across the river and into the purple hills without the carefree air that usually accompanied their evening rides. Sunset and the picnic passed in near silence as though some dark fog pooled between them. As the stars spread their blanket across the night sky, a breeze blew out of the north touched with night chill. Ty wrapped an arm around her. She rested her head on his chest.

"You know I have to do this."

"I know you think you do. I only pray that when it's done, it's enough."

"What do you mean enough?"

"Enough to set you free. Your heart's married to a ghost, Ty. Every time that one-eyed monster pops up somewhere, you're off on another chase. Tomorrow you'll be gone and I'll be left here to wait and wonder. If anything happens to you, I might never know."

"Lucy, darlin', that's no way to talk."

"Maybe so, but it's the sad truth."

"We're gonna get him this time. I can feel it."

Lucy looked up to him. Tears welled in the starlight. "I hope you do, Ty, I truly hope you do. I want you rid of that demon because it's plain enough, I can't have you until he's done tormenting you."

Ty hated the sight of sorrow in those eyes. That he put it there pained him even more. He kissed her tears dry, tasting salty sadness. She nuzzled against him, soft and warm. Her lips found his. They floated on the night breeze, drifting slowly, slowly to earth like falling autumn leaves locked in embrace. He'd been careful not to let things get away from him out of respect for her desire for a proper courting. Somewhere in the back of his mind he reckoned the fortress of those good intentions was under serious assault.

Night music cloaked them in light and shadow. The give-and-take of the kiss, the press of her body, slowly sapped the strength of higher purpose. He rose on one elbow, resting her on the blanket beneath. His hand caressed her cheek, her shoulder, her arm. He paused at her tiny waist. She pulled back, eyes half lidded. Her breath rose and fell, caught somewhere between desire and reason. Her fingers found his shirt collar button.

"Is this what you want, Lucy?"

"Yes."

"No."

"I don't know. I thought I wanted a shiny knight, but that only happens in fairytales. It's the silly notion of a foolish girl. I'm no girl anymore, Ty." She kissed him again, hard and urgent.

He held her close. "I'm no shiny knight."

"You can say that if you want. I still think you are."

"So much for fairytales."

"Oh I think this one's just begun. Once, upon a time." Her words trailed off in a flurry of gingham and denim.

Candlelight cast her shadow across the room. She stared at the blank page, uncertain of her feelings, less so in how she might record them. She fingered the pen, letting her mind return to that hillside, to the blanket of stars and the feel of him. It had been truly special. True feelings once exposed couldn't be hidden. She gave him her feelings. He'd accepted them. He gave something in return. How much? How deep? Was it enough? She couldn't be sure. She trembled with the echo of him. He truly was special. She wanted more. Did he? Did he have it to give?

She'd changed things between them. She'd convinced herself she wanted a proper courtship out of some girlish notion. A fine man like Ty Ledger would have respected that if she hadn't led him on. In the end, she was the one who changed things. She didn't have the strength of her own conviction. Did it matter? He was a man after all. Men weren't burdened by foolish notions like lost innocence. Or were they? Might he think less of her for what happened between them? Only time would reveal that. She hoped not. He'd known her for who she was from the first time they met. She picked up the pen, dipped the tip in the ink pot and set it to the blank yellow glow.

Things changed tonight. Marshal Widenmann brought word. Patch attacked a woman at South Spring. Ty will be off after him in the morning. We took our picnic to the hillside west of town. That killer haunts him. I think she does too. I hope he gets him this time. I hope it puts her to rest. For better or worse, we gave up the masquerade tonight. I gave up the masquerade. I hope he can love the honest truth.

Chapter Twenty-Eight

Seven Rivers

Chisum called a halt on a rise overlooking the Evans ranch. Roth drew up beside him. The boys fanned out along the crest of the hill, making no attempt to conceal themselves or their numbers. Chisum had his best guns with him. Frank McNab, Doc Scurlock, Bill McCloskey, Charlie Bowdre, Tom O'Folliard and Jose Chavez, all heavily armed. A hot wind whipped hats and bandannas as they looked over their rival's stronghold.

Chisum eased back in his saddle. "How do you want to play this, Johnny?"

Roth scratched the stubble on his chin, squinting in thought. "Don't suppose we'd be welcomed if we just rode in there. Same for me if I rode in alone. Let's ease on down there. Show 'em your firepower, John. I'll go in for a parley. See if I can get Evans to give him up."

"Lead on."

Buckshot Roberts hefted a forkful of hay and froze. He had a bird's-eye view from the barn loft. Eight he counted. "Riders comin', Jesse!"

Evans clumped out to the front porch followed by Frank Baker. Buck Morton wiped his hands on a dirty apron and stepped out of the cookshack into the sun-soaked yard. "Best take cover, boys, till we figure what the hell this is about."

"Frank, bring me a rifle." Roberts's short-barreled shotgun

was better suited to close range.

Baker grabbed two Winchesters and a box of shells from the rack inside the house and ran to the barn. Morton returned to the shelter of the cookshack. Evans watched the riders. They drew a halt at two hundred yards or so, close enough to identify Chisum and his hired guns. One rider separated from the group and rode in, empty hands in plain sight. He drew rein at the yard gate. Evans recognized him.

"What do you want, Roth? Why the hell did you bring that bunch with you?"

"Afternoon, Jesse, nice to see you too. We're lookin' for Patch."

"He ain't here."

"You wouldn't be hidin' him would you?"

"What for?"

"He's wanted for murder."

"You the law?"

"No. There's a bounty on his head."

Evans laughed. "You'd better hurry if you plan to catch him while he still has his hair."

"What do you mean?"

"Chero and his band jumped the reservation. Patch has some kind of score to settle with him. He lit out of here as soon as he heard about it. If he ain't dead already, he's probably somewhere in Comanche country."

Roth eased back in his saddle. "You wouldn't lie to me would you, Jesse?"

"For a no-account half-breed with all them guns at your back, why would I? He ain't worth spillin' blood over. You're welcome to him, if the C'manch don't get the both of you for your trouble."

Roth didn't like it, but it had the ring of truth to it. "All right Jesse, my friends and I will be on our way. If I find out you're lyin', we'll be back. In the meantime, let me do you a favor. Chisum's got a competent crew lookin' after his cattle. You'd do well to keep that in mind."

Evans scowled. It had the ring of good advice.

Roth wheeled the black and squeezed up a lope back to Chisum and his men. He drew up beside the rancher.

"Well, what's the story?"

"He's not here. Chero and his band jumped the reservation. Evans says Patch has some sort of score to settle with him. He's gone off after the C'manch."

"You believe him?"

"No reason for him to lie about such a thing."

"I can think of one."

"What's that?"

"Send you off on a wild-goose chase in hostile country."

"If that's it, he got it right."

"You're not thinkin' of goin' after him are you?"

"I am."

"Hell, Johnny, if Evans's story is true, you can kiss your killer's sorry ass good-bye. That son of a bitch Chero will butcher him."

"Seems like folks of all stripes around here hold the same opinion of ol' Chero."

"He cut a bloody path through these parts before the rangers finally corralled him. If he's off the reservation we all best keep our eyes peeled. Hopefully he's headed back to his old hunting grounds in Texas. We got no use for him here."

"That's likely where I'll find our boy, then."

"No amount of bounty's worth runnin' into Chero."

"It's not just the bounty, John. After what he tried to do to Dawn Sky, I understand why Ty wants him so bad. It's got kind of personal."

"You won't do her no good if you go get skinned alive. Them

C'manch know how to kill so death's a mercy."

Roth looked off to the east. "I doubt I can find Patch's trail, but he'll be lookin' for Chero's trail. It's harder to hide a whole village."

"You're crazy, Johnny."

Roth cut his eyes to Chisum and shifted the Colts on his hips. "Just take care of Dawn till I get back."

"That might never happen."

"I'll rest easier knowin' she's cared for." He squeezed up a lope to Texas.

Texas

The trail led southwest toward the Pecos. Chero would camp near the river close to his old hunting grounds. Patch found an abandon campsite where they struck the river. From there the trail followed the river west. He felt the presence of the witch grow strong. Soon he would find her. He rode into the hills north of the river valley. Here he had the best chance to see the village before any of the band saw him. He followed the river valley for three days. Early one evening smoke sign smudged the purple sky in the distance. He rode on, cautious of the hills and gullies around him. As the sign drew near he found a thicket of cottonwood trees along the banks of a small stream. The creek spilled its way through the hills down to the river. He picketed his pony in the trees and melted into the gloaming hills for a closer look.

Hidden in the rocks overlooking the valley he made out the village in the fading light. Thirty tepees spread along the riverbank at a gentle bend where shallow water made good bathing and washing. The ponies were picketed along the grassy bottom east of the village. Cook fires pricked the gathering shadows. One cook fire was the fire of a witch. He must find that fire. Then he would wet his blade in her blood. He would break her curse with vengeance.

He returned to his pony and made a cold camp. He would wait and watch until she showed him his chance.

Each day he went to his place in the rocks to watch the village. On the morning of the fourth day Chero and his warriors rode out to hunt. They followed the river east searching for game that came to the river to drink. With the warriors away he had his chance.

Later that morning women and children left the village. They climbed into the hills carrying berry baskets. As they came toward him, he saw her among the women. Hard years bent her frame. She moved slowly. The bad medicine she carried still hung at her belt. Rage rose in his breast. His breath came short and tight. He fingered the hilt of his knife. He felt it cut. A blood-red vision swam before his eyes. Not here. Not now. Too many were with her. He would find her at night, alone in her lodge, Chero's lodge. Yes there, in the devil's own lodge he would spill the witch's blood.

He slipped back from the rocks, away from the approaching gatherers. He hurried to his pony. He must leave for now, or risk being discovered. This day he would hunt game. The meager supplies he'd taken from Seven Rivers were nearly gone. He would return at the end of the day to learn the lodge where he would find her.

South Spring

Ty pushed the steel dust out of the hills. South Spring sprawled across the valley below bathed in bright afternoon sun. He'd made good time on the ride down from Lincoln. He angled south to the gate and jogged up the road to the house. He spotted Chisum talking with Caneris at the corral. They turned to watch him ride in.

"Afternoon, John, Wade." He stepped down.

Chisum lifted his hat and wiped sweat from his forehead on a bandanna gone damp with the work. "Afternoon, Ty. Figured you'd be along about now."

"I came as soon as I got the word from Marshal Widenmann. Where's Johnny?"

"Gone to Texas after your boy."

"Texas?"

"Seems old Patch has a score to settle with a renegade C'manch named Chero. Chero jumped the reservation up in Oklahoma Territory and headed back to his old hunting grounds. Patch left Seven Rivers to go after him. We picked up his trail at Seven Rivers. Johnny went after him."

"Alone?"

Chisum nodded. "I tried to talk him out of it."

"What the hell made him do a fool thing like that?"

"Patch tried to attack Dawn Sky. Johnny took it personal. Kind of like you he said."

Ty shook his head.

"What are you gonna do?"

He glanced off to the south and thought for a moment. "If you'll stake me to some supplies, John, I'll be goin' after him."

"That makes two of you."

"Two of us?"

"Crazy."

Chapter Twenty-Nine

Texas

Hot wind and dust followed dust and hot wind. Roth cut his trail southeast, grinding out mile after mile. If the Comanche planned on surviving out here somewhere south of the Canadian, it had to be near the Pecos. That guess was a gamble. Patch had several days head start and likely some idea of where he was headed. Anticipating the band might gain him some ground. Then again it just might lose the whole play. There were times a man had to trust his gut. He wheeled the black south and squeezed up a short lope.

With afternoon sun slanting out of the west he began to look for a campsite. Another day of oven-baked rolling hills, sand and scrub offered little in the way of hospitable prospects. An ever-shifting sea of desolate, dry scrub stretched as far as the eye could see in all directions. Jump a reservation for this? Things there must be poor beyond imagining.

All at once the black pricked up his ears. His nostrils flared to the breeze. He quickened his step. He'd caught the scent of something. It could be trouble, but Roth doubted it. More likely it was water. He expected to strike the Pecos anytime now. He let the black have his head at a brisk trot. He kept his eyes peeled, alert to his surroundings.

Twenty minutes later the black mounted a rise. A gently sloping valley fell away below them. Patches of green appeared in the distance, springing up along a river bottom. The black gave a snort at the strong scent of water. Roth eased the horse down the valley wall to the river bottom. He picked up an easy lope to the riverbank. The prospect of grass and water and a little shade lifted the spirit. It promised relief from the harsh conditions of recent days. It'd be near as welcome as a first-rate hotel.

The riverbank brought more than respite from the heat, dust and wind. He'd crossed plenty of trail sign to get there. The trail had long gone cold, but a goodly amount still remained. Even if some of the sign had been lost he saw enough to suggest a large party headed west. He found the remains of a campsite on the riverbank.

He stepped down and ground tied the black. As he walked along the riverbank among the scrub oak he counted the scorches of some twenty lodge fires. He found pony sign along the riverbank, all of it dry and hard, all of it but one. He knelt to examine that pile of dung. It was more recent than the rest. It had not yet dried to dust. Someone had been here and not that long ago. Someone was following the larger party. He stood and squinted along the river winding its way southwest where the setting sun flared orange atop distant purple hills. *Patch,* the name resolved a determined set to his jaw.

He unsaddled the black and picketed him in a grove of cottonwoods near the river. He gathered firewood in the purple shadows, advancing out of the east at sunset. He built a small fire and set a pot of coffee to boil while he spread his blanket. Supper consisted of hardtack and jerky with a little coffee to wash it down.

He'd tracked the killer for months by hunch and the bloody remains of his victims. Finally he had a trail he knew would lead to him. He'd thought about waiting for Ty to come down from Lincoln, but now that he had the trail he knew he'd been right to go on alone. Knowing Ty, he was probably not far behind. The important thing was that they get Patch. The breed had left a long trail of death and sorrow. He understood Ty's grief. He understood his desire for vengeance. The attack on Dawn Sky had given him his own stake in seeing the bastard dead.

He gazed past the circle of firelight. He could almost see her in the darkness beyond. What was it about her? He'd known lots of women, had his way with more than a few. He never had a problem picking up and moving on. What was it about this one that made her so different? She was pretty. Others were too. Her visions and feelings about things you couldn't explain were unusual and a mite unsettling. Her eyes were part of it. They spoke a language all their own. A language he somehow understood. Black as night pools they could reach out and hold him it seemed whenever she set her mind to it. They gave him a powerful urge to hold on to her in a way he'd never felt for any of the others. She came to him now, the sweet taste of her lips, a hint of cinnamon mingled with mesquite smoke. She felt good and warm and part of him in a way he couldn't explain.

Part of him, that's the difference.

Ty picked up Roth's trail east of Seven Rivers just as Chisum had suggested. The week-old trail had faded some, but Roth made it plain enough for him to follow without much trouble. West Texas spread out in a seemingly endless sea of windswept sand and scrub, a land so harsh it favored Comanche killers.

With his eyes fixed on the trail and the steel dust picking his way, he let his thoughts wander. He was no shiny knight. Now they both knew it. The heat of that moment hit with the force of a mule kick. Reason gone lost in a fiery moment, swept away in a flood. He'd held her then, sweet and soft and delicate as the night breeze against his skin. She wanted him to love her. Maybe he would one day. He had feelings for her sure enough. It took time for that with Victoria, so long ago. Back then he'd just been a man doing a job. He didn't have the heavy sense of loss that haunted him now. He'd kill the man responsible for that loss, but that wouldn't make up for it. Where did that leave Lucy? He'd let his head get away from him. That made the situation more complicated. She deserved better than that. *Damn!*

The trail took an abrupt turn south for no apparent reason. Ty drew the steel dust up. He squinted south against the sun shimmering over waves of rolling scrub. He'd seen no sign of the Comanche trail. *What made Johnny turn south?* Southeast made sense. That should cross any trail coming down from the north. Either Roth had seen something or he'd figured out where they were headed. In the end he could only shrug and nose the steel dust over to the south.

Pecos River

Chero and his warriors rode through the hills north of the river, returning to the village with their kill. White men killed the buffalo. Now the Comanche must eat the white man's cattle. Morning sun climbed high and warm as they passed above a campsite they'd used on the way to their homelands.

Chero lifted his eyes, following the trail home to the horizon. A strong hot breeze ruffled the loose hair at his shoulders. Gray wisps shot through his once-black mane, a concession to his many summers. His body retained the lean wiry muscle of a man in his vigor, though the passing seasons etched deep lines in his copper features. Freedom surrounded him here, freedom to feed his people, freedom to be a man. Freedom until the soldiers came to take them back to the reservation in the north. This time they would not take him back. This time he would find the freedom to die.

He drew his pony up, signaling a halt. He pointed to a dark speck, moving along the riverbank in the distance. A lone rider, Chero smiled crookedly. He exchanged glances with Singing

Coyote. "The women will have meat for their bellies and a white man to amuse them." Coyote nodded. Chero squeezed up a lope, closing the distance on the rider.

Hot sun climbed to mid afternoon. Roth checked his back trail for the third time in an hour. He scanned the horizon north of the river from east to west. He couldn't shake the feeling he wasn't alone. He eased the black over to the riverbank and stepped down. The horse dropped his nose to the water and drank.

High overhead buzzards circled lazily in the burning blue sky. Roth checked the south riverbank as he fished a hardtack biscuit out of his saddlebag and took a bite. The wide valley bottom rolled away for a good mile. No place to hide other than the cottonwood groves and scrub along the bank. He pulled the cork on his canteen and took a swallow to soften the biscuit. If anyone was following him it had to be from the north. He checked again, no sign of movement.

Finished with his drink, the black blew his nose and turned his attention to cropping river grass. Roth sat on the bank and took another bite of biscuit. He figured he'd gained some time on Patch with his guess on the river. How much he couldn't say. He guessed he'd find the Comanche soon enough. Would Patch be with them? Likely not, if he had a score to settle. Chances are he'd be stalking Chero while Roth stalked him. He glanced at the sun. Another good three hours to sunset. Time enough to put some distance between himself and his back trail, if need be.

Roth scanned the horizon as day settled into evening shadow. No sign of smoke. He pitched camp along the riverbank. A little hot coffee flavored and warmed the tasteless hardtack. He reckoned it safe enough to risk a small fire. An easy breeze out of the northwest would send the smoke down his back trail. He'd watched that all afternoon. He'd seen nothing. At the last he shrugged off his unease. Just a case of nerves brought on by the knowledge he was getting close.

The moon came up bright and clear only to disappear behind a curtain of low running cloud. He settled down to an uneasy attempt at sleep as the fire burned low. Night sounds seemed noisier than usual, or was that too all in his head? Somewhere a coyote barked. Another answered. Roth shifted his head on his saddle. It made a damn poor pillow. His eyes slowly drifted behind a light veil of sleep.

He jerked awake. His face slammed into the dirt beside his saddle. Strong hands pinned his arms behind his back. Leather thongs bit his wrists. The sour tang of unwashed bodies clotted his nose. Shadows moved everywhere, swift and silent. Here and there he heard a guttural word. *Comanche,* the realization turned an icy ball in his gut. He'd been right. He wasn't alone. He'd gotten careless. *Damn fool.* They jerked him to his feet. His knees turned to water. *How long would it take to die?*

Short powerful dark shadows held him hard and fast. One of them stepped out of the warriors swarming over the campsite. A dark mask with bright black pits sneered up at him behind a twisted foul-smelling grin. He made some unintelligible grunt. The warriors holding Roth drove him toward his waiting black. He guessed the fire-eyed one for Chero. They threw him up on his horse and tied his ankles under the black's belly.

Ponies appeared. Roth guessed there might be twenty or so. Warriors began to mount. One took the black's lead. The stocky one with the fierce eyes circled his horse, waiting for his warriors to mount. Satisfied they were ready, he wheeled away to the west along the riverbank.

Chapter Thirty

Comanche Village

Day after day he passed the heat in a rock crevice overlooking the camp. She went about her daily chores with a younger woman. This woman had children. He took her for Chero's younger wife. She had her own lodge. The old wife lived in another. He knew the one. For this she would die alone. He thought about killing the younger wife too. The children made too great a risk. Someone would sound the alarm. No he would put an end to the witch who tormented him and take his satisfaction in that. If Chero were foolish enough to come after him, the father would pay the debt of his worthless son.

Evening settled over the camp. Cook fires dotted the village, islands of light among the tepees. Smoke sign drifted into deepening shadows in the night sky. Women, children and old ones floated among the tepees. They settled in circles around the fires taking their meals.

Patch watched and waited. The witch's lodge stood in the center of the village near the riverbank, the younger wife's lodge beside it to the east. According to custom the lodges opened east to the morning sun. He planned his attack. Circle the village to the west. Leave his pony in the trees along the river west of the village. He would enter the village from the cover of the riverbank until he reached her lodge. If he took her quietly he could return to his pony and make his escape before the villagers awakened at dawn.

As the moon rose higher children began to disappear, leaving the women to clear away the remains of the evening meal. Old men sat at fires smoking and telling stories of the days before the white man's reservation. One by one they drifted off to their lodges as the fires burned low. The moon crossed over the sleeping village.

He left his place in the rocks and returned to the thicket. He stripped to breechclout and moccasins. If he were seen, he could be taken for one of their own. He collected his pony and rode west past the village out of sight in the hills. Pale moonlight painted the land a ghostly white. The somber mood of the land suited his purpose. He did not feel the strong urge that drove his usual hunt. Vengeance filled him. Deep and still, it smoldered in his blood like the coals of a slow burning fire. This kill would quench a flame the others could not.

West of the village he rode south out of the hills. He crossed the river bottom to a stand of trees along the bank. The current snaked toward the village, black and silent, ripples frosted in moonlight. He followed the bank to the east. The village appeared as a jagged cluster of shadows dotted in the orange glow of dying embers. He drew rein in a grove of cottonwood and scrub oak a short distance from the western most tepee. He slipped down and tethered his pony to a sapling in the darkness among the trees. He followed the sandy riverbank, clinging to the tree line, a shadow moving among shadows.

As he approached the first tepee, he dropped to his knees. He listened. The village slept among peaceful night sounds. He started forward, using the soft soil to cushion his moccasins. Off to the left a dark figure emerged from a nearby tepee. Patch dropped into the cover of darkness among the trees. His heart quickened in his chest. He had seen no sign of warriors since Chero and the hunting party left. The bent figure shuffled. An old man, Patch breathed. The old one made his way to the river. He made water, splashing in the soft mud. He shuffled back to his lodge and disappeared inside. The village fell silent once more.

Patch moved cautiously, pausing in the cover of rocks or trees to listen until he drew level with the witch's lodge. He gripped the hilt of his blade, gathering the sense of her like an intoxicating potion. Familiar hatred warmed his blood. Moonlight splashed the scrub leading from the river to the tepee shadow. He must cross it, exposed for a time. He searched for movement among the lodges. He saw none. Gentle night breeze off the river chilled his flesh. He shivered in anticipation. He took a breath and expelled it before trusting himself to move into the open. He crossed the short span of open ground swiftly and silently to the dark near side of the lodge.

He crouched in the shadows at the tepee entrance, listening. Steady breathing came from the darkness within. He drew his blade. It would silence her breathing. He slipped through the entrance flap and stood. Moonlight from the smoke hole pooled on the lodge floor and peeked around the edges of the tepee where the hides were raised to catch the evening breeze. He made out the dark sleeping form. He crossed the lodge on the paws of a cougar and stood over her.

She lay on her sleeping robe naked to the heat. Shadow hid her face. He pictured her watching them drive him away, her fingers stroking the evil medicine bag. She deserved a slow and painful death, an amusement he could not afford. Regrettably it must be swift and silent. Still she must know it for her own evil deeds.

He stepped astride her and dropped like a great mountain cat falling on its prey. His hand clamped her mouth tight, her eyes shot wide with surprise, bright white in dim light and shadow. Recognition flickered, followed by flashes of fear and anger. She struggled. She remained surprisingly strong in spite of her advancing years. He held her fast. He savored her fear for an instant before she jerked a knee into his groin. His vision exploded in a white flash of pain. His hand slipped on her mouth. She bit hard. A short scream burst from her throat. He slashed it to gurgling silence. Gouts of blood covered his chest, his belly and his arms. Her body jerked beneath him, its lifeless reflexes voiding the remains in death's final dance. She went still. He sat back on his haunches feeding fiery pain to his rage. Somewhere a camp dog barked an alarm. He must run. But, first, he watched. The blood-coated blade opened her. The witch poured out her torment, dead to him.

Confused voices outside joined the howling dogs. The sound of danger called him back from his fascination. He wriggled under the side of the tepee and crawled to the shelter of the trees along the riverbank. He slipped into the shadows and crouched, tense to what might come from the village. No one seemed to have noticed him. He backed away, moving as quietly as he could up the riverbank to his pony. Behind him the commotion in the village grew louder. Soon they would notice she was missing. Soon they would know the evil had come to an end.

They'd ridden all night. At mid morning tepees came into view. The village rambled along the river some thirty lodges in all. Seeing it Roth understood how a condemned man must feel, watching his executioners construct a gallows. He'd heard stories of how the Comanche tortured their captives, most of it left to the women. The old ones instructed the younger ones. Death became a mercy the torturers held out of reach. He closed his mind to the stories as the band rode into camp.

People crowded around a lodge near the center of the village. They sang a keening wail he did not understand. They melted back at the approach of the warriors, revealing what looked like a body wrapped in a blanket.

The one Roth took for Chero leaped down from his pony and went to the body. An old woman pulled the blanket aside. The mutilated remains of a woman cast unseeing eyes to the sky. Roth recognized the handiwork. Patch must have settled his debt.

Chero turned away, dark with rage. "Who killed Winter Moon?" He swept the circle of his people, looking for answers.

Roth couldn't make out the Comanche palaver, but he understood the woman must have meant something to Chero.

"A man came in the night. We heard Winter Moon scream. We found sign behind her lodge."

"Show Chero this sign."

An old man led him around the tepee where the crowd gathered. Roth watched them walk to the riverbank. As they turned west one of the warriors untied his feet. Rough hands jerked him off his horse and threw him to the ground. The women began to murmur among themselves as if noticing him for the first time. The old one who attended the body rose. She straightened her bent frame and came to stand over him. She looked down at him, her sun-hardened features etched in deep lines. Her eyes glittered, enflamed by the memory of an old way brought back by the presence of a white captive. She spoke in a raspy wheeze.

"Stake him."

Warriors jerked him to his feet. Roth's gut cramped in a sour knot. He fought a powerful urge to loose his bowels. They stripped him to the altogether as the whole of the village watched. They tied his wrists and ankles to wooden stakes and spread him on sun-baked ground. They stretched his arms and legs wide and drove the stakes into the hard packed dirt. Leather thongs cut his ankles and wrists. Hard cracked ground cut the flesh at his buttocks and back. The sun turned his vision to a bright red yellow haze. Shadowy figures moved about him, chattering in low tones hushed with excitement. Roth felt totally exposed, wondering where and when the first cut would come.

Suddenly a sharp voice rose over the crowd babble. Roth recognized Chero's commanding voice.

"Leave this one until we bring back Winter Moon's killer. He can watch this one to better know his own death. Come!" He shouted to his warriors. "We have good sign to follow."

Roth heard horses being mounted. He felt the ground shake as the warriors rode out of the village. He sensed the villagers drift away until only the curious young remained dark shapes beyond the veil of sunlight and thirst. They left him to await the unknown. Cutting he expected. This he did not. What might it mean? Nothing good.

Chapter Thirty-One

Lincoln
September 1877

Lincoln wasn't big enough for a stranger to remain unnoticed for long, especially if he was the handsome, well-turned-out English gentleman Lucy collided with coming out of Dolan's store. The parcels she carried scattered across the boardwalk.

"Beg your pardon, missus." The stranger bent to gather her bundles.

"No, no, it's my fault. I should have watched where I was going."

He straightened up and smiled a boyish grin. "Nonsense, dreadfully clumsy of me, I do hope you will forgive me." His voice trailed off as he handed Lucy her packages, first noticing her for more than a gingham cloud. "John Tunstall at your service, missus." He said with a stiff little bow.

Amused at his accent and stilted manners she mocked a curtsey. "Lucy Sample and it's miss." The word sounded forced. She could feel her cheeks flush in response to his dark-brown-eyed gaze.

"If I've damaged anything, I shall more than happily replace it."

"It's only dry goods and sewing supplies. I'm sure it's all fine."

"May I carry it somewhere for you, then?"

"You don't have to do that."

"Oh, but I simply must make some amends for the inconvenience I caused you." He smiled, reaching to take her bundles.

Lucy returned the smile and let him take her packages. *Charming manners, a gentleman, what's he doing in Lincoln?*

"Where to, then?" he asked.

"Mrs. O'Hara's house on the east end of town."

"Splendid. Lead on, then, Miss Sample."

She smiled again. "Please, call me Lucy, everyone does."

"Lucy it is, then, and you must call me John."

She led the way down the boardwalk in the bright morning sun.

"You're new in town."

"I am. I arrived only yesterday from Santa Fe."

"Do you have business in Lincoln?"

"Not yet, though, I believe I see an opportunity or two."

"Then you're planning to stay in town for a while."

"I should say. I quite fancy starting a business here."

"What sort of business?"

"J. J. Dolan & Company, I notice, have no competition in the mercantile business. That doesn't seem terribly sporting to me, does it to you?"

"They do charge a dear price for everything."

"There's a clever girl, my point exactly. I met a chap from Lincoln in Santa Fe a few weeks ago. He suggested I might find opportunity here. I plan to look him up and tell him I quite agree. He's a barrister. Perhaps you know him?"

Lucy wrinkled her nose. "Bar-ris-ter?"

"You know." He groped for the word. "A lawyer."

"Oh that must be Mr. McSween. He has his shingle out just down the block."

"Shingle?"

"You know, his license to practice law."

"Oh yes, quite so. You colonials are so quaint. You are correct, though, Alexander McSween is the very chap I met."

"Had to be. He's the only lawyer in town."

She turned in at the gate to a picket fence. "Well this is it. Thank you for carrying my packages, John. It was really very sweet of you."

"No trouble at all. And a fairly clever way to make the acquaintance of the prettiest girl in Lincoln, don't you think?"

She blushed.

"May I call on you another time?"

Ty cast a brief shadow at the back of her mind. She smiled up at the handsome Englishman undecided what to say.

He returned her smile. "I'll take that for a yes, then. Good day to you, Lucy."

He turned on his heel and strode purposefully back up the street the way they'd just come. *John Tunstall,* she wondered. The man surely had a confident way about him. He'd need that and more if he planned to take on Jimmy Dolan.

Next Morning

McSween maintained a storefront office across the street and down the block from J. J. Dolan & Company. He lived upstairs with his wife, Susan, who served as his assistant when anything needed assisting. This morning, like most mornings, he sat with his cup of coffee brushing up on some facet of his law training he hoped to employ one day in the service of a client. Today he'd chosen federal land grants, claims and deed registration. One thing Lincoln County had was land and lots of it. Sooner or later he reasoned somebody would want to own some of it.

The visitor bell clanged, announcing an arrival. A dark figure stepped out of the bright sunlight beyond the door.

"Alex, Remember me? John Tunstall, recently of Santa Fe."

McSween set his book aside and rose with a smile. He rounded the desk and offered his hand. "Of course, John, good to see you again. I'm pleased you decided to come down here to have a look at Lincoln."

"No surprise there, I said I'd come and as you will soon see I am, indeed, a man of his word."

"Come in, come in, have a seat." He gestured to a barrel-backed chair beside the desk and took his seat. "When did you arrive?"

"Day before yesterday, I took the liberty of having a look around before coming to see you. Your description of the situation here quite correctly points out the opportunity we discussed. J. J. Dolan & Company monopolize mercantile commerce. Their prices border on larceny. I can already see the merits of your idea. The use of a bank is a most ingenious twist on the mercantile. It also suits my thoughts on land speculation."

Footsteps sounded on the stairs to the residence. Susan McSween swept into the room on a flounce of green and white gingham.

"Oh, excuse me, dear, I didn't know you had a visitor. I've just brewed some fresh coffee. Perhaps you and your guest would care for some."

"Mr. Tunstall, this is my wife Susan. Susan, meet John Tunstall. This is the man from Santa Fe I told you about."

Tunstall stood and made a slight bow. "Mrs. McSween, a pleasure, I'm charmed." A twinkle in the serious young man's eye said he didn't miss the fact that Susan McSween had a stunning figure and fresh cream complexion topped off in a rich fall of auburn curls. Tunstall didn't read it in her soft hazel eyes, but all that proper femininity cloaked the hardy appetites of a woman with enough starch to take what she wanted whenever she saw it.

"Very nice to meet you, Mr. Tunstall. Alex told of your meeting in Santa Fe. I hope you find Lincoln up to your expectations for the journey." She eyed the Englishman. *Milquetoast.*

"I've just been telling Alex how pleased I am by what I've discovered."

"Splendid. Now about that coffee?"

"More a tea drinker myself, I'm afraid. Though I suppose if I'm to make my way among you colonials I shall have to learn to drink the stuff." He smiled. "Cream and two sugars, if you please."

She suppressed an amused smile. "I'm afraid our sugar doesn't come in lumps. I'll do my best to sweeten it properly."

"I'm sure it will be perfect."

"I'll have a cup too dear. Thank you."

She climbed the residence steps to fetch the coffee.

"Now John, what sort of land speculation did you have in mind?"

"Ranching initially, I think."

"Ranching, I must say you don't strike me as the type."

"Oh, I don't mean to become a rancher. I shall hire someone to do that. I mean to own it and run it as a business. I shall be far too busy with other aspects of our enterprise to do more than that."

McSween rocked back in his chair as Susan descended the stairs with two cups of coffee. She set the cups on the desk.

"That is a rather bold plan all at once, John. It will require significant amounts of capital."

"Yes, I quite understand. My father has rather substantial business interests across the British Empire. I am assured of his backing in these ventures. Cheers." He hoisted his coffee and took a sip.

Susan stepped away from the desk, scarcely believing what she'd heard.

Alex made a steeple of his fingertips. "You know, John, you'll be taking on The House if you do this. Dolan's not likely to take kindly to any part of your plan."

"Yes, well, you see that is precisely what appeals to me about this particular opportunity. The lack of competition strikes me as terribly unsporting. It renders this Dolan chap ripe for a takeover. So much the more so if he's impoverished of cash as you suspect."

"I doubt Jimmy Dolan will consider any of this 'sporting.' He'll play rough."

"That of course is what courts are for; but have no fear I'm not planning anything remotely illegal. As my solicitor, you will see to that for both of our sakes."

"When I say rough, I'm not talking about the law. I'm talking gunplay."

"Oh my, what a dreadful thought, I'm far too civilized to engage in violence. The only battle I'm interested in winning is in business. Should you join me in this endeavor as we discussed, you shall see I am quite good at it."

"I'm sure you are. I just want to make sure you know what you're getting into."

"Then you've reservations about joining me?"

"Just common sense."

Susan cleared her throat. Both men turned remembering she was still in the room. "Alex, Dolan has a stranglehold on this whole county. You've said as much yourself. The kind of competition you propose, Mr. Tunstall, comes at very high risk. In fact, risk understates it. James Dolan will shoot first and consider the consequences later." She held her husband's eyes letting her words sink in.

"Now, now, my dear, don't you think you are being a bit of an alarmist. John proposes a very generous and lucrative opportunity here. My only purpose in bringing up the possibilities is to be sure he is properly advised. Perhaps you should run along and leave such matters to men."

Her eyes flashed. One corner of her mouth curled. "Of course, dear." She turned on her heel.

Tunstall broke into a broad grin. "Good girl! There's the spirit. He's right you know."

She glanced over her shoulder at the Englishman. "Ganging up on me, are you?"

"Nonsense, I would never do such a thing. Unless of course it were necessary."

"I see. Perhaps you and James Dolan will get on better than I expect." She lifted her chin and left.

"Now, Alex, where were we?"

"I believe we were discussing ranch land."

"Quite so, yes, indeed."

Chapter Thirty-Two

Texas

Ty crossed the trail in the hills north of the river. He drew rein and stepped down. He put the sign at twenty unshod ponies, tracking the river west and not long ago by the look of it. *Comanche,* an uneasy feeling collected in his gut. They'd crossed Roth's back trail or damn close to it. He stepped back up on the steel dust and picked up a lope west with the sign.

Three hours later they'd come to a stop. He stepped down and ground tied the steel dust. Fresh pony sign said they'd waited here for some time. No sign of a fire. It hadn't been a campsite. They'd just waited. *Ambush?* He looked down toward the river. He collected the steel dust and rode down to a willow break at the riverbank. Sure enough, the trail picked up there.

The ashes of a small fire marked a campsite. His uneasy feeling took a turn for the worse. He drew rein short of the fire site, so as not to disturb the sign. He stepped down with a strong sense of foreboding at what he might find. Hoofprints mingled with moccasin prints. He crouched beside the fire. The embers were faintly warm. Nearby, he found the distinct print of a boot heel among the moccasins. They'd gotten Roth, sure as hell. Damn, nothing good about this.

He examined the ground around the heel print. He found the prints of one shod horse among the unshod prints. No sign of blood, yet. Small comfort, he thought, as he collected his horse and remounted. The trail led out, following the riverbank. Ty squeezed up a lope.

He pushed the steel dust as hard as he dared through the course of the day. All the while he fought the gut feeling he might be too late. Even if he found him alive, how the hell was he going to rescue him against those odds?

Smoke sign smudged the late afternoon sky in the west. He wheeled the steel dust north and climbed into the hills above the river bottom. He found a cottonwood thicket east of the village where a lazy little creek wandered down to the river. He tethered the steel dust out of sight near graze and water. He drew his Winchester from the saddle boot and headed out on foot to scout the village.

He found a shadow-filled notch in the rocks overlooking the village. He crawled into the notch and spotted him instantly. A naked white man staked out in the center of the village. It had to be Roth. No blood yet, that much he could see. He cut his eyes across the rest of the scene. Children played in small knots at the east end of the village, their laughter punctuated by yapping camp dogs. Women tended cook fires scattered among the lodges. Something was missing. Young men, he didn't see any. Only a few horses stood at the picket line near the river, Roth's black among them. There were too few for a village this size. The warriors he reckoned must be off on a hunt. If he had any hope of getting Roth out of this alive, he better do it fast.

Once the village settled down for the night he'd need to deal with the dogs. He reckoned he could use a west wind to get close upwind of the picket line. He had a little jerky left in his saddlebags. It wasn't much to get him the rest of the way to where they had Roth staked. It'd have to do.

★ ★ ★ ★ ★

A pale silver moon climbed the night sky over the sleeping village. Ty let the steel dust pick his way through the hills east of the village. He circled south toward the river well out of sight and sound of the village. He struck the river and turned west, working his way toward the village in the shadows of the tree line. A gentle westerly breeze wafted his scent away from the village undercover of the ponies on the picket line. With luck that should hide him from the camp dogs for a time.

He drew rein short of the village and stepped down. He tethered his horse to a tree. He rummaged in his saddlebags, found a small sack and filled his shirt pocket with the remaining jerky. He untied his blanket roll and tucked it under his arm. He followed the riverbank to the village, moving swiftly and silently through the tree line. He found Roth's black tethered at the end of the picket line. He lifted his nose, curious at first until he recognized a familiar scent. Ty stroked his neck. One unshod pony stomped a hoof. The rest dozed or found no threat in him.

At the center of the village he paused in the shadows to watch and listen. The village lay quiet, the tepees little more than dark shapes against the night sky. He could see Roth staked out on the moon-washed ground in the center of the village. The last thirty yards to reach him would be crossed in plain sight.

He dropped to his belly and crawled forward, keeping low in ground shadow as he moved among the tepees. He reached the cover of the last lodge before the open ground leading to Roth. A low growl challenged him from the darkness off to his right, the dog no more than a shadow brightened by moonlit eyes. Ty's heart hammered at the back of his throat. He tossed a strip of jerky in the direction of the shadow. The dog went quiet. The village remained undisturbed. The moon dimmed behind a thin layer of running cloud. Maybe the Good Lord had a hand in on their side.

He wrapped himself in the blanket. It didn't make for much of a disguise, but it might fool a child or someone roused from deep sleep. He crossed the open center of the village. Roth snapped alert at his approach. He lifted a finger to his lips and knelt beside his friend. Roth blinked wide-eyed in recognition.

Ty drew his knife and slit the thongs binding Roth's wrists. "Lay still till I finish," he hissed. He cut Roth's ankles loose. He checked the circle of tepees. Still quiet. "Can you stand?" Roth nodded. Ty tossed him the blanket. "Follow me."

Roth struggled to rise. Ty wrapped an arm around him and helped him to his feet. He led the way around the nearest tepee, slowed by Roth's unsteady legs. They melted into the shadows and moved on to the next. Off to the left a dark figure emerged from the trees at the riverbank. Ty froze. The man walked back to the village and disappeared in a lodge beyond where they hid. Ty waited and listened. Nothing. He caught Roth's eyes and lifted his chin to the tree line.

They moved more quickly now, Roth's legs slowly growing steady. They reached the trees and paused in the shadows. The village remained quiet. Ty led the way east along the riverbank. They reached the picket line without incident.

"You got any water?" Roth's voice cracked a dry whisper.

"On my horse. He's tethered a bit further downstream."

Roth's black greeted him with a nuzzle.

Ty stripped his lead from the picket line and led the horse while Roth hung on to his blanket. The steel dust quietly cropped river grass. Ty handed Roth the black's lead and pulled the canteen from his saddle. "Be quick about it. We need to get trackin' out of here."

Roth choked on a swallow.

"Ease a little of it down. Can you mount?"

Roth nodded, grumbling, "No saddle, no rig, bare-ass neked."

"I'll get you my spare shirt and pants once we get clear of here."

Roth attempted to swing up on the black, but in the end he needed a leg up. Ty stepped into his saddle and led the way east along the river.

They cleared the village and turned north into the hills before swinging out to the northwest. Ty set an easy pace, taking opportunities wherever he could to cover their trail. They rode in grim silence for a mile or more, each man a mixture of relief at having gotten away and wary for any sign of pursuit.

"You sure as hell are a sight for sore eyes. I thought I was a gonner. Gone in a hell of a bad way too by the way them squaws was a lookin' at me."

"Oh, they was just sizin' up your marriageable prospects."

Roth scowled. "Not them ugly old crones. More likely they was pickin' over the parts they most fancied cuttin' first."

"I've heard stories. You owe me, assuming we get away."

"I expect."

"How the hell'd you let yourself get caught like that?"

"Don't ask."

"I got a pretty good idea just readin' the sign at your camp. Have you seen our boy?"

"Not exactly, the C'manche was fixin' to bury his latest victim when ole' Chero brought me into the village. Apparently our boy's score involved one of his women. Lucky for me I suppose. I reckon I'd be buzzard bait by now if they hadn't had better things to do. Patch has got way worse than us on his trail now. If they get him before we do, there may not be enough of him left to collect bounty on."

"It'd pleasure me to put a bullet in the son of a bitch for what he done, but he might get real justice from what the C'manche do to him. Where do you suppose he went?"

"I heard Chero and his warriors ride off. Sounded northwest to me."

"Most likely he's headed for Seven Rivers."

"If we go after him, it'll put us on Chero's trail too."

"Likely so."

"We far enough clear we might stop for them clothes?"

Ty drew rein.

Patch rode hard through the night he left the village. Killing the witch lifted a burning rage from his heart. He felt refreshed. His medicine felt strong, as though nothing could touch him. He paid some heed to covering his tracks more out of habit than any fear of being followed. By the end of the second day he decided he'd put good distance between himself and any pursuit. He slowed his pace and drifted northwest toward Seven Rivers. Late on the afternoon of the third day a shallow creek crossed his trail. A cluster of scrub oak spread along the grassy banks. Graze and water provided a good place to camp. These comforts were always in scarce supply in lands as harsh as these. A few more miles under the remaining sun promised little advantage. He turned upstream to the grove of trees.

He picketed his pony on the creek bank and gathered wood for a small fire. He spread his blanket in the shelter of the trees before the setting sun. He watched the fiery ball dance on the featureless horizon. It disappeared, lighting the cloud billows orange and red, purple and black. He lit a fire and munched thin strips of smoked jerky. The fire crackled and popped, sending sparks to the velvet blanket of night sky. A bright sliver of moon rose to watch over the drift of his thoughts.

Killing the witch released a demon that tormented him from boyhood. Other demons remained in her place. He thought of the woman and the big hacienda. He pictured her bathing in the creek, glistening in the sun. The urge to hunt stirred his medicine. She would make a fine prize. Twice she'd escaped him. The demon witch mocked him no more. Now he could be a patient hunter. He could wait to spring his trap when she had no escape.

Lincoln

Lucy gazed at the darkness beyond her window. Candle glow illuminated the journal page awaiting her thoughts. *Ty. Where was he? When would he come back? Would he come back? He would unless . . .* She banished that thought. No, he would return. She couldn't bear the thought any other way. *Would vengeance be enough?* That was the ugly question. That is the question that loomed like a dark cloud on the horizon. Vengeance and grief, one might hide the other; but could vengeance release grief? Doubt gnawed at that unknown. Time would tell, if he returned. She dipped her pen in ink.

Texas

"Smoke sign," the wolf grunted leaping down from his pony.

Chero's eyes glittered in the pale moonlight. "Where?"

"There." The scout pointed northwest.

Chero turned to the shadowy band of warriors and ponies resting in the dry wash. "Lead us," he said over his shoulder as he strode to his pony and leaped to his back.

Patch sat before the remains of his fire, glowing embers slowly dying. The night songs were soft and quiet save the distant howl of a lonely coyote. His good eye drooped heavy. His head nodded to his chest. Pale moonlight dusted the sand and rocks beyond the fire glow. It painted white ripples on the surface of the creek that became lost in shadowy scrub oak. Silence spread around him with the darkness.

He snapped awake suddenly aware of a presence. Dark figures

emerged from the thicket. They surrounded him. He cursed his carelessness as he reached for his gun. Too late, iron hands pinned his arms to his back. He struggled. They were too many to resist. A familiar smell turned watery recognition in his gut. They jerked him to his feet. His knees turned weak unable to support him. Familiar fierce hard features appeared out of the shadows painted in moonlight.

"You," Chero hissed. "First a son, now a wife, I should have killed you when you were a whelp. This time you will wish I had. You can watch the white eyes scream for his death and know you are next. Tie him to a tree. We return to the village at sunup."

Chapter Thirty-Three

Lincoln

A sharp rap sounded at the front door. Mrs. O'Hara looked up from her sewing. "Now who could that be?" Lucy set her sewing in her lap with a blank expression that said she had no idea. The knock sounded again. "Coming," Mrs. O'Hara called. She set the dress she was hemming on the parlor settee and hefted herself to her feet. She crossed to the green door and opened it.

The young Baker boy who did odd jobs and errands around town for anyone with the price of a quarter stood on the porch. He shifted from one bare foot to the other, holding an envelope. "For Miss Lucy." He held it out. "I'm to wait for her reply."

"Lucy, it's for you, dear."

Lucy came to the door. She took the envelope from the lad with a puzzled expression. She tore it open. The card inside was written in an even hand. Mrs. O'Hara read over her shoulder.

Might you do me the honor of joining me for supper this evening? Shall we say seven?

J. Tunstall.

Lucy hesitated. The charming Englishman amused her. Ty's rugged rough shave waited somewhere beyond nearby. Her doubts stacked the space between them. She put her reservations aside. It's only supper.

"Yes, tell Mr. Tunstall that would be very nice."

Standing behind her Mrs. O'Hara's jaw dropped.

Boots sounded on the front porch at seven sharp. A knock at the door followed. Lucy waited in the parlor. Mrs. O'Hara had retired to her room seemingly afflicted by some unspoken dyspepsia. The kindly, pleasant widow acted standoffish from the moment she'd accepted John's invitation to supper. *It's only supper. It's not like she was engaged to Ty.* She opened the door.

He looked handsome in a soft gray suit, starched collar and black satin tie. His brown eyes went deep and dark at the sight of her. She'd turned herself out in her best yellow dress with the nicely cut neckline and flounce to accent the trim shape of her waist. She favored him with a smile.

"You look positively stunning, my dear."

Flattery rolled off his tongue effortlessly, accented in cultured tones that sounded so much the better by the simple saying of them. She blushed and made a small curtsey.

"Why thank you, Mr. Tunstall. That's very kind of you."

"No kindness at all, merely the statement of fact." He offered his arm. "Now, you know, you promised to call me John."

"So I did." She took his arm, closing the green door behind her.

"I thought we might stroll up to the Wortley dining room. It serves common fare but a tablecloth makes it the best Lincoln has to offer."

"The Wortley is very nice." Tunstall turned out the gate and guided her up the street toward the hotel. Early evening settled a quiet dark mantle over Lincoln. Lamplight spilled out windows, pooling on the boardwalk. Somewhere in one of the saloons a piano man plunked out a tune, familiar to the sound of piano tunes heard in saloons everywhere.

"Perhaps when my business is established, I shall retain a

chef and open a proper restaurant."

"You'd end up your own best customer. I doubt you could count on Dolan for a regular guest. Not many others in these parts go in for fine dining."

"Hmm, I suppose you're right. Lovely and with a head for business, I like that in a woman."

Lucy blushed, catching his eye in the corner of hers.

"Perhaps I shall find a position for you in one of my new enterprises, or are you completely pleased being a seamstress assistant?"

"Mrs. O'Hara has been very kind to me. What sort of businesses are you planning?"

"I shall have a mercantile and a bank to start. Lately, I've been looking at ranch land. The cattle business offers some opportunities that might properly be exploited. But enough dull talk of business. The evening is far too pleasant and the company far too enchanting to prattle on about such things."

Tunstall held the door to the Wortley dining room. Table for two he signaled. The proprietor, waiter, bartender, cook led them to a quiet corner table with a red checked tablecloth. Tunstall held her chair then took the one across from her. The waiter lit the stub of a single candle warming the dim corner in a soft yellow glow.

"I say, my good man, might you have a bottle of champagne?"

The proprietor arched a brow, scratched the stubble on his chin and nodded.

"Would you care for a glass, Lucy?"

"That would be very nice."

"Splendid. Bring us a bottle of your best."

"Ain't got but one to choose from."

Tunstall pursed his lips. "I'm sure then that shall serve as your best."

The waiter ambled off to the bar.

"Tell me, Lucy, how long have you been in Lincoln?"

"I only arrived this past summer."

"And where did you arrive from?"

"Denver." *He wanted her story, how much should she give him?*

"Oh my, that's quite a journey. How did you manage that?"

"I booked passage on a freighter over Raton Pass to Santa Fe." *Now what?* "I, ah, met an old friend in Santa Fe. He and his partner were headed this way. They let me ride along with them."

"How exciting, and is this old friend of yours still here?"

The waiter returned with a chilled bottle of champagne and two glasses. He set the glasses on the table and popped the cork. The elegance of chilled champagne made stark contrast to the cook pouring it in a stained apron. The waiter left the bottle and went back to his kitchen.

Tunstall lifted his glass. "To a lovely evening and an even lovelier companion."

Lucy felt herself blush again. She couldn't remember she'd ever done so much of that in the span of an hour. The champagne tickled her nose. She sipped, hoping the conversation might turn in some new direction.

"Not bad." Tunstall returned his glass to the table. "Where were we, then? Oh yes, your traveling companion, is he still here?"

"No, he's on the trail of a killer."

"Oh my, that sounds perilous. Is he a sheriff?"

"Ty, Ty Ledger's his name. He was sheriff in Cheyenne. The man he's after killed his wife."

"I'm so sorry, what a terrible pity."

"Now he's a deputy US marshal. His partner's a bounty hunter. They're after the same man. Ty wants revenge. Johnny, Johnny Roth, that's his partner, wants the bounty."

"And this killer, is he known to be here about?"

"He killed a woman over at Fort Stanton, attacked another down at the Chisum ranch."

"You must be quite careful with a man like that about preying on women."

"Oh, I've already had my run in with him up in Denver. Shot him too, I did. Too bad I didn't kill him."

"Shot him? Good heavens! A beautiful woman with a head for business and a markswoman too, is there no end to your surprises?"

"Out here a girl best learn to take care of herself."

"Yes, I quite admire that. I shall be sure to mind my manners on the off chance you may still possess a gun." A twinkle flickered in Tunstall's eye as he raised his glass again.

The waiter returned from his kitchen. "Well, what'll it be folks? The special's roast beef, fried potatoes, steamed greens and fresh biscuits with chokecherry pie for dessert."

"Lucy?"

"I'll have the special."

"Make that two."

"Have it up in no time." The waiter headed off to the kitchen.

Tunstall topped up their glasses. "You mentioned John Chisum's place."

"Yes, Mr. Chisum is quite an influential rancher in these parts. He may not be as powerful as The House, but he's a big man in the Pecos valley."

"Does everyone in Lincoln County bend their knee to this Dolan crowd?"

"They got all the commercial and political power from here to Santa Fe. Rumor says they're even in tight with the Santa Fe Ring."

"Santa Fe Ring?"

"Republicans up in Santa Fe, they control territorial government. Not much happens around here unless The House or the

Santa Fe Ring want it to."

"Interesting, what about John Chisum, where does he stand?"

"He isn't a Dolan man, so that puts him on the outside looking in."

"I surmised as much. I think I must get to know Mr. Chisum."

The waiter arrived with their plates.

Tunstall opened the gate, to the usual rusty complaint more noticeable in the evening stillness. They walked arm in arm to the porch. The top step groaned its telltale welcome. Lucy paused at the door.

"I had a wonderful evening, John, thank you."

He locked her eyes in his. "The pleasure was all mine. Would you do me the honor of a drive on Saturday?"

Lucy hesitated for a moment. Ty clouded her mind again. Well, they'd made no commitments. "That would be lovely. I'll pack a picnic lunch."

"Splendid," the word trailed off. The air between them felt thick and warm. Starlight sparkled in her eyes. He lifted her hand to his lips. "Until Saturday, then."

His kiss felt soft and warm. She shuddered. "Until Saturday." She opened the green door quickly and let herself in.

A single lamp burned in the parlor. Mrs. O'Hara looked up from her book. "Did you have a pleasant evening, dear?"

Lucy paused at the foot of the stairs. "Yes, I did. John is quite the refined gentleman. He has some rather ambitious business plans too."

"More ambitious than catching a killer?"

"Yes. I mean no, just different. That's all. His ambitions leave time for, other things."

"You mean other things like you."

Lucy knit her brow. "Yes, I suppose so."

"And what are Mr. Tunstall's ambitions?"

"He plans to open a mercantile and a bank."

"He plans to take on James Dolan you mean."

"Yes, he does."

She closed her book, marking her place with a finger. "Be careful, Lucy, dear. He may be a fine gentleman, but James Dolan is not. He won't take kindly to Mr. Tunstall's ambition. He and his men will chew your gentleman up and spit him out. You don't want to be caught in the middle of that."

Lucy pressed her lips in a frown. "He's very smart."

"I'm not talking about smart. I'm talking about tough. Marshal Ledger might be tough enough to take on Dolan. John Tunstall is not."

"Ty can't see past avenging his wife's murder. It doesn't leave time for other things."

"Be patient, dear. Good things take time."

"I am patient. My fear is that he will get his killer, only to find that vengeance isn't enough."

"And John Tunstall looks the safer choice."

Lucy lowered her eyes and said nothing.

"Be careful what you wish for, dear."

She left by the sound of a stair creak.

Chapter Thirty-Four

Texas

They cut Chero's trail the next morning. Twenty ponies were easier to follow than one and Chero wasn't trying to cover his tracks.

"I expect we're gainin' on 'em," Ty observed. "See here, they slowed down to look for sign. Then they pick up the pace there when they're back on his trail."

Roth flicked his gaze to the horizon. "Keep a sharp eye peeled, Ty. You don't want no part of even comin' close to a C'manch skinnin' knife."

"The voice of experience speaks. That would have been good advice for you before you lit out on our boy's trail alone."

Roth cocked an eye. "And s'pose I'd waited for you to come along. Likely we'd both be staked out for skinnin'."

"Put like that I reckon I'm the one owes you a favor."

"Well, maybe not exactly."

"I thought as much."

Morning wore into midday. The sun rode high and hot overhead. Not long past high noon Roth pointed to the hills ahead. "Dust sign."

Ty drew rein. "Sure enough and comin' this way."

Roth twisted in his saddle searching for a hiding place. "There." He pointed to a dark crack off to the north. He wheeled the black and put his heels to him, expecting Ty to follow. The crevice he'd spotted from a distance turned out to be the dry wash he'd hoped for. The black slid down the steep bank with the steel dust close behind. Roth pulled up out of sight and swung down. He scrambled up the bank to the rim. Ty followed, Winchester in hand. They had a good view of the cloud, drawing closer.

Moments later dark specks resolved out of the shimmering heat haze. As they drew closer the specks grew to silhouettes. Horses and riders came into view, moving southeast headed back to the village at an easy lope. They passed strung out in file, Chero in the lead, a bound captive with an eye patch near the center.

Ty set his jaw hard as steel at the sight of the man who'd killed Victoria. He levered a round into the Winchester. Roth wheeled rattler-quick in warning.

"What the hell do you think you're doin'?"

"Fixin' to kill that son of a bitch."

"No, you're not. He's as good as dead already, and mean dead at that. You take a shot at him now you'll get us both killed. Put that rifle up and let 'em by."

Ty pulled the rifle off his firing line and watched the band pass.

As they rode away Roth blew out a deep breath. "That was close."

"Not close enough to the one I want."

"Revenge won't do you no good if you're dead. With that bunch you'd likely wind up dead before you got close enough to kill the son of a bitch. We know where they're goin.' Best we give 'em a few hours and just follow along. Maybe we get a chance to snatch him, or maybe we just let the C'manch take your revenge for you."

"What about your bounty?"

"All I need is proof he's dead. There's lots a ways to get that without gettin' skinned."

"Now he gets careful."

"A man's judgment improves with age."

"Hell, then you must have done some serious agin' in the past couple days."

Chero's Village

Ty circled east through the hills north of the village. They reached the cottonwood thicket with its clear running stream near mid afternoon. Sunlight filtered through the trees dappled the stream and grassy bank in ripples of light and shadow. They picketed the horses on the creek bank near graze.

"I reckon we're no more than three or four hours behind them." Roth kept his voice low and hushed.

Ty nodded. "There's a spot in the rocks up yonder where we can get a good look at the village." He led them out, moving low and cautious, keeping below the crest of the hills. He found the notch in the rocks and slipped into the shadows. He crawled to the opening overlooking the village.

The village was a beehive of activity at the return of the warriors. A festive crowd milled around the captive staked out in the fashion they'd held Roth in. Children taunted him. Young girls gawked and wondered at the ways of torture they would learn. Women prepared food for a feast to celebrate the return of the warriors and the entertainment Winter Moon's one-eyed son would soon provide.

Ty pulled back to let Johnny have a look. Roth climbed into his place. The scene in the village made a chill stir in the pit of his stomach. "Been there," he said turning away. "If it wasn't for all he done . . ." He cut himself off.

"You could almost feel sorry for the son of a bitch," Ty finished. "I might, if he screams loud enough. Then again, I doubt it."

"The festivities won't start until tonight. Let's go back to the horses and get out of the sun."

Patch remembered little of his short time with the band, but he did remember the night the women did their work on a hated Apache captive. The Apache were known for their cunning and courage. Taking one captive caused much celebration. Breaking his spirit with torture was a source of much pride. They did their work by turns, beginning from the oldest to the younger ones. The old ones were skilled with firebrands and knives. They burned and cut slowly. The man showed courage at first, winning grudging respect from his tormentors. Long into the night when his medicine broke, they cut out his tongue to silence his screams. The worst of it came after that, the burning, the skinning, the cutting. They took his eyes, his ears, his nose, his lips, his man parts. In the morning light they cut out his heart. It still beat, a little.

That memory formed his defense. Chero was old. Hatred and pride were his weaknesses. Patch was young. His medicine was strong, stronger than Chero's hatred. If he could catch the old chief in his medicine, he might yet escape.

"Wake up." Ty nudged Roth with the toe of his boot. He snapped awake, instinctively reaching for the gun he didn't have. Early evening shadow shrouded the thicket in deep purple. "It won't be long now. Time we head up to the notch."

Cook fires dotted the village. Dark figures gathered around their evening meals or moved among the lodges. Roth watched Chero's lodge. He expected the signal would come from there. Presently a bent figure rose from the circle at his fire. She lit a torch and shuffled toward the center of the village. There she lit a new fire illuminating the staked killer in orange light and shadow. The fire summoned villagers to the spectacle.

"Looks like the fun's about to start."

Ty scrambled up the bank beside Roth. Across the camp villagers left their fires, shadows moved silently among the tepees. They gathered in the circle of firelight, a ghostly specter surrounded the pegged captive.

It sounded softly at first. It drifted out of the village on a light breeze. A throaty sound, oddly out of place, broke the silence. Someone laughed. The sound grew louder, long and mocking. Telltale shaking told it for Patch laughing.

"The son of a bitch is laughin' at 'em," Roth hissed. "He's either got cannonballs or he's crazy."

"Crazy I'd wager."

Chero burst into the center of the assembled people. The laughter broke into a heated exchange of Comanche lingo neither Roth nor Ty understood.

"White-eye dog shit will not find our knives funny."

"I do not find the knives funny. I find Chero funny. Chero sends women to kill his enemy. The reservation has made an old woman of him. He can no longer face an enemy in battle. The witch Winter Moon took my father's manhood for her medicine bag. She must have filled it with Chero's stones too."

"Silence filthy dog or you will eat your withered stalk and stones for a last meal."

"The words of a woman spoken to a man staked to the ground. Do it, then. Let your women kill your enemy. Let your people see you no longer have the stomach for a fight. What will you do when the bluecoats come? Squat and make water for them? Cut me loose and fight like a man if you are one!"

Roth turned to Ty. "What the hell's goin' on down there?"

Ledger shrugged. "Beats me."

Chero drew his knife, the blade flashed orange yellow light.

He bent over Patch. Suddenly he jumped back, wiping spit from his face with a curse. He stepped back. He barked an order. Two warriors stepped into the circle. They squatted on either side of Patch and cut him loose.

Patch rose slowly rubbing his wrists. One of the warriors handed him a knife.

Roth cut his eyes to Ty. "Looks like he's goaded Chero into a fight."

"If he don't get killed we might get him yet."

Patch crouched, his knife in the familiar attack position. Chero circled away from the blade. Patch pressed forward, his circumstance gone from certain death to predator stalking yet another kill. Anger and pride delivered him from his would-be torturers. Anger and pride would impale the old renegade on his blade.

They circled. Patch feinted a slashing cut and stepped back, hoping to draw Chero to charge. He did not. Fear, he could smell it on the old man. Patch pressed forward.

Chero circled back crouching low. His free hand snaked out and grasped one of the firebrands intended for torture. He sprang from his crouch swinging the stout club in a shower of sparks from the glowing red knob.

Patch dropped to his side with a wide sweeping kick that caught Chero behind the knee. He fell back, hitting the hard packed ground with a grunt. Patch bounced to his feet, delivering a killing cut aimed at his fallen adversary.

Chero rolled away from the blade with surprising agility. He leaped to his feet with his own slashing cut.

Patch fell back, narrowly avoiding the fire-lit blade. Chero staggered behind the force of his stroke. Patch rolled to a crouch and sprang at his adversary behind a vicious cut. Chero twisted his body in a vain attempt to avoid the blade. The cut found its mark, slicing the old chief's side. A deep cut opened. Red darkened stain spilled slick down his thigh in the firelight.

The Comanche grabbed his side and fell back, avoiding a second killing cut. He countered, slashing wildly. Patch caught his knife hand at the wrist. He jerked it behind the renegade's back with a crack that separated arm from shoulder. The knife slipped from his fingers. Patch stepped behind the old chief and laid his blade at the Comanche's throat.

"Now walk me to my pony. If any of these warriors move, you go to meet your ancestors."

"Let him go." He croaked through teeth clenched against the pain of his ruined arm.

Patch paused at Chero's lodge on the way to the picket line. He took Chero's rifle and cartridge belt. He found Roth's double rig beside the rifle and threw it over his shoulder. At the picket line, he stripped Chero of his breechclout, belt and knife sheath. He threw the clothing on the back of the paint and swung up behind. He cocked the Winchester and leveled the barrel between Chero's eyes. Black pits glittered with rage.

"You drove me away for the worthless life of the one who took my eye. The filthy witch watched. Now I have won. I could kill you old fool. Better to leave you to your people, a bleeding old woman. Follow me and you will be the first to die." He wheeled the paint away and galloped into the night.

Chapter Thirty-Five

Roth watched in disbelief as the killer made his way to the picket line shielded by the Comanche chief. "The son of a bitch is gonna get himself out of this."

"Not for long, get the horses." Ty led the way as they scrambled down from the notch and raced back to the thicket. He threw his blanket and saddle on the steel dust and hitched up the cinch. He swung into the saddle and wheeled away to the north and west with Roth seconds behind.

Gullies and washes gashed the land in shadow, slowing their pace. Roth pushed the black up beside the steel dust. "How the hell do you expect to track him at night?"

"I don't. We know where he's headed."

Roth shook his head and rode on in silence.

In the small hours of the night, Patch paused to rest and water the paint in a thicket beside a spring-fed pool. Wounded as the old renegade was, he doubted he would mount a pursuit before daybreak if he pursued him at all. He used the time to dress in Chero's loincloth and check his weapons. He had plenty of firepower and ammunition with the Winchester and double rig. The pistols were a nicely balanced, matched set of .44s. Someone must have paid dearly for the renegade to have these.

Chero the old fool, he'd made it easy. He was no match for Patch's medicine. He'd disgraced the man before his people.

Such a thing might be more painful than death for one with such pride.

Ty pushed through the night. Hour after hour they rode north and west, matching their pace to the terrain. At last the eastern sky began to gray at the approach of dawn. He threw up a hand and drew a halt. He stood in his stirrups and squinted into the dim light.

"You see something?" Roth held his voice to a whisper.

Ty nodded. "I think so. There." He pointed to a dark grove of trees, signaling the presence of water.

"I don't see a thing."

"That paint horse has white markings on his butt. I seen something white move in them trees."

"What makes you think it's him?"

"Just a hunch."

Roth shook his head. "He'd be a fool to stop now."

"Probably figures Chero won't be comin' after him so soon." Ty studied the terrain to the east and west. "OK, here's what we do. I'll circle round and come into that grove of trees from the east. Give me ten minutes to get started. Then you ride off to the northwest with my horse. Make yourself known. He'll stay put figurin' he's well hidden. I should be able to jump him before he knows what hit him." Ty stepped down and handed Roth the steel dust's lead.

Johnny locked Ty's eyes. "You gonna kill him?"

"If he gives me cause, it'd pleasure me. If he gives up, I'll see him hang." He disappeared in predawn ground shadow.

Something struck a rock nearby. Patch froze. He recognized the distinctive metallic sound of a horseshoe striking a rock. Two horses, he could hear them clearly now. He took the Winchester and moved cautiously to the edge of the thicket. He could barely make out the shadow of a rider leading a second horse off to the west. A packhorse? He saw no pack. A spare mount? It could be. The man had horses, supplies for the trail and proper clothing. Things he needed to ease his travels. A slow smile parted his lips.

A pistol cock sounded behind him. "Drop the rifle and put your hands where I can see them or you're a dead man."

Patch hesitated, judging the man's position in the trees behind him.

"Go ahead, asshole. Make a play. After what you done to my wife and child, nothing would please me more than watchin' you bleed to death. I was kind of lookin' forward to seein' what the C'manche might do to you."

Patch dropped the rifle.

"Now the pistol belt, slow and easy, any sudden move and I blow your sorry ass down the high road to hell." Patch unbuckled the rig. "Now the knife." The knife clattered to the ground. "Step away from the weapons." He did. "Drop to your knees, hands behind your back." Ty stepped up behind him and snapped handcuffs on his wrists.

"Got him, Johnny!"

Moments later, Roth rode up to the thicket as Ty collected the half-breed's weapons. "Say these look like yours." He held out the rig.

"Sure are. Much obliged." Roth walked over to the kneeling killer. "Not much to him when he ain't killin' women or old men."

Patch fixed him with a surly glare.

"Best mind your manners. You're worth bounty to me dead or alive. My partner here would just as soon kill you himself as see you hang. All totaled, your life ain't worth a pinch of shit to either of us."

"We'll water and rest the horses here for a spell. Shackle him to a tree. We'll head out once the sun is up."

Day dawned hot and dry. Ty led the way northwest, a lead rope to Patch's paint dallied to his saddle horn. Roth brought up the rear keeping an eye on the prisoner.

"Where do you figure to turn him in?"

Ty considered the question. "I ain't got much use for Sheriff Brady after the stories Chisum told us. Marshal Widenmann will take him if he's still in Lincoln. If he's not we may have to haul his sorry ass all the way to Marshal Sherman in Santa Fe."

"He ain't that good a company. I say we just shoot the son of a bitch and be done with it."

"Don't tempt me."

Roth laughed.

The trail cut a small stream at midday. They stopped to water and rest the horses. Patch sat with his back to a rock, head nodding on his chest. Roth squatted in the shade of a rock ledge cleaning his guns. Ty dozed nearby, hat pulled low over his eyes. Neither noticed Patch come awake.

His eye darted southeast. He squinted against sun glare, checking their back trail. Off in the distance a feint hint of dust sign disappeared in the wind. They were coming. He expected they would. Left to his own he would have escaped. As things stood, it looked like a choice between Comanche knives and a hangman's noose. Not much choice. Chero would be madder than a wounded bear. He'd take his chances with the hangman. These two white men might yet make a mistake.

"Comanche come."

Roth looked up. "Where?"

He pointed with his chin. "Dust sign on back trail."

"Ty, wake up. Did you hear that? Patch says we got C'manch on our back trail."

Ty sat up and pushed his hat brim above his eyes. "How far back?"

Roth looked to Patch.

"A mile, maybe two."

"Let's get out of here." Ty stalked off to collect the steel dust and the paint. He pulled Patch to his feet and helped him mount.

"Take handcuffs off. You're gonna need another gun."

"Nice try, buck." Ty stepped into his saddle.

Roth swung up beside him. "We're gonna need a place to fort up before nightfall."

Ty set his jaw and picked up a trot up the creek bed. If they found a good stony place to leave the stream, they'd buy some time or just maybe throw the Comanche off their trail.

South Spring

Caneris rode in under a slanting afternoon sun. A fresh breeze cooled the remnants of late summer heat. Deacon Swain and Jose Chavez rode with him. They drew rein at the corral and stepped down. Chisum stepped off the porch and sauntered across the yard.

"How'd it go, Wade?"

"No trouble. We moved the river valley herd ten miles further north. They're close enough again that we can put a watch on 'em. That won't stop strays from wanderin' off, but at least they won't wind up on Seven Rivers range."

"Good. That might not stop them thievin' skunks, but if they come callin' they'll sure as hell wish they hadn't."

"Speakin' of callin,' you expectin' company?" Caneris lifted his chin to the northwest. Two riders jogged out of the hills. "Recognize either of 'em?"

"The big one looks like Dick Brewer. I don't recognize whoever's ridin' with him."

"Might be a preacher or an undertaker by the look of him."

"Pretty fancy trail duds."

Brewer and the stranger drew rein and stepped down. "Mr. Chisum, Wade." Brewer offered his hand.

"Dick, what brings you all the way down here?" Chisum eyed the stranger.

"I do, Mr. Chisum. John Tunstall at your service."

"Pleased to meet you, Mr. Tunstall. This here's my foreman, Wade Caneris." Tunstall and Caneris exchanged nods. "I take it you're not from around these parts, Mr. Tunstall, what brings you to South Spring?"

Tunstall chuckled. "Quite observant of you there and please call me John."

Chisum nodded. "They call me John too."

"Dick has been showing me some ranch land I may purchase southwest of here. I've learned enough of the area to admire your operation. I thought it might be best to meet a prospective new neighbor and perhaps discuss a bit of business."

Chisum measured the greenhorn. Nothing about him appeared made of the mettle for ranching. "What sort of business?"

"I see commercial opportunities up in Lincoln. I'd like to discuss them with you."

"Business in Lincoln means Dolan."

"So it seems. Precisely the opportunity I would like to discuss."

Chisum considered the reed of a man. No mettle for ranching, less so if it came to taking on Dolan. If the man had balls enough to think about it, he might be worth hearing out. "Come on up to the house. We'll find some refreshment and you can tell me all about these 'opportunities' of yours."

★ ★ ★ ★ ★

The house smelled of cinnamon. Dawn Sky had a fresh-baked apple pie cooling for supper. Chisom and Tunstall settled into cushioned chairs arranged around the fireplace. Chisum poured two glasses of whiskey, handed one to Tunstall and set the bottle on the table between them. He lifted his glass. "Welcome to South Spring, John."

"My thanks and cheers."

"Now tell me about these 'opportunities' you see in Lincoln."

Tunstall set his glass on the table and composed a serious expression. "The lack of competition is at the root of it. Dolan runs the only mercantile in the county. He sets the price of everything and extracts whatever premium he chooses from people who have no alternative. He sells on credit so the landholders and other businesses are indebted to him. No one dares oppose anything he does. It is quite a tidy little arrangement really and altogether legal."

"Put the law in his back pocket and he controls everything in the county, legal and not so legal. So where do you see opportunity in all that?"

"When it comes to the mercantile, two can play at that game."

"You think you can open a mercantile and compete with Dolan?"

"I'm quite sure of it."

"That would take a great deal of money."

"Money is not a problem. My family has rather substantial financial resources to establish the enterprise initially. The bank will provide credit facilities after that."

"Bank?"

"Of course, don't you see? All that credit Dolan extends takes cash. Cash is his weakness. Our bank will give us the upper hand in that."

"You think Dolan will take that lying down?"

"I don't expect Dolan to accept defeat graciously. That's why I've engaged Alexander McSween to stand for me."

"McSween's a lawyer."

"Quite so and everything I propose to do is perfectly legal."

"Maybe so, but Dolan don't play by those rules."

"That's what Alex keeps telling me. And that's why I'm here. You have the largest cattle ranch in the region. Unfortunately you do not control the cattle business."

"Thanks to the small ranchers rustlin' my stock. Dolan provides a ready market for them to feed his government contracts."

"Those contracts should rightfully belong to you and at vastly different prices."

"I might agree with that, but if that's the way you see it, why are you looking at ranch land?"

"Ah, that." Tunstall smiled like a cat eying a canary. He tossed off his drink. Chisum poured another round. "You have the largest herds, free range and plenty of water, yet the small ranchers hang on. They hold down the price of your beef, legally and illegally. They rely on others for fodder and water."

Chisum knit his brow. "Graze in some cases, but I don't see water."

"Water comes from somewhere. Should a landowner choose to conserve his water, others may find it less plentiful. They may be forced to pay for it. They might also find they are paying more for feed. As their costs rise in a depressed market, the price of beef should rise as well. I should think you might find advantage in that."

"I might, but I don't see where you are going with this."

A small smile creased the corners of the Englishman's eyes. They took on a conspiratorial cast. "As circumstances unfold it may be difficult for some of these small ranchers to stay in business. Pity that, but then those little ranches go up for sale. A man with capital might buy up rather a lot of land at what are sure to be attractive prices. That land stands to be worth a fortune one day."

"Well, I'll be." Chisum sat back with a newfound respect for the Englishman.

"You see, John, you are a rancher. I've no plan to play that game. I intend to pursue the cattle business as a means to an end. Done as I see it, I should think the market will deliver those government contracts to you at just the right price."

"So what's my part in this?"

"Very perceptive, I like that. Your part is quite simple at first. When I open the bank, you open an account. People around here respect you. It will give them confidence to do the same. When the mercantile opens with prices lower than our competitor, people will come to us for their needs. As long as we stay competitive, people will favor us with their business out of their dislike for Dolan."

"Dolan won't let you run him out of business."

"Legally, there is nothing he can do."

"The law hasn't stopped him before."

"Alex also said that. You have professional gunmen I believe. Dick tells me I shall need some of my own. Should Dolan's tactics become . . . shall we say, uncivil . . . together, we should be up to the task."

"Uncivil is it?" Chisum laughed. He knit his brows and studied the Englishman. "An hour ago I thought you were a funeral lookin' for someplace to happen. Now I'm not so sure. This just might work, Tunstall. This just might work." He lifted his glass. "As you say, cheers."

Chapter Thirty-Six

Texas

Chero halted his band at the stream. Fresh pony sign said they were close. The sign also spoke of three ponies. The one-eyed devil had friends. The trail ended at the stream. They used the stream to cover their tracks.

"Yellow Dog, look for the trail upstream. Coyote look downstream."

The wolves rode off to scout the creek bed. The rest of the band dismounted to water their ponies and wait.

Chero's wound burned. They'd stopped the bleeding with a hot knife and a few ragged stitches taken in dried gut. The burn fed his rage. He would feed the one-eyed devil his stalk and stones before they took his remaining eye. No woman would have the pleasure of this. He may not be a young man, but the white dog spawn would know his blade. Winter Moon's half-breed whelp would beg for death before he finished with him. Those foolish enough to ride with him would suffer the same end.

The sun passed midday when Yellow Dog rode in. He slipped down from his pony. "Has Coyote returned?"

Chero shook his head. "Have you found their sign?"

Yellow Dog shrugged. "I found a stony bank. It would make a good place to leave the stream. If Coyote finds no sign of them we might search further from there."

Chero ground his teeth.

The sun sank toward earth mother when Coyote returned. He reported no sign.

Chero set his jaw. The one-eyed devil vanished like a cloud of smoke. "Ride upstream to this stony place."

Covering their tracks made for a slow pace, much depended on leaving no sign where they left the stream. As the sun drew low in late afternoon, they mounted a rock-strewn rise. Near the summit a gully gashed the hillside from north to south fed by the trickle of a small creek. Ty measured the remaining daylight. They could cover a few more miles, but they might not find a position as defensible as this if they needed defending. He turned to Roth.

"Let's fort up here for the night, if we lost 'em, a few more miles don't matter. If we didn't lose 'em, cover and water could be the difference."

Roth nodded. They picked their way down the gully wall. The gully offered shelter for the horses and cover if cover were needed. The creek provided water to sustain man and animal. Roth and Ledger dismounted. Johnny took care of the horses while Ty hauled Patch down. He settled the killer beside a rock at the bottom of the gully.

"Johnny, I'm gonna cuff his hands in front of him so he can eat. Keep an eye on him. If he makes any sudden moves, shoot him."

Roth dropped his hands to the butts of his .44s and watched as Ty unlocked the prisoner's handcuffs and fastened them again with his arms in front of him.

"What about a fire?" Patch asked. "It'll get cold when the sun goes down."

Ty stood up. "No fire. I shouldn't think you'd want to put up any smoke sign for your friends to see. My guess is Chero has big plans if he can get his hands on you. There's hardtack in my saddlebags. We can fill the canteens in the creek."

Ty took his hardtack and canteen and climbed the gully's east wall. He sat beside a large boulder where he could watch their back trail in the fading light of early evening. As the sun sank behind him, a spark of light flashed in the distance. Sunlight caught some shiny surface. The flash disappeared into shadow and was lost. Ty slid down to the gully floor.

"We didn't lose 'em."

Roth looked up, munching a bite of hardtack. Patch turned his good eye to Ledger.

"I seen something move on our back trail."

"A critter maybe?"

"Critters don't carry shiny things that catch the sun."

Roth popped the remaining hardtack into his mouth and checked the Winchester he'd taken from Patch.

The killer lifted his wrists to Ty. "Turn Patch loose. You need another gun."

"You better hope we don't. I'll take first watch, Johnny." Ty drew his rifle from its saddle boot and a box of shells from his saddlebag. He climbed the gully wall and took up his position, the Winchester cradled in the crook of his left arm.

Coyote knelt to examine the sign. He shaded his eyes against the slanting sun, searching the plain to the northwest. The land rose in the distance. High ground, the sort of place a man might hide if he were being pursued. He swung up on his pony and wheeled away back to rejoin Chero and the rest of the band.

Chero listened to Coyote's report. He gazed off to the northwest. The one-eye thought he could hide. They would find him.

"Come, my brothers. Coyote show us this sign."

The scout led the band back to the sign. Chero slipped down from his pony to examine his wolf's work. Little could gauge the age of this sign. It could not be old. They must be close. Night would fall soon. He remounted his pony and rode on to last light. If they could get close before dark, they might catch them in the morning.

Lincoln

The buggy clattered out of town into the setting sun and wheeled southwest along the riverbank. Lucy pushed her bonnet to the back of her head and let the breeze play through her hair. She caught Tunstall's profile in the corner of her eye. Charming to the point of disarming she thought. Between his accent and manners he could make any girl's head swim, let alone one who traveled with a mule skinner because he called her *miss*. The fact he was rich didn't hurt, either.

A mile south of town the riverbank spread out to embrace a willow break with a grove of white oak. Lucy remembered the place. She'd ridden here with Ty a time or two. *Ty*. The thought of him prickled her skin. She wondered where he was. Had he gotten his killer? Did it matter? Was he coming back? She set the questions aside. What more could she do?

"There, John, that looks like a nice spot."

"Whatever you say, my dear." Tunstall guided the chestnut gelding into the long shadows and drew rein in the shade of a white oak bent with age. He stepped down from the buggy and came around to help her off. She took the offered hand, gathered her skirt and took her place beside him. He held her hand a fraction longer than necessary. The air felt warm and close, silence broken by the buzzing of a fly.

"I'll get the basket," she said.

He spread a blanket beside the tree while she busied herself behind the buggy seat. Moments later they sat down to a picnic of smoky ham sandwiches made with fresh baked bread, pickles, lemonade and chokecherry pie.

"Nothing makes a meal more special than the great outdoors, unless it is a perfectly lovely companion."

Lucy felt her cheeks redden. Perhaps he wouldn't notice in the glaring shafts of sunset. "I'm glad you like it."

"The outdoors, the picnic or my lovely companion?"

"Oh, John, you know what I mean. You are such an unmerciful tease."

"Only for the pretty way it causes you to blush."

She shrugged in despair. "How was your visit with Mr. Chisum?"

"He is quite the stalwart chap, you know. We got on famously. He saw the merit of my plan straight away. I think he shall be only too happy to take his part in it."

"What part is that?"

"When we open the bank, he has agreed to open an account."

"That doesn't seem like much."

"Oh, but it is. People here respect John Chisum. Putting his faith in the bank will give others the confidence to do likewise. The bank will bring in deposits, cash that can be loaned out to worthy purposes such as funding mercantile inventory and receivables. That is where you can help."

"Me?"

"You." He smiled. "I should very much like it if you came to work in the store."

"I don't know the first thing about keeping shop."

"Neither do I, but between the two of us I expect we can muddle through. You know people. You can start out assisting them with their needs. Susan McSween knows something of stocking she tells me. I can do the accounts. What more could we possibly need? Why in no time at all you and Susan will run the whole place, whilst I toddle off to the bank and cattle businesses."

"It's a very kind offer, John. I've never considered taking up storekeeping."

"Please do consider it, Lucy. It is a splendid opportunity." He broke off and held her eyes. "It is really only the beginning of what I have to offer."

He leaned forward. She felt his breath. He took her lips in his.

Chapter Thirty-Seven

Roth watched their back trail from the east gully wall. Purple haze settled behind the fading light. Sometimes the mind played tricks, imagining what you couldn't see. He had a feeling he couldn't shake. Chero was coming. Times like these gave a man pause to think. He'd come damn close to meeting the bad end of a Comanche skinning knife. He knew that for a fact. He'd about given himself up for dead by the time Ty came along. He'd come to the realization he might never see Dawn Sky again. He hadn't realized how much that part hurt until Ty pulled him back from certain death. He had a second chance. He meant to make the most of it. He meant to get back to that dark-eyed girl with the cinnamon scent in her hair. He meant to grab hold of her and never let go. If she'd have him, that is.

Somewhere in the darkness a coyote barked. Another returned the call.

"The wolves talk among themselves." Patch grunted.

Scouts, Ty thought. He eased up beside Roth, peering into the darkness.

"Coyotes was real noisy the night they took me."

"They're lookin' for us."

Roth laid down his Winchester. He drew the knife he'd taken from Patch. "You stay here with him. I can do a little bit of scoutin' too."

Ty caught his arm. "Are you sure about this, Johnny?"

"If anybody gets close, I'll put 'em away nice and quiet like."

Patch spat. "White man who plays a Comanche wolf at his game is a fool. Give Patch the knife. Let a wolf catch the wolf."

Roth shook his head. "He keeps tryin', don't he?" He climbed over the gully wall and melted into the shadows beyond.

Moonbeams flickered in the breaks between a thick cover of low running cloud. He worked his way down the slope to a large rock stand. He crouched in the shadows and listened. Night sounds covered him like a soft blanket. Dry scents of dust and grass flavored the air. He worked his eyes from north to south and back again. No movement disturbed the shadows. He slowed his breathing and his heart, his senses alert to sight, sound and scent. Time passed.

Off to the north a soft scratch disturbed the silence. Roth's senses pounced on the sound. It might have been some night critter dislodging a stone. His gut told him no. He searched the shadows and waited. A light north breeze played at his nostrils tainted with a sour tang. He tasted the scent. He remembered the smell of captivity. He remembered it much stronger then, close and overpowering. Here it came to him as a light telltale sign. He fingered the hilt of the knife, resting in his lap. He searched the darkness, alert to movement, a shadow or shape that didn't belong. He fixed on a nearby boulder. It breathed. The shadows deceived his eyes. The shadow moved. It inched along the ground, spreading darkness before it.

He slowed his breath, quieting the pounding in his chest. The shadow continued toward him, inching along silent as a pool of ground fog. A small smile tugged at the corner of his mouth. The hunter became the hunted. He strained his senses. Where there was one, there could be more. He cut his eyes to the north and south. Nothing came to him, only the ghostly shadow approaching the rocks where he waited. The scent grew stronger. The breeze hid Roth. Chero's wolf passed within a few feet of his position.

He gathered himself, like a predator stalking its prey. Silently he sprang through the air. He landed on the scout's back. His blade flashed a lightning strike across the renegade's throat. Life force burst from the raw gash, blood pumped in black gouts. The body jerked in violent reflex and went still beneath him, expelling its last in a faint gurgle.

In an instant silence returned. Roth scuttled back to his hiding place. He resumed his watch. He listened, intent to the soft night sounds. Nothing. No one came to investigate the sound of the struggle. A coyote barked off to the southwest. This time no mate answered.

Lincoln

Candle glow washed the journal page golden. The entry read *John Tunstall.* Lucy sat at the small table, her chin resting in the palm of one hand her pen in the other. *"It is really only the beginning of what I have to offer."* What might that mean? What was a girl alone in a frontier town to make of that? A dashing English gentleman, a shiny knight she'd disappointed and a crosscurrent of emotion that wouldn't hold still. She'd made a mess of it now for sure. What was she to do? If she knew the answer to that, she'd have an entry for this stupid journal. Sometimes writing it could be downright irritating. That's when it helped most. It made her think.

What was she to do about his offer? She could use a job that paid something more than board and keep. That part was plain enough. They'd spend their days side by side in the store. That was the part she needed to sort out. That part and Ty. She knew enough of men to know John Tunstall had more on his mind than a shopgirl for hire. How did she feel about that? It wouldn't be honest to lead him on if she weren't prepared to answer that question. That should be easy enough for a girl in her circumstances given all he had to offer. It should be easy. Yet, it wasn't.

She glanced at her reflection in the window and clenched her jaw. She'd been looking after herself a long time now.

Lucy Sample, get a hold of yourself. You're acting like a foolish schoolgirl again. You've been offered a very good job, nothing more than that, yet. That shiny knight you fancy pining for isn't here. He could be dead for all you know. You might never see him again. And if you do, who's to say there will be anything left of him for you? Well, a very substantial, proper gentleman is here. He's made you a very fine offer that might promise something more.

She put her pen to the page.

John Tunstall offered me a position working in his store tonight. I'm going to accept.

P.S. He kissed me.

Texas

The eastern sky turned gray, as night crept toward the western horizon, making way for first light. Yellow Dog did not return. He did not answer Coyote's call. The one-eye's knife spoke to Chero from the hillside in the distance. His warriors waited, stony silent dark shadows. He turned to his pony.

Roth crawled over the gully rim and slid down the bank.

"Where the hell have you been all night?"

"Coyote hunting. I got one too."

"I thought they might have got you."

"I wasn't far away. One of 'em got damn close. Maybe others too. When the one I left out there doesn't come back, you can bet they'll be comin' for us."

"Can we make a run for it?"

"They're close. We wouldn't get far in open country. Forted up here at least we've got a fighting chance. We got cover and water. The hillside makes for a good field of fire. If we make 'em pay dear enough, maybe we can run 'em off."

The half-breed shifted his seat. "Give Patch a gun."

"Shut up!" Ty clenched his jaw. He rummaged in his saddlebag for three hardtack biscuits. "We better have a quick bite before things heat up." He tossed one to the prisoner and joined Roth at the rim of the gully.

Roth munched his biscuit, watching the horizon grow light. They'll wait for first light. Let the sun cover them. A splinter of light broke over the skyline. A glow, a shaft, an edge of the fiery ball spilled bright light across the horizon. He squinted into the glare. Dark shapes appeared. A line of riders advanced toward them strung out along a broad front. "Here they come." He pointed into the sunrise.

Ty studied the shadowy line as it approached. "We'll set up a cross fire. I'll take the north rim. You take the south. Let 'em come in close enough to make our first shots count."

Roth nodded. "The way they're comin' the center of that line is gonna find the body of the one I killed. It'll be sixty or seventy yards out there. That'll likely stop 'em and give us some good shots. Let Chero show himself. Wherever he is in there, he'll go to the body. Take him down and maybe we take the fight out of them red devils fast." He slid down the gully wall and moved off south along the creek bed.

Patch sat beside his boulder watching and listening. They'd left his hands cuffed in front of him. From there he could make a move. The question was when. He would not let Chero take him. The fight would distract his captors. Sooner or later he would see his chance.

Chero and his warriors approached slowly, dark silhouettes against bright sunlight wary of the unseen. Ty sighted his Winchester and counted, nineteen. He waited. Minutes passed. Fingers of nerve clenched a fist in his gut. Tension parched the back of his throat. Comanche were dangerous fighters and vicious victors. They were not a fight to be taken lightly. He remembered the stories told by old Texas Rangers. Veterans made sure they kept one bullet in reserve. A man might need it at the end of a C'manch fight.

At seventy yards, the center of the line came upon the body of the dead scout. They drew a halt. Two riders dismounted and approached the body. One of them turned and said something to the rest of the band. Disciplined soldiers would have held their line. The Comanche did not. They rode into the center to have a look at their fallen brother. Some dismounted and knotted around the body. At this range in blinding light there was no way to pick out the renegade leader. They'd have to trust to luck. He looked down the gully and caught Roth's eye. He nodded. Both men raised their rifles and dropped them on line.

The first shots caught the band by surprise. Two warriors fell beside the body of the first. Ty worked the Winchester action, lever, exhale, squeeze. The rifle bucked. Lever, exhale, squeeze. Off to his right Roth stitched a deadly seam, raking the scrambling warrior band fighting to control a melee of spooked ponies. A few Comanche returned fire, shooting wildly. Their bullets whined harmlessly overhead. Two more fell trying to remount. Chero and the rest of the band regained control of their ponies, swung to their backs and galloped away.

Ty put up his rifle. "Save your ammunition."

Roth put up his rifle. Four ponies galloped after the retreating warriors, their fallen riders lay unseen in the underbrush and rocks. "We put a pretty good lick on 'em."

Fifteen Ty counted. "Opening dance, they'll be back."

Morning sun burned Chero's gaze to a black rage. The one-eye found another to join him. At least two fought from the hillside. He folded his arms across his chest. Anyone with the one-eye would die for his treachery. His warriors waited. He crouched and scratched a line in the sand. "Gully here." He stuck the point of the stick at each end making a hole. "Men shoot here and here." Two, trail sign say three, he wondered why. He looked around the circle of his brothers. "Coyote, Man Who Eats His Enemy's Heart."

Two warriors stepped forward. "Go here." He traced a line in the sand to the north end of the gully. "Get behind them. Kill whoever helps the one-eye when we attack. Do not kill the one-eye. He belongs to Chero." Man Who Eats His Enemy's Heart frowned. Chero caught his eye and spat. "The one-eye's heart is not fit to feed wild pigs. That one will watch his heart die in Chero's hand. Now go. We give you to high sun before we ride."

Morning sun reflected off rock walls, baking the gully like an earthen oven. Shimmering heat rose in waves from the gentle slope and broad plain below. Roth and Ledger sweated by turns at the watch. The Comanche took refuge in a wash at the base of the hillside out of sight of their prey. Time passed. Sweat soaked Ty's shirt and lined his face. His bandanna grew damp from keeping his eyes clear. He wondered if they might have given up and slipped away. Tempting as that thought might be, he discarded the notion. That kind of thinking got a man killed.

As the sun climbed toward high noon, shadows appeared amid the heat waves off to the east. They rode in single file toward his end of the gully.

"Here they come."

Roth climbed to his position on the south wall and chambered a round.

Ty squinted against the sun glare. "Looks like they mean to take a run at us. Hold your fire. Let 'em get close."

Patch flattened himself against the boulder, listening for movement above. He meant to be ready when the wolves came.

The Comanche broke into a gallop. They lifted their voices in a chorus of war cries trailed by dust clouds. Ty leveled his Winchester and waited. Roth did the same.

Chero and the leaders opened fire as they climbed toward the gully. They wheeled south, riders slumped over the sides of their galloping ponies firing across the horses' backs.

Ty lit 'em up, raking the line with steady action. Bullets spit and whined, stinging the rocks and buzzing away like angry wasps. He squeezed off three shots before it hit him. Something wasn't right. *Thirteen* shit! He drew his Colt and spun around to the Comanche in the rocks behind him. He dove to his right as the rifle exploded a shower of rock chips. He fired his pistol twice, one muzzle flash eclipsing the other in clouds of blue smoke.

Man Who Eats His Enemy's Heart rose from behind the rock where he hid, silhouetted against the bright blue sky. He toppled forward down the rocky bank into the gully below nearly falling on Patch. His rifle skittered across the stony ground to the creek.

Patch eyed the Winchester while his captor watched the rocks above looking for another attacker. *Damn* he'd never make it. It could as easily have fallen into his lap. He rolled away from the boulder, looking up as though in fear. He bumped against the dead Comanche.

There in the rocks above Roth's position. Ty fired again. Nothing moved.

Patch scuttled back to his place beside the boulder the renegade's knife tucked in the folds of his loincloth.

Roth turned away from the retreating warriors. "Unexpected company?"

"I saw sign of another one. Keep a sharp eye." He tossed the Comanche's rifle to Roth and climbed the west gully wall into the rocks above. He drew his pistol and searched the length of the rim, but saw no sign of the second attacker. "Keep an eye on the main bunch Johnny. I'll keep a lookout up here."

"I gotta piss."

Roth cut his eyes right to Patch. "Piss yourself for all I care."

Patch stood. He pulled his loincloth aside holding the blade concealed in the folds. He relieved himself where he stood. When he finished, he walked around to Roth's side of the boulder and sank to the ground. He stroked the haft of the knife. He was ready. He had only to wait for his chance.

Chapter Thirty-Eight

Coyote jogged into the south end of the wash his glistening body soaked in sweat. He headed straight for Chero.

"The one-eye is the prisoner of two white men. The one we captured and another who must have helped him escape."

Chero knit his brow. "How do you know the one-eye is their prisoner?"

"Coyote has seen him. His hands are tied with steel."

"These men must be white man's law." He pursed his lips in thought. "Maybe they will make trade, their lives for a worthless dog."

Blazing sun rode high across the cloudless western sky, turning the afternoon to suffocating heat. Roth dozed near his post on the south wall. Ty sat watch in the rocks above the north end.

"Here they come."

Roth snapped awake. He climbed into position. The Comanche rode in file along their first line of attack. They approached to a couple hundred yards and drew a halt. One rider came forward, his hands held open unarmed.

"Looks like they want to parley," Roth said over his shoulder.

Ty scrambled down from the rocks.

The rider drew rein at seventy yards near the bodies of his fallen brothers. "Give us the one-eye," he shouted. "Chero will let you go free."

"Seems like a fair enough trade to me." Roth pushed away

from the gully wall and waded across the creek to their sullen prisoner. He snatched the patch covering the prisoner's empty socket. "You won't be needin' this much longer." He turned back to Ty. "I got what I need to collect the bounty on this sorry son of a bitch. I say we let the C'manche have him. They cut him up and we save decent folks the cost of a hangin'."

Ty stood silent. Roth had a point. The trail of blood the half-breed left behind destroyed his family. The man might just as well have cut out his heart. If the Comanche returned the favor, it would serve the son of a bitch right. The way he killed deserved death, maybe even savage death. The Comanche sure had that in mind.

Patch sat, leaning against the boulder, defiant.

"For what you done to my wife and baby." The words hung in stifling stillness.

A twinge of fear clutched the breed's gut. He knew what he'd do if he were in the white man's place, even without a dead wife to avenge. He felt the knife. If he could not escape, he might escape Chero's death for a bullet. He might even take the nearest one with him.

Ty glanced at Roth. Time stood motionless. Loss and duty clawed at conscience and right. It would be easy. Vengeance finished. Justice served in a bad way. Vengeance wasn't justice. Comanche torture wasn't justice.

"I can't do it, Johnny. I been a lawman too long."

"You think that scum's worth dyin' for?"

"Who says we're gonna die?"

"Two of us and thirteen of them?"

"Yeah, I know. But we done all right so far. Besides we're bad-ass sons a bitches." Ty stalked off to the north end of the gully and took up his position.

Roth followed him with a glare. "Hey, don't I get a say here? The son of a bitch ain't worth dyin' for, Ty. Turn him over to the C'manche and let's get the hell out of here with our skins."

"You were the one who wanted a lawman for a partner. Well now you got one." Ty climbed the gully wall to glare at the waiting messenger. "I'm a deputy US marshal. This man's my prisoner. Tell Chero he can go to hell."

The rider wheeled away with a whoop, returning to the band. War cries split the stillness. Chero and his warriors surged forward to the attack.

Ty levered a round into his rifle chamber and took aim. At seventy yards he exhaled slowly and squeezed. The Winchester bucked. The lead pony broke away to the south, the other riders falling in line. *Shit!* He counted eight.

Where the hell are they? "We got trouble, Johnny."

"No shit." A volley of rifle fire raked the gully wall spraying rock chips and whining lead overhead.

"I don't mean them. I mean the five we don't see."

"They gotta be movin' in somewhere while we're pinned down here like sitting ducks." Roth popped up to the top of the wall and squeezed off two quick shots. "You sure you don't want to let 'em have our woman-killer friend here?"

Ty wiped sweat from his face on his sleeve, furiously jamming fresh cartridges into his rifle. In the rocks above the gully he wouldn't be much help fighting off the attackers. He might be able to cover their back, but even then it'd be damn hard to see trouble before it found you.

"Here they come again."

"Take our back, Johnny. I'll take the charge. When they pass my position, you take the charge and I'll take the back." War cries and rifle fire sounded on the slope below. Ty swung into firing position and levered a round into his rifle.

They'd use the charge to occupy them and then . . . Roth let the thought trail off as the silhouette of a rifle appeared in the rocks above Ledger, the shooter's head pressed to the stock, taking aim. Roth swung his Winchester on line and squeezed. The rifle charged, and the skull of the shooter exploded. He pitched forward. His rifle clattered down the rocks into the gully. *Four.*

Patch measured the distance from his place at the boulder to the fallen weapon. This time the rifle might be within reach.

"Got it." Ty took back watch.

Roth swung his rifle to the attackers and cracked off two shots as the band swept past. He turned to the back watch as a rifle shot exploded from the rocks above him. The shooter missed. The ricochet sang off a boulder at his left shoulder. Powder smoke gave up the shooter's position. Ty poured two rounds into the rocks with no sign of a hit. Roth's rifle charged followed by a grunt behind Ty's right shoulder. The dead renegade toppled into the gully two steps from him.

"Nice shot." *Three.*

"We're even."

"I got one up here in the rocks somewhere."

"My turn." Roth crossed the creek and scrambled up the west wall into the rocks above.

Ty guessed. He trained his rifle on Roth's position at the south face of the gully. The instant Johnny climbed out of the gully the renegade appeared. Ty fired. The heavy .44 round lifted the Comanche up and threw him backward. He disappeared from sight. *Two.*

As suddenly as the attack began, the shooting stopped. Ty turned back to the hillside. Chero and the main body withdrew.

"They're pullin' back, Johnny." He couldn't see Roth in the rocks above the gully.

"I'll clear things up here, just to make sure they all pulled back."

Ty checked their prisoner. A fallen Comanche rifle lay in the gully too close for comfort. He climbed down and claimed it.

The killer eyed him from an empty socket. "Night comes. Release Patch to guard against coyotes."

"Don't waste your breath."

"You cannot win this alone."

"You better hope we can. You'll be poor pickin's for the buzzards if we don't."

Roth wiped sweat from his eyes, as he worked his way north through the rocks above the gully. He moved cautiously, gun drawn. He saw no sign of the two unaccounted Comanche. He reached the north end of the gully wall. He saw movement off to the northeast in the trees along the creek bank. He waited. *One, two* they scuttled east toward the main body on foot. He stood.

"They're gone."

"You sure?"

"Seen 'em go." He climbed down to the gully floor.

"Now what?"

"Night's comin' on. Our boy here says their coyotes will be out tonight."

"Likely so. What do we do about it?"

"We make 'em a warm welcome."

"How we gonna do that? I figure north, south and east. That gives 'em three ways in. There's only two of us. How do we cover all three?"

"We don't. I got the north rocks. You got the south rocks."

"What about the east slope?"

"If they come that way, we'll know soon enough."

"What makes you so sure?"

"Our boy there, he'll be screamin'."

★ ★ ★ ★ ★

Shadow crept over the western gully wall. Ledger stood watch on the north end of the east wall. Roth sat with his back to the wall cleaning his guns. Patch sat across the creek with his back to the west wall. Finished cleaning his guns, Roth opened his saddlebags, drew out a box of cartridges and began reloading his belt.

"How's your ammunition holding out?" Ty asked.

Roth glanced up. "Sixteen and one."

"You mean seventeen."

"No I mean sixteen and the last one. You best have one too."

"Ok, make mine fifteen and one."

"Thirty-one rounds, we best make them count."

"There's only ten of them left."

"Maybe so, but they've got bullets too."

"I like our odds as long as we see them coming."

"Don't count on just seeing them. When coyotes come out in the dark, sometimes you have to smell them."

"I'll remember that."

Chero addressed his warriors in the gathering gloom. He drew a line in the dirt from northeast to southwest.

"Coyote will lead my wolves here, here and here." He stabbed each end of the line and the east slope in the middle with his finger. "Kill the white eyes. Leave the one-eye for me." He fixed each man with his order. Each nodded in turn.

Roth and Ledger climbed the west wall into the rocks at opposite ends of the gully. Cloud cover muted the moon to a shifting patchwork of soft light and shadow.

Patch sat hunched against the west wall of the gully. Moonlight flickered here and there on the surface of the creek. He considered his chances of slipping out of the gully and escaping into the night. With his wrists in handcuffs he doubted he'd get far or last long if he did. He might free his pony, but that would only give away his attempt at escape. Still he might find an opportunity if the wolves attacked. He clutched the knife. It would be his only defense if Chero's wolves made it past his foolish captors. He wished for a gun. The knife would have to do. Chero's wolf would come over the east wall. He would find Patch alone and bound. His orders would spare Patch for Chero. The old man's vanity and vengeance would spare him again.

Roth found a crevice near the crest at the south end of the gully. Here the hillside was boulder-strewn, bristling with mesquite, sage and creosote bush. He wasted little attention to far seeing. With so many places to hide and ground shadow affording additional cover, an intruder would be all but upon him before his presence were known.

Ty lay in the shadow of a large bolder, looking north where he could see the slope climb toward him. Ground shadow and cloud-filtered moonlight gave the scene a ghostly appearance. It promised a long tense night. Time passed. He fought sleep's tug on his eyes. Battle fatigue, loss of sleep and hunger conspired to pull him into the comfort of darkness. Capturing the one-eyed killer had proven a daunting task. Simple vengeance was there for the talking. He hadn't taken it. Victoria would not have been surprised. Now all of it might exact a dear price if Chero and his warriors had their way. He drifted.

No wait! Something moved. There by that sage bush. He blinked hard. His eyes might have tricked him. He cradled his gun in the crook of his arm and slowed his breathing. The bush moved again. No trick this time. He marked the ground shadow and played his gaze over the hillside. Where there was one, there could be more. A shot might bring on an attack. *Fifteen and one,* make every shot count.

Mesquite scented a soft night breeze. Roth saw nothing. He tasted it, close and coming closer. He studied the rugged terrain, searching for movement where there should be none.

Something moved at the rim of the east wall. Patch held still in the shadow. The wolf did not move. He might be confused. He expected to find three men. Instead he found none. Patch gripped the hilt of his knife. If the wolf climbed down he would find for a prisoner a scorpion with a sting. He would also give up a weapon.

He had to be there, but where? Roth slowed his breathing. *Patience,* he'll make a fatal move.

A single gunshot exploded at the north end of the gully. Ty got one, he hoped. That should flush this one, but where? He waited. Nothing moved. Then he noticed something. The sour scent on the breeze softened to mesquite.

He'd gotten close, real close. Ty shot him point-blank. No one attacked. The hillside stood silent and still. One counted, *fourteen.* The Comanche count stood at nine.

The wolf at the rim of the east wall pulled back. They were gone. The small hours this night would pass with no further disturbance. Patch closed his eye to sleep. His captors would not.

Chapter Thirty-Nine

Roth and Ty climbed down into the gully in the gray light of predawn. The prisoner slept soundly.

Ty shook his head. "Look at the son of a bitch, sleepin' like he ain't got a care in the world."

"Why not? He had us up all night keepin' watch."

"Wolves go away when you know they are here."

"Look who's come out of hibernation. I reckon you knew that all along," Ty said.

The breed favored him with smug disdain.

"Well, since you're so savvy about Comanche ways, what's next?"

"Attack at sunrise."

"Do the wolves come back?"

"I would send them."

"Looks like we'll be fightin' on two fronts again," Roth said.

"There's nine of 'em left. Make every shot count."

"Even then we may not have enough ammunition to hold them off for a day."

"Then we make them last two count." Ty glanced at the one-eyed killer. "You best hope we don't have to use those two bullets. If we do, you're Comanche buzzard bait."

"I'll climb up the south end and keep an eye on things," Roth said.

★ ★ ★ ★ ★

Time passed. The sky brightened. The sun perched a fiery ball on the horizon.

"Here they come."

Ty scrambled into position on the north end of the gully.

Chero and the main body of warriors rode out of the sun in file.

"Ok, Johnny, same plan. I'll take 'em on this end. You watch our back. Then we switch."

Roth turned to the rocks in the west wall above.

Ty jacked a round into his Winchester as the renegade band galloped out of the sun. Ty shouldered the rifle and sighted the lead rider. They swung into the charge raining fire on his position. He fired, *seven.*

"Two up top, Johnny. You got this bunch." Roth swung his rifle into the charge. Ty swept his gaze across the western wall. *Nothing, why?*

Distant gunfire halted Red Tail Horse in his tracks. He'd searched for many days now. He found no sign. This sign found him. He put his pony into a lope southwest toward the battle sounds. Less than a mile distant he mounted a rise. A line of warriors circled two men fighting from a rocky hillside. A crooked smile cracked chiseled features. He wheeled his pony away to the northeast at a gallop.

"They're circling for another pass," Roth said.

"No sign of 'em up above. How's your ammunition?"

"Thirteen and one. How about you?"

"Twelve and one. Did you get any in that last pass?"

"No. You?"

"No."

"Here they come again. Take 'em, Ty. I got our back."

Ty squeezed off a shot as the lead rider galloped across his field of fire. He fired a second time, counting his shots down to ten and one. Off to his right a shot exploded at the south end of the gully. A second and third followed. He swung around as a rifle clattered to the creek bank followed by the body of its shooter. Roth spun back to the charge as it passed south of his position and circled east.

"There's one more up top, Ty. I'm goin' up after him. You'll have to hold the next charge."

"Did you burn all three shots?"

"Just two, our friend there had the other one."

Ty turned back to the east. "Make 'em count."

"I hear you." Roth started his climb.

"Here they come," Ty said. He levered a round into his rifle chamber, shouldered the weapon and sighted the lead pony. The Winchester bucked. The pony bellowed and toppled to its knees, pitching its rider onto the hillside. The rest of the party swept by, raining bullets and rock chips on Ty's position. The down warrior swung up behind the last renegade as they galloped away to the south. *Eight and that one,* Ty thought watching his attackers circle.

Just then the hot breeze rang with the sweetest sound Ty ever heard, the clarion call of a bugle and the heart-lifting bars of the charge. Off to the northeast a blue line swept out of the hills, the Stars and Stripes unfurled, the red-and-white unit pennant straight in the wind. Chero and his warriors broke the attack and galloped away to the south.

Patch moved cat-quick and silent. He scooped up the fallen rifle and leveled it at Ty's back. "Drop gun."

Ty glanced over his shoulder and cussed his own foolishness. He dropped his rifle.

"Now pistol."

Ty lifted the Colt from his holster and dropped it on the ground.

"Climb down. Now keys."

Ty gritted his teeth. He couldn't let the son of a bitch get away, not after all this. He dropped the keys.

The killer waved him away from his weapons with the rifle muzzle.

Ty stepped aside.

The breed crossed the creek, his eye locked on Ledger, the Winchester leveled at his chest. He squatted and picked up the keys. He fumbled for the lock. His attention never wavered. The handcuff clicked open and dropped from his wrist. He didn't bother with the second cuff. He slipped the key ring in his waistband.

Ty sensed movement in the rocks above. He glanced at the shadow.

Patch caught the gesture. A flicker of doubt crossed his eye.

Roth edged to a notch in the rocks. He listened. The cavalry took care of Chero, but they still had one Comanche prowling up here. A shot rang out up toward the north end of the gully.

Patch staggered. Ty kicked the rifle out of his hands. The half-breed grunted, shook his head and recovered his survival instinct. The knife appeared from nowhere poised to strike. Blood slicked the shoulder of his still-cuffed free hand. Pain twisted grotesque features. He crouched, the blade menacing as he advanced to the kill. He lunged at Ty with a vicious cut.

Ty jumped back from the blade, stumbled on the rocky creek bank and fell on his back. Patch pounced. Ty rolled away. The half-breed sprawled on the ground. Ty bounced to his feet and delivered a powerful kick to the half-breed's ribs. He stomped the hand holding the knife. Patch shrieked an animal mixture of rage and pain. The knife skittered from his hand. Ty scooped it up.

The killer tried to rise. Ty shattered the bridge of his nose with a kick that snapped his head back senseless. He hefted the blade. His mind ran red with his last vision of Victoria. Her killer's vitals lay exposed to the blade.

One to go, Roth thought. The last of the Comanche lurked somewhere up ahead. He circled a line of boulders and began to climb. Slowly, cautiously he scaled higher, searching for his quarry below. Toward the center of the gully he paused. From his position he could see Ty standing over Patch with a knife. The cavalry column approached from the east face of the slope.

Something moved in the rocks below. Roth considered an easy kill shot. *Let the son of a bitch decide for himself.* He levered a round into the Winchester's chamber, the metallic action announced his presence. The shadow froze. The length of a rifle appeared overhead in a sign of surrender. The warrior stepped out in the open.

"Drop it." No telling if the buck spoke English. Roth doubted he did, but in the universal language of defeat the rifle clattered onto the rocks at his feet. "Step away." He emphasized the command with the barrel of his rifle. The renegade moved aside. Roth made his way down from his position, rifle leveled at his captive. He picked up the renegade's weapon and motioned him down the rocks to the gully.

Ty turned at the sound of the lone Comanche captive sliding into the gully at Roth's gunpoint. The intrusion brought him back from a long-distant place with smoldering ruins and the hollow sound of dirt falling on pine. He looked at the unbloodied knife as though disappointed by what he saw. He tossed it to the ground.

"Yo, the gully." Authority rang from beyond the east wall.

Ty picked up his gun as if remembering himself and holstered it. He turned to the east gully wall.

Patch stirred. Blood smeared his shoulder. His shattered nose flattened below his empty eye socket. Fire raged in his ribs.

The cavalry column halted some twenty yards down the slope. An officer wearing colonel's pips stepped down and walked to the rim of the gully.

"Lieutenant Colonel Nathan Augustus Monroe Dudley at your service, sir."

"And right grateful we are for it, Colonel. I'm Deputy US Marshal Ty Ledger. This here's my partner Johnny Roth. You came along just in time. They had us outnumbered pretty good."

"Judging by the bodies over yonder and the ones layin' down there, I'd say you boys gave a good account of yourselves. My troop is out of Fort Stanton. We've been tracking Chero's band since they jumped the reservation in Oklahoma Territory. Our orders are to round them up and take 'em back where they belong. You boys were a big help in finding them."

"It wasn't voluntary duty."

"Looks like you've got a couple of captives I can take off your hands."

"Just this one." Roth nudged the warrior forward with the muzzle of his rifle. "That one's a half-breed wanted for murder. He belongs to us." Roth pushed the renegade past Ty, forcing him to climb the gully wall.

"Sergeant Caleb, prisoner detail front and center!" Dudley called. Three troopers rode forward, dismounted and took control of the prisoner. "You sure about keepin' that one?"

Ty nodded. "He's wanted on rape and murder charges from Lincoln to Deadwood. They'll have to draw straws to see who gets to stretch his worthless neck, but I'll be there to watch him swing."

Dudley knit his brow. "Sounds personal."

Roth spoke up for Ty. "It is."

Patch wanted no part of a hangin.' He'd rid himself of the

witch. Her demons still haunted him. He escaped Chero's knives, only to be caught in the hatred of a man whose wife he'd killed. That man had a right to kill him if he could, but it didn't have to be at the end of a rope. His hand closed over the hilt of the discarded knife. He leaped to his feet and sprang at Ty's back.

"Look out!" Dudley roared.

Ty spun. His gun filled his hand and fired in a single motion. Muzzle flash and powder smoke bloomed in front of the killer. The report rang down the gully like a thunderclap. The bullet caught the half-breed in the groin. He screamed, dropping the knife. Gouts of blood spouted from the wound. He sank to his knees.

Ty stood over him, listening to the man's stifled groans as the powder smoke drifted away.

Patch looked up, his face masked in his own gore, his one eye twisted in pain.

Roth broke the silence. "You gonna let him bleed out gut shot like that?"

Ty stood silent, staring. His voice cracked. "I should for what he done."

"Finish the son of a bitch, or I will."

Ty thumbed the hammer. A round rolled into firing position. He leveled the muzzle at the half-breed's good eye. "Her name was Victoria. She carried our child. You took her life. You take that to whatever hell's awaitin' you. This bullet's better than you deserve." The flash exploded, filling the gully with the final vengeance report. Acrid blue smoke clouded the splatter of blood and bone behind the ruined eye. Patch pitched back as the smoke drifted away. Ty holstered his gun. *It's done.*

Dudley broke the silence. "Sergeant Caleb, burial detail front and center."

Chapter Forty

Lincoln

Lucy stared into the darkened ceiling alone in her room. She pictured herself sitting across the candlelit supper table from John. *Tepid,* it seemed an odd word. Like so many of the odd words he used. He said it when his thin, milky tea went cold in the cup. Tepid fit. John Tunstall's kiss was tepid. If a girl wanted thunder and lightning, it took a man like Ty Ledger.

Her thoughts filled with Ty's chiseled features, rough shave and steely eyes. The vision made her legs feel long. The choice couldn't be clearer, tepid and safe, or haunted thunder. What was a girl to do?

Where is he? Off chasing his ghost killer somewhere. He could be dead for all she knew. She might never see him again. John was steady and ambitious. He was rich and likely to get even richer. The job in his store held promise. Good clean work far removed from the sporting life. Tepid maybe, but he was sweet on her just the same. Who knew where that might lead?

She sat up in bed. Two futures stretched out before her, one solid and sure, the other romantic and uncertain. She hadn't written that to her journal. Sometimes that helped. She fumbled on the night table for a lucifer, struck it and touched the bright sulfur glow to the lamp wick. She climbed out of bed, trimmed the lamp and carried it to her seat at the small writing table. The leather bound journal lay on the table attended by inkpot and pen. She opened the book and took up her pen.

John took me to dinner again this evening . . .

South Spring Ranch
October 1877

A north breeze cut a sharp edge against Roth's cheek. Late afternoon sun did little to soften the chill. Shelter for the night and a warm fire would feel damn good. And then there was the promise of Dawn Sky. The thought of her warmed him against the cold wind. It felt as though he'd been away for a long time. Part of him had been missing the whole time. The empty space never left him. Nothing like a brush or two with death to make a man understand what was important. He'd been a man on the move his whole life. He'd never given it a second thought. Settling down was something other people did. Now it tugged at him like the onset of an unfamiliar illness. No, Dawn Sky tugged at him. What would settling down mean? Would she even have him? Whatever feelings she might have for him surely conflicted with her loyalty to Chisum and the only home she'd ever known. What would come of that? He didn't know. He'd find out soon enough. They'd make the ranch by nightfall.

Up ahead, Ty brooded. He thought killing Patch would finish it. He thought avenging the loss of Victoria and their child would free him from his bitter anger. He expected he'd want to hurry back to Lincoln to see what could be made of his feelings for Lucy. He'd expected that, but somehow vengeance wasn't enough to chase all his demons. He had a void the killer's cold corpse couldn't fill. Lincoln loomed like a dark heavy cloud to the north. If he couldn't rid himself of these feelings by the time he got there, what would he tell Lucy?

Smoke from the hacienda chimney rose against the dusk sky. The sign heralded the end of the trail. Roth squeezed up a lope. Ty fell in behind. Lengthening purple shadow draped the hacienda up the road beyond the bunkhouse, barn and corrals.

Lamp-lit windows reflected warm welcoming light. Roth smiled as he rode. He'd missed her. He knew that, but the promise of ending the separation warmed him in a way that surprised him.

The kitchen smelled of fresh bread and the savory aroma of a roast in the woodstove. She'd sensed the need to make enough for guests. She wiped her hands on her apron and hung it on its peg at the sound of hoofbeats approaching fast. She set off for the front door through the dining room so as not to disturb Mr. Chisum. She reached the doorway and paused, waiting for the knock to come. Her heartbeat climbed the back of her throat. She looked in the window glass and smoothed her long black hair.

Horses drew rein beyond the door. She heard the creak of saddle leather as the riders stepped down. A boot scraped the front porch. She threw open the door and ran into the arms of a surprised shadow.

Johnny swept her off her feet and held her crushingly tight, the moment frozen between them. She scarcely heard the muffled voice call knowingly from the parlor.

"Dawn Sky, do we have guests?" Chisum couldn't help but notice her behavior that day. He knew her well enough to read her uncanny ability to anticipate things. He wasn't at all surprised they had visitors and he didn't need to go to the door to know who one of them was.

Johnny set her down, eyes locked in unspoken exchange. A light scent of cinnamon welcomed him home. *Home,* funny it felt like that. Chisum filled the lighted doorway.

"Ty, Johnny, welcome back." He extended his hand in greeting. "Come in, come in." He ushered them into the warmly lit parlor with a cheery fire crackling in the great stone fireplace. Light mesquite scent colored the air. "I expect you boys have some stories to tell. How about a drink?"

Roth spoke for both of them. "That sounds mighty good, John."

"Dawn Sky was just fixin' us some supper. I think she just might have enough for the two of you to join us. That right, Dawn?"

She lowered her eyes, her copper skin flushed.

"I'll fetch the boys a drink while you put a couple of extra places on the table."

"No need," she said. "I'll fetch the whiskey."

He shook his head with a chuckle. "Then join us, I expect you'll want to hear what they have to say too."

She hurried off to the dining-room sideboard.

"Sit down boys and make yourselves at home."

Dawn Sky returned with a bottle and glasses. She set them on the table before the settee and poured. When they were settled Chisum lifted his glass. "Well, here's to the both of you. When you went off like you did with Chero's band on the loose, I wasn't sure we'd see either one of you again." He took a sip.

Roth took a pull on his drink. "I wasn't so sure about that a couple of times myself."

"You got him, then?"

Johnny caught Dawn Sky's eye as she took her seat across the room.

"We did. I got my bounty and Ty got . . ." He paused. ". . . got what he came after."

Chisum nodded. "This country will be a better place without the likes of him. Did you have any trouble with Chero?"

"Oh yeah, I managed to get myself caught by the C'manch. Ty here pulled me out of there before they got around to skinning me."

Dawn gasped.

"You're real lucky young fella. Not many men live to tell that tale."

"Don't think that thought didn't cross my mind. It's funny in a way. If Patch hadn't killed one of Chero's women, they probably would have cut me up before Ty got there. He got to me while Chero was off chasin' Patch."

"If you got him, I guess Chero didn't."

"Nope, Chero got him all right. Patch goaded Chero into a knife fight while they was fixin' to cut him up. Patch won the fight and got away. That's when we caught him."

"Well I'll be. That's a hell of a story."

"It'd be enough for most but there's more."

"Then that calls for another drink." Chisum refilled their glasses.

Ty sat silently, lost in thought as Roth told the story.

"We was headed back to Lincoln with the prisoner when Chero and his bunch caught up with us. We forted up and had us one hell of a fight. They'd likely have got us too if the cavalry hadn't come along."

"Cavalry?"

"A column out of Fort Stanton lookin' for Chero."

"Did they take the half-breed?"

"No, Patch made a play to escape. Ty shot him in self-defense. I get my bounty, dead or alive."

"That's some story. 'Bout enough to give a man an appetite. How about let's eat?"

Roast beef, biscuits, gravy and greens made a feast for men fed on hardtack, jerky and canned tomatoes for weeks. Dawn Sky watched Johnny eat. Chisum watched her watch him. Roth turned to conversation for diversion. "What's the news around these parts while we been gone? Them Seven Rivers boys behavin' themselves?"

"My gut says no, but I cain't prove nothin.' I think they're pickin' off my strays. Nothin' big, we just ain't caught 'em at it. Those boys are a small part of the problem. Dolan's the real problem in this county, him and that bunch up in Santa Fe who let him and his crowd get away with anything they like. It'll take more than me standin' up to 'em to put a stop to it. But that just might happen."

Roth cocked an eye. "What makes you think so?"

"Young English feller name of Tunstall showed up in Lincoln. He's got pockets full of money and a head full of big ideas. He's fixin' to take on Dolan at his own game."

"You keep sayin' Dolan, what happened to Murphy?"

"Sold out to Dolan on account of poor health."

"So you think this Englishman can beat Dolan at his own game?"

"Damned if I know. I'll tell you one thing: he's got a plan that sure enough could work, unless he gets himself killed first. But enough of that, what do you boys plan to do now?"

Roth turned to Ty for his answer.

Ty paused, a forkful of roast beef dripping gravy over his plate. "I haven't thought past gettin' back to Lincoln."

"What about you, Johnny?"

Chisum asked the question, but Roth could feel Dawn's eyes waiting for his answer. "I don't know exactly. I kind a like it in these parts." Dawn lowered her lashes at his answer.

Chisum glanced at her too. "I can see that."

"Maybe I'll look for work up in Lincoln."

Chisum settled back in his chair. His eyes darted from Dawn to Roth under furrowed brows. He knew what he was up against. There were some things a man couldn't fight even if he was John Chisum. "I could probably use another gun around here until the Dolan business is settled. How might that suit you?"

Dawn's eyes popped open wide and round.

Roth smiled a half smile. "Why, John, that'd suit me just fine."

Chisum pulled a frown over a knowing twinkle. "I thought it might."

Dawn Sky began clearing dinner plates away as though the matter were settled.

Roth lay awake, remembering another night he and Ty bunked in Chisum's barn. This time he knew why he couldn't sleep. Nearby he could hear Ty's steady breathing. He'd been afraid for a time the sound of his heartbeat might keep his partner awake. Looking up into the inky blackness he could see a silver sliver of moon through the loft door. Its pale light lit the garden behind the darkened hacienda he could see through the open barn door. Finally her shadow appeared in the soft light.

He tossed back his blanket and rose as quietly as he could.

"Just don't get yourself fired the first night on your new job," Ty said.

"Good thought. Don't wait up for me." He headed for the garden.

She waited as she had that first night, her face tilted to the sky, washed softly in starlight. She turned at the sound of his boot on the garden path and ran to his arms. She shivered against the night chill, soft and warm against him. He'd never touch a slice of apple pie again without being reminded of her. He found her lips with his. The night stood still. She wrapped her arms around his neck and held on as though she might never let go.

"Dawn Sky did not think you would stay."

Her throaty whisper felt warm and moist on his neck. "I never gave a thought to leavin', as long as you'd have me."

Her eyes turned liquid in his. She held him tight by way of a reply. She looked up, starlight glistened in her eyes. "Come." She took his hand and led him down the garden path to the creek. An owl hooted over the gurgle of the creek.

He slipped an arm around her. She came to his embrace. He found her lips in his and let his head go light. She took his breath away, exposing his inner hunger. He'd known desire before. This was different. This was more. He held her, running his hand over the soft curve of her back. Passion mixed with possession and a sense of completion he'd never experienced before. He ached for her in a way he'd have to do something about before he did something that got him worse than fired. "Dawn." He whispered into her cinnamon scent. "Would you, I mean, could you?" He choked on the words.

She smiled up at him misty eyed with starlight. "Padre Bernardino."

He smiled. "I'll take that for a yes."

She kissed him.

He was in love with her. That much would be plain to a blind man. Ty tossed restlessly in his blanket spread over a pile of sweet-smelling straw. Chisum had given Roth more than a job, whether he knew it or not. Imagine that, Johnny Roth ground tied by a slip of a Navajo girl. It reminded him of Victoria. Such feelings were special. How many chances did a man get to have that? He didn't know for sure, but not many; and that brought him back to Lucy.

The prospect of seeing her hung over him like a cloud. What was he to make of it? He'd felt the physical connection the moment he met her in that Dodge saloon, so young, so pretty, so out of place. Back then, there'd been Victoria. He'd felt it again in Denver. It only became stronger in Santa Fe and then again on that creek bank on the ride down to Lincoln. It sure as hell got away from both of them on that hill above Lincoln. He thought it was only a matter of avenging Victoria's death. Patch was dead. His feelings for Victoria were not. Lucy could give him things a man wanted. Could he give her the things she deserved? That was the question that troubled him. He didn't have a ready answer for that one. Only time would tell. Best take it slow.

Night chill clung to the early morning light. Autumn hinted at the arrival of winter. Ty tugged the cinch snug. The steel dust blew his nose. "I'll send the telegram when I get to Lincoln."

Roth nodded. "Much obliged. You gonna stay around long enough I might get paid?"

Ty dropped his head. "I don't know, Johnny."

"I thought you and Lucy . . ." He let the question trail off unfinished.

"I don't know. If Widenmann needs help I might stay around. If I don't stay, check with Widenmann or that no-account sheriff. Best I can do."

"I understand. Maybe I'll see you in Lincoln, then."

"Maybe." He stepped into the saddle.

Roth extended his hand. "Best of luck, pard. Next time I got renegade C'manche fixin' to skin my ass I'll be lookin' for you."

"Do us both a favor and stay clear of renegade C'manche."

"I expect you're right."

"You be good to that girl."

"Count on it. Till next time, then."

Ty wheeled away.

Chapter Forty-One

Lincoln

The last long rays of sunset faded out of Lincoln, leaving a deep purple curtain. The steel dust picked its way along the east end of town, sensing his rider's hesitation. He turned toward a familiar picket fence at a light touch of right knee.

Ty stepped down in front of the neat white house with the green door. He remembered that first night, the sudden realization that he was calling on a woman. The gate hinge creaked a familiar protest. His boots crunched the path to the porch. He paused.

He'd spent the long ride from South Spring grappling with his doubts. What should he do? What should he say? For all of that, he still had no answers. He could climb back on his horse and simply ride on, but where? He'd broken his ties to Cheyenne. It held nothing for him but painful memories. He could find someplace new, California maybe, but to what end? New Mexico was new enough. Running away solved nothing. Time had a way of healing things. Maybe time would mend his loss. Time and a girl for whom he still felt a special connection. It wasn't much to offer. He hoped it would be enough.

His boots scraped the porch step, shattering his private silence. He rapped on the door and waited. He brooded over a mixture of uncertainty and frustration. Muffled footsteps within dismissed the feeling. The door swung open.

Lucy's eyes went round and wide. "Ty."

He'd expected she might rush into his arms. She didn't. He took off his hat. "You sure look pretty."

"When did you get back?"

"I just rode in."

"Lucy, girl, have you lost your manners?" Mrs. O'Hara called from the kitchen. "Are you going to invite Marshal Ledger in or keep him standing on the porch all night?"

"I, ah, oh, I'm sorry, Ty, come in please." She stepped back to let him pass and closed the door.

They stood staring for an awkward moment until Lucy found her voice. "Did you get him?"

He nodded.

"And?" The question hung in the air, silent except for the jangle of carriage harness drawing up at the gate. The ghost in his eye said more than words ever could.

The gate creaked. Boots crunched the front path and clumped the porch, announcing a visitor. The knock at the door sounded like a pistol shot. Lucy jumped. She met Ty's eyes for a nervous moment before opening the door.

"Good evening, my dear." Tunstall bowed. "You look positively fetching." He straightened, his attention shifting to Ty. "Oh, I say, forgive me. I didn't know you had company."

"John, this is Marshal Ty Ledger. Ty this is John Tunstall."

"Ah, this must be the friend I recall you telling me about."

Ty took the offered hand. Clearly the Englishman had come calling. The way Lucy was gussied up, she'd expected him. She hadn't let any grass grow under her feet while he'd been away. *So much for frettin' over what to say to her.* It should have made things easier. It didn't.

"John just moved to Lincoln, Ty." Lucy fumbled to fill the awkward silence as the two men sized each other like two roosters, each caught in the other's henhouse. "He's fixin' to open a business."

"Chisum mentioned something about that."

"Ah you know Mr. Chisum. Jolly good fellow, quite stalwart by my estimation I should say."

"How do you know him?"

"Mr. Chisum and I have discussed a business opportunity or two."

"What sort of business was it again?"

Tunstall pursed his lips, considering the pertinence of the question. He half smiled for Lucy's benefit. "A mercantile, perhaps a ranch to go with it."

Ty hooked a thumb behind the hammer of his pistol. "That's right. He said you was plannin' to take on Dolan."

Tunstall wrinkled his brow. "More like a little friendly competition."

"Competition ain't likely to be friendly where Dolan's concerned."

"I'm sure we shall keep things above the borders of civility and within the law."

Lucy took a half step between them to change the subject. "Ty just returned from tracking down a vile murderer."

Tunstall looked from Lucy to Ty. "Congratulations, Marshal. That sounds like a true service to Lincoln's law-abiding citizenry."

Ty met Lucy's eyes. "I best be goin'."

"Will you, will you be staying in Lincoln, Ty?"

"I don't know. I'll let you know. Tunstall." He replaced his hat and stepped into the night.

"My pleasure, old chap, good evening to you."

Ty checked into the Wortley and headed for the bar. He found Widenmann nursing a beer.

"Ty Ledger, well I'll be." He stood to shake hands. "I was beginning to think the Comanche got the two of you."

"They damn near did."

"Where's Roth?"

"Workin' for Chisum."

"Then I take it you got your man."

"We did."

"You boys have been busy. Sit down, have a drink. I want to hear all about it."

The owner, waiter, bartender, cook appeared in an apron that hadn't seen the inside of a washtub since the last time Ty saw it. "What'll it be?"

"You got anything left to eat in the kitchen."

"Fried chicken, biscuits and gravy."

"I'll have an order of that and a whiskey. Bring the bottle."

"Bring me another beer." The waiter hurried off. "Comanche and a killer, sounds like a hell of a story."

"Closer to hell a few times than I care to come."

Ty began his story, interrupted by the waiter delivering their order. He continued around a mouthful of chicken. He didn't notice the waiter greet two new guests at the door behind him. He finished his tale with the last bite of biscuit soaked in gravy.

"Well I was right about one thing. That's a hell of a story. You had a chance to tell it to her yet?" He tilted his chin over Ty's shoulder.

He glanced back. He didn't need to. Lucy and Tunstall sat at a candlelit corner table. He shrugged. "I told her some."

"Been a pretty regular thing since Tunstall hit town."

"So I gather. Who the hell is he?"

"English gent, hails from money to hear him tell it. Claims he plans to start a business in Lincoln. He's been talkin' some with that lawyer Alex McSween. No tellin' what that's about."

"A mercantile, maybe ranchin,' he says."

"You know him?"

Ty shook his head. "Lucy introduced us when he come callin'."

"Sorry about that, Ty."

"Don't be. Probably wasn't gonna work out anyway."

"A mercantile huh, Dolan won't take kindly to that notion. If Tunstall takes him on, he better have friends. Dolan plays rough."

"You're right about Dolan. I hope Lucy don't get herself mixed up in that kind of trouble."

"She's a big girl. So what about you? You fixin' to stay around, or move on?"

He glanced over his shoulder again. "I don't know, Rob. I thought I might stay around for a while. Now I'm not so sure. With Patch dead my marshalin' job's done. I'll help Johnny collect his bounty, I reckon. I should have a notion by then."

"Well if you've a mind to stay, I expect I could persuade Marshal Sherman I need some help down here. The Seven Rivers boys have been quiet, but South Spring's still an armed camp. I smell trouble between Tunstall and Dolan. Tunstall may be green, but he's no fool. If he decides to take on Dolan he'll be lookin' for help. Dick Brewer took him down to South Spring to meet Chisum a while back."

"Chisum said they'd talked about a couple of opportunities, whatever that means."

"Don't matter. There's no love lost between Chisum and Dolan. If Chisum decides he's got a dog in the Tunstall fight, all hell could break loose. If it does, Sheriff Brady will disappear behind Dolan's coattails."

"Hmm." Ty scratched his chin. "You know, Rob, I just might take you up on that."

Widenmann stretched his hand across the table. "I'd be damn glad of the help."

★ ★ ★ ★ ★

Lincoln
November 1877
The black-clad vaquero rode out of the hills into the west end of Lincoln. Sunlight flashed on his silver-concho-studded hatband. Silver spur rowels jingled as his flashy black stallion pranced up the deserted street. Matched ivory-handled Colts rode low on his hips. Dark eyes darted left and right under a prominent brow. A hawk-like nose defined lean carved features. A knife scar slashed his left cheek. A thin black mustache turned down in a scowl around the stub of a cigarillo tucked between thin cruel lips.

He drew rein and stepped down at the rail fronting the Wortley saloon. A tumbleweed chased down the street followed by a dust devil as his boots clumped up the boardwalk to the saloon door. He stepped inside. The dimly lit bar smelled of smoke and stale beer. Two men sat at a back corner table. The proprietor, waiter, bartender, cook stood behind the bar, wiping it with a dirty rag.

"Afternoon, stranger, what can I get for you?"

"Tequila." His voice cracked hard, thickly accented in Spanish. The bartender set a glass on the bar and poured yellowish liquid from a dusty bottle. The stranger tossed a silver dollar on the bar and held up the glass. "Salute." He tossed it off, exhaled the bite and poured another.

"You're new in town."

"Sí."

"What brings you to Lincoln?"

The stranger's eyes narrowed to black slits. The scar on his cheek twitched. "I look for an hombre."

The bartender eased back, sensing the stranger meant trouble. "This hombre got a name?"

The stranger shook his head. "Tall, black double rig like

these." He eased his Colts forward in their holsters showing the handles. "Scar here." He sliced his lower lip with a fingernail.

The bartender furrowed bushy eyebrows. "That sounds like Johnny Roth."

Roth's name caught the attention of Ty Ledger, sitting at the back table with Rob Widenmann. He took in the black-clad vaquero with a vague sense of recognition. It couldn't be.

The stranger arched an eyebrow. "Where can I find this Johnny Roth?"

"Works for John Chisum down on South Spring these days. What do you want with Roth?"

The stranger knocked back his drink. "I owe him the return of a debt. Muchas gracias." He turned to leave.

"If I see him, who should I say is lookin' for him?"

The stranger paused in the doorway. "Tell him, Crystobal comes."

It couldn't be but it is.

Widenmann sensed Ledger's distraction. "Somethin' the matter?"

"Maybe." Ty pushed back his chair and followed the pistolero to the door. He watched Crystobal lead his horse across the street to Dolan's store. He looped a rein over the rail and climbed the boardwalk. Ledger returned to the table.

"What was that all about?"

"A ghost," Ty said lost in thought.

"A ghost, what the devil are you talkin' about?"

Ty came back to the moment. "That might be closer to it."

"You're talkin' in riddles, Ty."

"Devil I mean. That son of a bitch is trouble."

"You know him from somewhere?"

He nodded, remembering.

Widenmann waited patiently.

"Me and Roth crossed his trail up in Santa Fe last spring.

Roth made the mistake of gettin' friendly with a woman Crystobal considered his property. He made a play on Roth. Not smart. Johnny shot him bad. We left town figurin' him for good as dead."

"Looks like he wasn't that good."

"Dead or fast?"

"Neither."

"Well he sure enough ain't dead. I'd best figure a way to warn Johnny. That sidewinder might try back shootin' this time."

The Mexican pistolero made Jasper nervous. The mousy little clerk in Dolan's store hurried to fill his order figuring it for the fastest way to get shut of a man who looked like nothing but trouble. The door to Dolan's office at the back of the store opened.

"We'll take care of it." Jesse Evans closed the door. He stopped short, transfixed as if he'd seen a ghost.

"Crystobal?"

The gunman dropped a hand and turned to the voice behind him. He cracked a half smile in recognition.

"We heard you was dead?"

"Who says Crystobal is dead?"

"That Roth feller you sent down to us last summer."

"Crystobal did not send him."

"Just as well, he's ended up workin' for Chisum."

"Then you know where to find him."

"Sure. What's it to you?"

"Crystobal comes to kill him."

Jasper blanched and shrank back from the counter behind the stranger.

"So he did shoot you like he said."

"Sí."

"Tell you what, come on down to Seven Rivers. Me and the

boys got some business that's likely to flush Chisum and his guns out in the open. Roth'll be with 'em. You can have it out with him then without takin' on Chisum's whole outfit by yourself."

Silver conchos bobbed agreement.

EPILOGUE

Las Vegas, New Mexico

Rick placed a scrap of paper between the yellowed pages to hold his place. He closed the cracked leather cover and set the journal aside. He removed his glasses and rubbed his eyes at the bridge of his nose against the strain of the faded even hand. Great-great-grandma Lucy's journal continued, right along with the history. Great-great-grandpa Ty had his vengeance all right. In the end he and Great-great-grandma Lucy had gotten to town just in time for the big show. Historians recorded most of what's come to be called the Lincoln County War. Ty's story took in bounty and vengeance. The war that followed had a bounty too, this time it was greed.

They say history is written by the winners. Likely it is. It's not a photograph or a documentary film. It's more like a point of view. A point of view that gets lost in the aura of fact. The journal didn't tell all of it, just some parts others never bothered with. He glanced at the clock and stretched. It was late, time for bed. He'd tell the rest of the story another time.

AUTHOR'S NOTE

While certain characters and events in these stories have a basis in historical fact, the author has taken creative license in characterizing them to suit the story. Where there is any conflict between historical fact and the author's interpretation, it is the author's intent to present a fictional account for the enjoyment of the reader.

ABOUT THE AUTHOR

Paul Colt's critically acclaimed historical fiction crackles with authenticity. His analytical insight, investigative research and genuine horse sense bring history to life. His characters walk off the pages of history into the reader's imagination in a style that blends Jeff Shaara's historical dramatizations with Robert B. Parker's gritty dialogue.

Paul's first book, *Grasshoppers in Summer,* received Finalist recognition in the Western Writers of America 2009 Spur Awards. *Boots and Saddles: A Call to Glory* received the Marilyn Brown Novel Award, presented by Utah Valley University.

To learn more visit www.paulcolt.com.